James Pattinson is a full-time author who, despite having travelled throughout the world, still lives in the remote village of East Harling in Norfolk where he grew up. He has written magazine articles, short stories and radio features as well as more than 100 novels.

ON DESPERATE SEAS

None of the crew is particularly gratified when the British tanker *Rosa Dartle* is chosen to carry a cargo of industrial alcohol from Philadelphia to Russia. For these are the dark days of World War II when convoys are receiving the full attention of U-boats and the Luftwaffe. And when six American seamen are embarked to take passage to Archangel there is concocted a human mixture as explosive as the liquid swilling in the tanks. After prolonged attacks, this motley collection of men must continue their fight for survival in an open boat and, later, on the mainland in pitiless Arctic conditions . . .

JAMES PATTINSON

◆

ON DESPERATE SEAS

Complete and Unabridged

ULVERSCROFT
Leicester

First published in Great Britain in 1961 by
Robert Hale Limited
London

First Large Print Edition
published 2002
by arrangement with
Robert Hale Limited
London

British Library CIP Data

Pattinson, James
    On desperate seas.—Large print ed.—
    Ulverscroft large print series: adventure & suspense
    1. Survival after airplane accidents, shipwrecks, etc.
    —Fiction 2. World War, *1939 – 1945* —Naval operations
    —Fiction 3. Sea stories 4. Large type books
    I. Title
    823.9'14 [F]

    ISBN 0–7089–4696–8

Published by
F. A. Thorpe (Publishing)
Anstey, Leicestershire

Set by Words & Graphics Ltd.
Anstey, Leicestershire
Printed and bound in Great Britain by
T. J. International Ltd., Padstow, Cornwall

This book is printed on acid-free paper

On desperate seas long wont to roam,
 Thy hyacinth hair, thy classic face,
Thy Naiad airs have brought me home
 To the glory that was Greece
 And the Grandeur that was Rome.

EDGAR ALLAN POE, To Helen

1

The 'Rosa Dartle'

It was early January, the fourth year of war, and a cold day in Philadelphia: freezing, overcast, with a threat of snow. Mr Thouless, chief mate of the British tanker *Rosa Dartle*, was on deck when the six American seamen who were taking passage to Archangel arrived. He watched them coming up the gangplank, and his thin lips tightened.

'Passengers!' he muttered. 'To hell with them!'

Mr Thouless, a tall, gaunt, bearded man of thirty-one, did not like passengers, least of all ones who were American seamen. But Mr Thouless had had no say in the matter; the authorities had decided that these men must be transported to Archangel. The *Rosa Dartle* was going there; therefore the men must travel in the *Rosa Dartle*. It was all very logical and all very displeasing to the mate, but it could not be avoided.

In Thouless's opinion it was an imposition, something that never should have been allowed. He had said as much to Captain Henderson, but Henderson, a thickset, heavy-shouldered man, twice as old as the mate, had taken the matter more philosophically. Henderson was philosophical about most things — about convoy regulations, about the dangers of being torpedoed with a cargo of several thousand tons of volatile spirit, about shortage of leave, about the undoubted shortcomings of his crew, and about an artificial right leg that was the creaking substitute for one that had been sliced off thirty-five years ago in a ridiculous road accident.

'We may be able to use them, Tom. We could maybe put them on gun watches.'

The tanker had six guns in all: a four-inch breech-loader on the poop; a twelve-pounder protected by a circular wall of plastic armour just forward of the squat, thick funnel, twenty-millimetre Oerlikons on either side of the afterdeck, and similar guns on each wing of the navigating bridge.

Thouless accepted Henderson's suggestion with a growl. 'They're Americans. They'll probably expect to be waited on like millionaires.'

He watched them gloomily now as they came up the gangplank, weighted down with their kit and, to judge by the expressions on

2

their faces, no happier about the embarkation than he.

They formed a mixed collection, and varied in size, in age, probably in upbringing. But they all looked tough — all except the last one, and he seemed out of place in the group; a small, plump man with a smooth, babyish face, china-blue eyes, and gold-rimmed spectacles. He looked like a studious schoolboy who had dressed himself in seaman's clothing and slipped past the dock police.

Thouless went to meet the men. Amidships the last of the big flexible pipes, through which the cargo of alcohol had flowed into the ship from the distillery tanks, was being disconnected. The *Rosa Dartle*'s deck had sunk closer to the waterline under the dead weight of this cargo; she was a steel skin separating the precious and deadly liquid within from the common but no less deadly liquid outside. Thouless sincerely hoped there would not come a time when the two would mix. He hoped that the skin would remain unpunctured.

The Americans had gathered in the waist near the head of the gangplank, a little huddle of men gazing around them with interest, perhaps with misgiving. Thouless came up to them.

'You're the draft for embarkation, I take it.' He addressed them as a group, not knowing which was the senior rating. A man with a face that might have been carved out of teak answered him.

'Yeah, yeah, we're the draft. My name's Carson. Bosun.' He let his gaze move round the ship, and his mouth twitched at the corners in the hint of a smile. 'Not aboard this packet, though.'

Looking at Carson, Thouless had the idea that it might have been no bad thing if this man were to change places with Jaggers, bosun of the *Rosa Dartle*. Jaggers was no asset, a slack-bodied man with a head like a turnip, a sagging belly, and a genius for moaning. If it came to the point not one of the deck crew was worth two pins, with the single exception of Gabriel Toresen, the carpenter. But this fellow Carson looked a real man, no doubt about that, even if he was an American and a passenger. He was no boy; about forty, perhaps, with shoulders like the ridge of a house, deep-set eyes, and a beak of a nose. Thouless wondered whether he had any North-American Indian blood in him; he looked that type. One of the other men took out a packet of cigarettes, shook one into his hand, and put it in his mouth.

4

Thouless said sharply: 'Put that away. This is a tanker.'

'Well, for God's sake!' the man said. He had a flattened, battered face, the face of an ex-prize-fighter, the nose squeezed out sideways, bent-ridged, the nostrils still, so it seemed, half blocked with clotted blood, so that you could hear the sound of the breath forcing its way through. Above his eyes was the discoloured lumpiness of scar tissue. He had taken some punishment in his time.

'You never learnt to read, Kline?' Carson said. Carson's voice was like a bear's growl. He jerked his head at a big painted notice hung up for all to see: 'No Smoking.'

'For God's sake!' Kline said again, but he put the cigarettes away.

'Some guys,' Carson said, 'you need to make a hole in the skull and knock it in with a hammer.'

Kline scowled. He looked as if he wanted to spit, but Thouless's eye was on him. 'Tankers! I never reckoned on no hell ship.'

'Experience for you,' Carson said. He stared bleakly at Kline. 'What's up with you, fella? Got cold feet or something? Wanna go home?'

'Cold feet, nothing. I don't take to being pushed around. That's all.'

'I'll bear that in mind. Mr Kline don't like

5

being pushed around.'

Kline shifted his feet and muttered: 'Wise guy.'

Mr Thouless spoke to Carson. 'I understand you're our passengers for this trip.'

'Yes, sir. That appears to be the set-up.'

It was not a set-up that particularly endeared itself to Carson, putting your life into the hands of a crew of Limeys. But the situation had to be accepted; no use kicking, no sense shooting your mouth off like that Kline. There was a man who would bear watching. The others he could handle easily enough; the one with glasses looked soft, but willing.

'No first-class cabins,' Thouless said. 'This isn't a pleasure cruise.'

'That's okay.' Carson gave a grin; it was like a ray of sunlight glancing through a cloud; one moment it was there, the next it had gone, leaving the face teak-hard again, the dark skin creased only by the permanent lines that the years, the wind, the rain, the salt spray, and the sun had engraved upon it. 'We don't look for luxury.' Then he added, giving a sardonic twist to the cliché, as though ridiculing it even as he used it: 'There's a war on.'

'So I have heard,' Thouless said.

A steward, grumbling in a constant

monotone, showed them their quarters
— bunks squeezed into odd little cabins that
might have been designed originally as
store-cupboards. Two of the men were to
sleep amidships, the rest aft in the crew's
accommodation. Muller, the small man with
the gold-rimmed spectacles, found himself
sharing the amidships cabin with Kline, not a
partner he would have taken from choice, but
that was how it turned out. Kline seemed to
be for ever smouldering with a sense of
injustice, a man burnt up with the fires of
distrust and envy and resentment.

'I don't know that it's legal. We could
maybe dig our toes in.'

'You mean refuse to sail?'

'What else?'

Muller could not see himself doing that. In
spite of Kline's contention, he did not
suppose there was anything illegal about it.
The Government had all sorts of emergency
powers. In any case, Muller was not of the
stuff of which rebels are made; he was the
kind of man who obeyed orders and did not
answer back, the sort of man who would
certainly give Stephen Carson no trouble.

'Sons-a-bitching tankers,' Kline said
viciously. 'You'd think they could've found
some other ship for us. I steered clear of
tankers all this time, and now they send me

to one. I'm letting out a howl about this, see if I ain't.'

Like Kline, Muller had never sailed in a tanker before. It had been a shock to him to discover what kind of a ship the *Rosa Dartle* was. Nobody in his right senses would have picked one of those jokers if he had been given the choice. But in this case there had been no choice. All the same, he could not see himself refusing to sail. He was scared, he admitted that to himself; but even if he had been given the chance to walk ashore now he did not believe that he would have taken it. You had to go through with these things to the end.

'Tankers,' Kline said. 'One torpedo. *Whoof-boom!* Up she goes. No missing. Helluva fine chance for us.'

'With gasoline,' Muller said. 'But this is alcohol. That's different, isn't it?'

'How different?' Kline's nostrils widened, drawing in air noisily. 'It'll burn, won't it? We'll burn too. You ever smell burnt flesh? Not nice.' Kline's lip curled, and the words seemed to tumble out of the side of his mouth. He took a cigarette and struck a match with his thumb-nail.

'It's all right to smoke in here, I suppose,' Muller said. He liked to be certain about the regulations.

Kline sucked smoke into his lungs as if they had been gasping for it. 'Sure, sure. Them no-smoking rules only apply on deck.' He sat down on the lower bunk and looked round the cabin. 'Don't give you room to throw your chest out, do they? Just what you'd expect in a Limey ship. No idea of decent living. Still in the last century.'

'You don't like the English?'

'I'll say not. Lot of pantywaists. Go get themselves a war, and then come crawling to Uncle Sam for help. We did it for 'em last time. Looks like we gotta do it again.'

Muller began to unpack his kit. He had no wish to get into an argument with Kline. He did not agree with Kline's views, but he did not feel like arguing. If Kline went around the ship talking like that he was likely to get himself a bloody nose before many days had passed. But that was his concern. Muller had already seen enough of him to look at the bloody-nose prospect with equanimity.

All he said was: 'You'd better watch your step.'

'Watch my step! What d'you mean?'

'It's all right in here,' Muller said, 'but if you go around talking about pantywaists and Limeys you're going to get yourself disliked.'

Kline laughed harshly. 'That should worry me. I ain't the guy to be pushed around, see?

9

I say what I like, where I like. If other guys take offence, let 'em.'

He had stripped off his coat, and under the blue jersey he was wearing Muller could see the solid, muscular torso of the man, beginning to bulge a little at the waist, but still tough even there. Kline was not tall, but he was extremely thick, with wide, sloping shoulders and long arms. He was not young either; the dark hair was going grey and thinning.

He lifted a clenched fist. It looked hard enough to hammer nails. 'I used to make a living with these, years back. I can still use 'em.'

'Boxing?'

'Sure, sure. Middle-weight. I had fights at the Garden. In line for a title one time. Things didn't pan out.'

He sucked at the cigarette, breath snuffling through his nose. 'That was the good time. I had dough then. I knocked around the smart joints; had fifty suits, yeah, fifty; handmade shoes. What's the use? The sharks get it from you in the end, and then you're back on your heels again.'

He pounded the bunk with his fist, thinking about that good time and resenting the loss of it. 'Now I'm on this goddamn Limey tanker. They better watch it though.

10

There ain't a Limey living that I couldn't take apart with my two bare hands and make into hamburger meat. No, sir.'

★ ★ ★

In the gunners' mess-room at the after end of the ship a discussion concerning the explosive qualities of industrial alcohol was also taking place. It was a subject that had a certain gruesome fascination.

A small, wizened, Army gunner named Bowie, with a sharp, ferret-like face, maintained that alcohol was as bad as petrol. He stabbed his forefinger at the blue-jerseyed chest of an Irish seaman-gunner, a black-haired man with a pleasant, boyish face.

'If you think this stuff is safe, Mr Michael Brennan, you want your brains testing. It'll go up like a bomb if we get a torpedo in the guts. You ask old Cookie.'

Reginald Tarbat, the cook, was a fat hill of a man with a stomach that hung over his belt like the inner tube of a lorry tyre. He was leaning back in a chair while his feet were attended to by a corn doctor. Tarbat had a lot of trouble with his feet. He made use of the gunners' mess-room because he hated the crew. They hated him too, so that made it even.

11

Tarbat gave the question his full consideration, then pronounced judgement.

'Not as bad as high octane; worse than crude oil. Best thing is to drink the lot. Be safer then.'

'Is it good to drink?' Brennan asked.

Tarbat winked ponderously. 'You ask the Russkies. You don't need to be a clairvoyant to guess what they'll do with it. Vodka, every last pint of it.'

There were three other men in the mess-room — Sergeant Grant, of the Maritime Royal Artillery, who was in charge of the ship's armament, Robert Rankin, a young petty officer, and another Army gunner, named Sime, who was stolidly eating his way through a corned-beef sandwich two inches thick. Grant had come on board only the previous day as a replacement for another sergeant who had got himself drunk, fallen down an open tank hatch, and smashed his head to pulp. He was still in the process of sizing up his men. Rankin, who had been on board the ship for a year, was able to give him some tips.

'You'd better watch Bowie. He's a twister.'

'I'll twist him if he tries any tricks,' Grant said. 'What about Sime? He looks dead from the neck up.'

'Another problem boy,' Rankin admitted.

'Seems to have only two objects in life — eating and sleeping. Women, too, of course. The lads call him Sharkgut. Fits him. Brennan's a good one; you won't have any trouble with him.'

In fact, Rankin did not think Grant would have much trouble with any of them; he looked hard enough to deal with any troublemakers. Rankin, none too sure of his own authority, was glad of the presence of a man who would know how to enforce discipline.

* * *

Outside, the afternoon light was fading. The *Rosa Dartle* lay motionless under a steel-grey sky, surrounded by a fringe of oil and scum, empty bottles, orange peel, bits of wood, corks, a half-saturated lifejacket, a loaf of bread, half a dozen beer cans. Now and then a ripple would pass, as though something were moving below the surface of the water, and the carpet of garbage would heave sluggishly, climbing a little higher up the grey side of the ship and then subsiding again. A few flakes of snow began to fall, appearing from the murk overhead and drifting silently down towards the deck.

Jaggers, the bosun, waddling across the

after catwalk, looked up at the sky and fancied there was more to come.

'All right then, send it down. All right.'

He put his hands under his belly and turned his gaze downward, down to the deck whose surface erupted into valves and tank hatches and pipes, all painted with that dull grey paint that had become the livery of merchant ships at war.

'Tomorrow,' Jaggers muttered, lifting his belly and lowering it again like a cook kneading dough.

Tomorrow the *Rosa Dartle* would be out of this dock and there would be nothing to mark the spot where she had been. Tomorrow would begin the long, long haul, the bitter days and the nights of terror, the waiting, waiting, waiting, and the cold worm of fear writhing inside you. Jaggers hated it; God, how he hated it! 'Them that started all this, why don't they come and do the dirty work?' Resentment burned in Jaggers. Why should he be made to endure it? Some day somebody was going to be made to pay for all that he had had to endure. Some day.

Jaggers shivered. He looked back towards the midcastle, half expecting to see Mr Thouless on his tail again. You never knew when the mate was going to spring out on you with his 'Why isn't this done? Why isn't that job finished?' To hell with Mr Thouless and all his works. There was enough trouble without having him for ever bawling you out.

But it was not Thouless he saw; it was Carson, the American bosun, one of the six taking passage to Archangel. Carson had his hands on the rail and was looking aft, perhaps sizing up the ship, seeing if there was any fault to be found. Even as he lounged there, Jaggers could see how tall the man was; he looked strong and lithe, the ridge of the nose prominent, a check cap on his head, with ear-flaps tied across the crown and a long peak.

'Damn Yankee,' Jaggers muttered. 'Passengers! You'd think there was enough without that. If they go poking their big snouts in my business there'll be trouble.'

He moved away aft. The snow began to gather in the angles of the ironwork like a white plague.

2

The High Seas

The *Rosa Dartle* came out of the dock stern first with the tugs fussing. She swung her length out into the stream and went down-river with a Philadelphian pilot on the bridge, a little leathery strip of a man with the wisdom of centuries in his eyes. She went with her keel deep and the water coming up towards the Plimsoll line marked on the hull. A wisp of smoke trailed from a squat, thick funnel, and a line of foam rippled at the bows. The Red Ensign was fluttering from her staff, and her signal halyards hummed in the breeze. Her cargo consisted of raw alcohol and a bunker of diesel oil, with six guns and some twenty thousand rounds of ammunition, with paravanes and smoke floats and a rocket projector that the gunners called a pig-trough. There was grey paint on her superstructure, and the name was obliterated from her stern. She went with a steady, ceaseless vibration, and the smell of the river drifting across her decks, the smell of mud and weed and rotting timber, of fish and smoke and tar. She went with the diesel driving her and the water dragging at the sides. She sailed with the hopes and fears and hates and ambitions of fifty-seven men, and from the safety in which she had lain for fourteen days into the deadly danger she would have to face for many weeks to come.

And the leathery pilot, as he stood with his legs braced on the scrubbed timber of the bridge, was thinking of nothing but the hazards of the Delaware that he knew as thoroughly as the contours of his own face.

'All right for him,' Bowie said. 'He'll be taken off and away home before we stick our nose into U-boat waters. Wouldn't I just like his job.'

'You couldn't do it,' Brennan said. 'You'd pile us up on a sand-bank.'

'If we was piled up on a sandbank for the rest of the war that'd suit me fine. I've had enough fighting for one lifetime.'

'You never did any yet.'

'I never did any!' Bowie was indignant. 'What you think that is?' He exhibited a scar on the back of his right hand, which Brennan had been told about at least a score of times before. According to Bowie, it had been inflicted by a shell splinter, but nobody ever believed that it was anything worse than a gash resulting from the slip of a knife, or

17

perhaps a cut from a broken bottle in a pub brawl. Nobody gave Bowie any credit for heroism, and it was noteworthy that he wore no wound stripe on his sleeve.

'Birthmark,' Brennan said. 'Cover it up before anybody sees it. And give a haul on this rope, can't you?'

They were swinging the boats out. There was a lifeboat on each side of the bridge-deck, and one on each side of the poop. Jaggers had collected a party of seamen and gunners and had got down to the regular shore-leaving job of making the boats ready for instant use.

'But don't let's be wanting you,' Brennan said. 'Sure, a lifeboat's an awful small craft in an awful big lot of water.' Surreptitiously he spat on his boat and rubbed his finger along its gunwale. He had no great faith in lifeboats. In a heavy sea he was afraid they would too easily capsize, even supposing you were able to get them away at all. It might be better to put your trust in one of the slatted rafts that were poised here and there about the ship, ready to slip into the water at the striking out of a pin. But it would be cold on a raft. 'No, no,' Brennan muttered. 'Let's be keeping the old ship afloat. Let's be doing that.'

Mr Thouless, that untiring man who

believed in leaving nothing to chance, had inspected each lifeboat before sailing. He had made sure that they were fully equipped with everything that the regulations prescribed: compasses, first-aid kits, sails, oars, bailers, hatchets . . .

They dropped the pilot and came out of Delaware Bay, out on to the high seas, heading northward unescorted. They would join a convoy that was gathering in New York roads, and then turn eastward on the long crossing; three thousand miles of ocean, with never any relaxation of vigilance, never any moment when a torpedo might not strike home. But at present the sea was calm, the sky was clean and blue, and away on the port side was the coast-line of the American continent that had never yet felt the weight of high explosive or incendiary bombs.

In Mr Thouless, striding with a springy rhythm back and forth on the wing of the navigating bridge, the day seemed to have injected an especial vigour. Though he would not have admitted the fact, Thouless was as near to happiness as a man of his sombre temperament could ever get. He peered down upon the long grey foredeck of the ship, and his gaze moved on to the forecastle, and beyond that to the smooth, scarcely rippled expanse of sea that gradually merged in a

19

curving line with the sky on the distant horizon. No other ship was visible, nothing upon the surface of the water but the glittering refraction of the frosty sun.

In the gun-box on the wing of the bridge Seaman-gunner Brennan was standing by the Oerlikon, not moving, just gazing straight ahead of him. The Oerlikon, uncovered, but not cocked in these waters where no hostile aircraft were to be expected, was pointing almost vertically at the sky, its black metalwork gleaming dully with the sheen of oil. A steel locker just outside the gun enclosure contained a supply of ready-filled magazines, but the clamps on the locker had not been loosened. Brennan was humming softly to himself and thinking of the next meal. Behind him he could hear the mate striding to and fro, but he kept his back turned. Mr Thouless was a stickler for discipline. If a gunner was on watch he expected him to keep watch, not to go to sleep or let his gaze wander inboard.

Brennan was surprised therefore to hear Mr Thouless apparently addressing him.

'What a day! Good to be alive, eh?'

Brennan turned cautiously and answered cautiously. 'Yes, sir; indeed it is.' It had never occurred to him that a man like Thouless would find any delight in being alive at all. To Brennan's eyes the mate appeared scarcely human, a kind of machine, a fault-finding machine devoid of all human emotion. Yet here he was making the kind of remark that any ordinary person might have made, a person sensitive to such natural phenomena as rain and sunshine, ugliness and beauty, things which Brennan would have supposed made no impression on the mate's steel-bright and efficient mind.

Thouless also had immediately been struck by the banality of the remark, and was impatient with himself for having made it. Moreover, he had again glanced down upon the foredeck and had seen Kline and Muller making their way towards the forecastle. The sight of the two Americans, and especially of Kline, had brought back that feeling of annoyance that he had experienced on first learning that the *Rosa Dartle* was to carry passengers.

His sudden change of mood made him growl at Brennan: 'Keep a sharp look-out, gunner. Ships have been sunk in these waters. Too many of them.'

Brennan noticed the change of tone and grinned to himself. This was more like the real Mr Thouless. He was back to normal. Brennan felt relieved, like one who notes the passing of a brief but worrying illness in a friend.

Kline, unaware of the resentment he was causing in the breast of Mr Thouless, was talking to Muller in his thick, snuffling, ex-pug's voice.

'That big son-of-a-bitch. There'll be real trouble between him and me if he don't watch out.'

Kline had mentioned no name, but Muller was uncomfortably aware who the 'big son-of-a-bitch' was: Gabriel Toresen, the ship's carpenter. Toresen was a solid, fair-haired young man, well over six feet tall, and of Anglo-Norwegian origin. Kline disliked all big men as a matter of principle, and he had soon clashed with Toresen.

It had occurred after a session of drill on the four-inch low-angle gun under the guidance of Petty Officer Rankin. Carson had agreed that his men should help to make up a crew on the gun, and though Kline had muttered and grumbled, he had obeyed Carson's orders to get down aft and stop belly-aching.

'Belly-ache, belly-ache, belly-ache,' Carson said. 'What you think this is — a pleasure cruise? Get moving.'

Kline breathed heavily through his flattened nose, but he got moving.

22

The four-inch-gun deck was a raised steel platform above the poop, with a low wire fence surrounding it, and there were metal stands fixed to the deck into which the shells could be pushed, nose downward, like coconuts in a coconut-shy. The gun was old, so old in fact that Brennan, while dismantling the breech mechanism, had discovered on one of the components the date 1897. Rankin said the gun was not as old as that, and that this was only a serial number, but Brennan was unconvinced. Certainly there was enough backlash in the traversing gear to make half a degree of difference to the laying; and scratched on the mounting in rather scrawling letters, painted over but still legible, was the inscription: 'To hell with Kaiser Bill — and Little Willie.'

When Kline looked at the gun he gave a throaty laugh. 'Holy Santa Maria! There's a chunk of old iron. What you do with this — throw it at a U-boat?'

'All right,' Rankin said, a little snappishly, 'have your laugh. Then we'll get down to it.'

'Okay,' Kline said. 'Let's get the fool stuff over with.'

He fell in with the others in a single line to the rear of the gun, and Rankin began to go through the drill as it was laid down in naval orders.

'Number!'

At the third attempt they numbered correctly. They scared Rankin; he had not supposed anybody could be so dense. He wondered whether they were being deliberately uncooperative. He began to detail duties. The drill dragged on, awkward, slow, the way all drill is at first. Rankin was patient, going through it again and again, picking out the best men, the ones who might make up a crew with a leavening of his own gunners.

He dismissed them at last. 'All right. That's the lot for now. We'll have another go tomorrow.'

'Damn waste of time with that iron,' Kline muttered. He went down the ladder from the gun-deck and saw Toresen grinning at him. Kline's head jerked up. 'What's so almighty funny?'

'You wouldn't know,' Toresen said. 'You couldn't see that drill. I just hope we don't have to shoot it out with a U-boat. Not with you boys on the job. I thought you Yanks were the lads for guns, but maybe this one's too big.'

'Listen, wise guy,' Kline said viciously. 'You're lookin' to get yourself hurt. Stow it. Stow it.'

Toresen still grinned. It amused him to bait this fiery, chunky American. It was like prodding a bear with a stick. Kline would have made a good bear — a small, rugged, bad-tempered bear, with wide shoulders and a flattened nose.

'Drill,' Toresen said. 'That sort of drill wouldn't get you into the Home Guard.'

Kline took a step towards the carpenter, threatening. Muller tugged at his arm. 'Come away, Joe. Don't take any notice. He's only kidding.'

Muller was thinking that he might have to do a lot of peace-making before the voyage was over. Or would the trouble come to a head and finish in one fierce explosion? Muller did not like explosions of any kind.

'He'd better watch that kidding,' Kline said. But he dropped his hands to his sides. This was not the place for a showdown, not with Carson hanging around. The showdown would come, but later, later. 'OK, son. Let's go.'

He went away with Muller, who, by reason of the chance that had made them cabin-mates, had become the unwilling companion of Joe Kline, ex-pug, killer, man with a fire burning in his chest.

Toresen watched them go, grinning. Kline amused him. You touched him with your finger and he snapped at it as if he would have bitten it off. Well, let him snap. It

25

relieved the monotony.

'One of these days,' Kline said to Muller, 'I'll make that big dumb-bell eat some of his own sawdust. I'll ram it down his goddam throat. Carpenters! I never came across a carpenter yet that wasn't wooden from the neck up — and maybe down too. No exception on this hooker.'

★ ★ ★

The sun went down in the landward sky, and night came with a cold wind from the north driving the sea against the cleaving stem of the tanker and sending little spurts of spray to damp and chill the look-out in the bows.

By the port-bridge Oerlikon Bowie stood with hunched shoulders, the hood of his duffle-coat giving him a gnome-like appearance. He stared gloomily towards the invisible coast-line, and saw the stars glittering, but they had no beauty in Bowie's eyes. He leaned against the covered Oerlikon and waited for the four slow hours of his watch to drag wearily away.

★ ★ ★

Captain Henderson was in his cabin, relaxing. He was sitting in an easy chair, his chewed-down pipe between his teeth, and a drawing-board resting across the arms of the chair. He was drawing a sailing-ship from memory, a square-rigger. Henderson was not sentimental about the passing of sail. He admitted that a full-rigged ship, a tea-clipper, or a schooner, was one of the most beautiful of man's creations, and he regretted that that kind of beauty was vanishing from the sea. But Henderson had served his apprenticeship in sail, and it had been a hard and bitter apprenticeship, and he for one had not been sorry to 'leave the sea and go into steam'. As a thing of beauty, he still loved the sailing-ship, but he had no wish to go back to it.

He was putting the finishing touches to the bowsprit when there was a knock at the cabin door.

'Come in,' Henderson called, and Mr Thouless, cap under arm, came smartly in.

Thouless glanced at the drawing and tightened his lips, as though he had discovered Captain Henderson pursuing some secret and reprehensible occupation.

Henderson raised his big head with its thick mass of white hair, and saw that the mate was in one of his tense moods. There was far too much tension about Thouless altogether. The poor devil never seemed able to relax. Did he have no interests in life other than ships and the sea? It was not good for a man to be so bound up in his work.

'Well, Tom,' Henderson said. 'What's the trouble now? It is trouble, I suppose?'

Mr Thouless said fiercely, bitterly, as if this were something that had been sent especially to annoy him:

'One of those damned Yanks has slit his throat with a carving-knife.'

★ ★ ★

Muller could never make up his mind as to whether Able Seaman Francini had done it on purpose. He knew only that Francini had been scared, that he had had no wish to go to Russia with Carson's draft, but had wanted to stay at home in New York, the city in which he had been born and in which he would have liked eventually to die.

'I been torpedoed once,' Francini said. 'That's one time too many for Tony.' He rolled his eyes, showing the whites. 'And now it's going to be bad again, huh? It's going to be a big flame maybe. Tony don't like that, not one bit, he don't.'

Francini was scared, sure enough. Muller was scared too, but with him there was no thought of trying to back out. This was the

28

path he had chosen and he would tread it to the end, into whatever horror it might lead him. But Francini was different, and that was why Muller could never be sure that it had really been an accident. Kline said there was no accident about it, that Francini had worked the whole thing out; but still Muller was not sure. Would a man, any man, take that way out? Muller did not know. He knew only what he had seen: the knife and the blood and Francini screaming, and soon not screaming any more.

They were in the crew's mess-room — he and Kline and Carson and Francini. They fed in there with the *Rosa Dartle*'s crew, and it was there that Francini boasted that he could swallow a sword.

'I do it all the time, one time. In a circus. Antonio Francini — sword-swallower. Me.'

'Damn liar,' Kline said. 'You're one big Wop liar. You couldn't swallow a carving-knife.'

The term 'Wop' did not please Francini. If Kline had been less tough he might have made something of it. But all he said was: 'I can swallow any carving-knife ever was made.'

It was Jaggers who went to fetch the knife from the galley. Muller thought Francini would climb down then. It was a big knife, long and sharp — razor-sharp.

'Here you are,' Jaggers said. 'Here's a nice tasty mouthful of cold steel for you. Make a meal out of that.' And Jaggers laughed nastily and threw the knife down on the table, where it lay under the electric light, shining with the bright sheen of honed steel. Jaggers sat down, nursing his belly. 'Best-quality Sheffield blade. None better. Taste it.' And he laughed again.

It was warm in the mess-room, stinking, smoky, with the blackout fug, deadlights clamped down over the portholes. There was silence, only the creak of timbers audible; that, and the engine thump and the rattle of a tin mug as the ship rolled. The other men stared at Francini and waited. And Francini moistened his lips with his tongue and looked at the knife, and a bead of sweat formed on his forehead, and he knew what he had to do.

He picked up the knife and stood up, balancing it in his hand as if testing its weight. He put his head back, right back as far as it would go, and opened his mouth. The blade of the knife went down into his throat.

'By God, he's doing it,' Jaggers said.

And then only the handle was visible, the bone handle, mottled, with a burn mark that it had acquired in falling on the galley stove.

There was Francini with his head back and

30

the knife handle sticking up out of his mouth. Muller felt sick. He wanted Francini to take the knife out. Enough was enough. He had made his point.

And then the ship rolled, and Francini lurched against the bulkhead, and the knife came out with blood on the blade. And Francini began to scream. And the blood bubbled up out of his mouth, the scarlet blood. And he stopped screaming suddenly. He stopped screaming, and stared at the carving-knife with the red blood staining it.

3

The Western Ocean

They weighed anchor and left New York in convoy with another seaman in place of Francini, a stolid, soft-spoken Cape Codder.

'That Francini,' Kline said to Muller, 'he slipped out of it pretty smart. Smart guy all right. He'll have a sore throat, but he don't have to sail in no Limey tanker. Oh, sure, he was smart.'

'You think he really did it on purpose?' Muller said. It was hard to believe that any man would thrust a knife down his throat to avoid unpleasant service. Surely the cure was worse than the disease. But Kline apparently had no doubts about the matter.

'Sure, he done it on purpose. Damn smart trick too. Job to pin that on him as a self-inflicted wound; he was just demonstrating his art. How'd he know the ship would roll? Anyhow, he's away ashore and us poor dumb bastards are left. Oh, Francini was the clever boy.'

It was what was known as a fast convoy, one that was planned to travel at an average speed of nine to ten knots, about five knots slower than the surface speed of many of the U-boats foraging in the North Atlantic at that time. Such a convoy would take more than two weeks on the crossing, and a lot could happen in two weeks.

There were some fifty merchant ships, and fifteen of these were tankers, sliding low through the water with their inflammable liquid cargoes.

'That's a nice number to choose from,' Grant said to Brennan, who was on watch on the starboard-bridge Oerlikon. 'So perhaps they'll let us sneak through.'

'I hope so,' Brennan said. 'I've never been to Russia. I'd like to have a dekko at Joe Stalin's paradise.'

Grant laughed. 'Some paradise. You should see Murmansk.'

'Maybe I will. It'll be good for me. Travel broadens the mind, so I've heard.'

'Yours should be pretty broad when you get back to Ireland. You might even be able to tolerate the North.'

'Sure now, there's limits to everything,' Brennan said.

Grant was going the round of the guns, making sure that all was in order. He left Brennan and went down from the bridge and along the after catwalk to the poop. There was a strong, cold wind blowing, and the *Rosa Dartle* was beginning to show how she could roll. She was shipping water over the after-deck, and as she rolled it swilled back and forth around the valves and tank hatches below the catwalk, sending up spurts of spray for the wind to catch.

The *Rosa Dartle* was near the middle of the convoy, and whichever way Grant looked he could see ships — big ships, small ships; steamships, motor-ships; coal-burners, oil-burners; ships of every description. They were all here, all herded into ranks and columns over five square miles of sea, all thrusting forward at a speed as close to the required value as the ingenuity of deck officers and engineers could make it, all intent on keeping with the convoy, on not becoming a straggler to be picked off unprotected.

Grant watched a Catalina flying-boat circling the convoy, keeping a look-out for submarines. It was never so bad when you were in range of the Cats, but those fellows could not stay with you all the way, and there was always a gap before Coastal Command picked you up on the other side. It was in the gap that you found trouble.

He moved along to the end of the catwalk and ran into Kline.

Kline said: 'Hey, Sarge, what's the odds we

don't stop a tinfish?'

'Fifty-fifty,' Grant said. 'Are you worried?'

'You bet I'm worried. I don't sleep nights, thinking about it.'

Kline laughed harshly.

'If you're looking for a night job, you could do gun watches.'

'Are you kidding? Me, I'm a passenger. No watches for this baby. No, sir.'

'Well, keep your lifejacket handy — and your asbestos suit. You may need both of them.'

'You can say that again,' Kline said. He grabbed the rail in one hard, scarred hand as the ship rolled. 'Hell, what is this — a log? What happens when we hit a real sea?'

'You'll find out,' Grant said.

He had no doubt about that. This was the North Atlantic and it was midwinter; if you wanted a gentle crossing you would choose a different time and a different place. There would be some rolling before this voyage was over. If that should prove the worst of their troubles there would be little cause to grumble.

★　★　★

Captain Henderson was standing on the starboard wing of the bridge, one hand on the teak rail in front of him. Ahead of the *Rosa Dartle* he could see a 'Fort' ship, one of the standard flush-deckers that the shipyards were turning out in the effort to keep pace with losses. To starboard was a Blue Funnel ship, one of the tribe with the classical names culled from the *Iliad* and the *Odyssey*.

He turned his head and gazed aft. Astern was another tanker, slowly closing the gap.

Henderson spoke sardonically to Thouless, who was standing beside him. 'There's enthusiasm for you.'

'We're going to have trouble with that blighter,' Thouless said gloomily. 'That's the *Evening Star*. I've seen her before. Never could keep station. We'll be lucky if she doesn't ram us.'

'We could threaten to put a four-inch shell into her. That ought to make her keep a respectable distance.'

'She's got a gun in her bows,' Thouless said.

★   ★   ★

It was the gun in the bows of the *Evening Star* that interested Grant. It gave him a stab of envy, for it was the kind of gun he would have liked — a Bofors forty-millimetre. You could not beat the Bofors for anti-aircraft work. The Oerlikon was good, but the Bofors was heavier and better.

So Grant stood on the poop of the *Rosa Dartle*, watching the *Evening Star* coming up, and he wondered what men were manning the Bofors. It would be a six-man team and might come from his own regiment. Scattered around the convoy were probably many men with whom he had drilled and been billeted if only he knew where to look for them.

The *Evening Star* came closer; he could see the foam bursting away from her bows and he could see streaks of rust staining her sides. She was an old ship, and gave somehow the impression of shabbiness, as if, being old, she no longer took any trouble with her appearance. Her single funnel aft was tall for a tanker, standing up very straight and thin like a linen-post.

The gap between the two ships continued to shrink.

'Trying to show us just how speedy she is,' Rankin said. 'Swanking. If she goes much faster she'll fall to pieces, an old tub like that.'

'If she goes much faster she'll boot us up the tail,' Grant said. 'I hope she's not going to try those tricks at night. Wouldn't be at all pleasant.'

The Bofors gun in the bows of the *Evening Star* was pointing upward in all its steely nakedness at an angle of forty-five degrees. Grant could see the trumpet-shaped flame-guard on the muzzle, and the brass cases of the rounds in the autoloader. That was the gun he loved; it was wasted on an old tanker like the *Evening Star*; Marlins and Lewis guns would have been more suited to her senility.

He could see three men standing by the Bofors and looking towards the stern of the *Rosa Dartle*. He borrowed a pair of binoculars from the look-out and lifted them to his eyes. A familiar face came into his line of sight, a face he was never likely to forget, since he had been with it on so many hectic pub crawls in Glasgow and other towns.

'Jock Dewar,' he muttered. 'Why, Jock, you old heathen, so it's you, is it?'

Of all the men in the regiment Dewar was Grant's especial friend, and he had not seen him for nearly a year; they had travelled different roads. And now, gazing across a stretch of broken water in the great expanse of the Atlantic, that face out of all others had swum into his vision. So Dewar was in the *Evening Star*; Dewar was sitting on his tail. Suddenly the vastness of the ocean seemed to shrink to the size of a regimental parade ground, to the comradeship of a sergeants' mess.

'Jock, my boy, it's good to see you.'

'Seen somebody you know?' Rankin asked.

'An old pal,' Grant said. 'I've got an interest in that ship now. They'd better not do anything to her, or I'll be annoyed.'

'That'll worry them.'

Grant saw Dewar lift his arm and throw his head back in a pantomime of the action of drinking, and then stagger about the deck as if drunk. He knew then that Dewar had recognized him also. He gave the thumbs-up sign.

He never saw Dewar so closely again. The *Evening Star* dropped back into her proper station and held it; but in the days that followed he would often glance across that strip of water that separated the two tankers, and gaze at the old sea-stained ship in which his friend was serving. He remembered Jock Dewar's bony, freckled face, his slow smile and dry humour; a good man, Jock, a good pal. It was frustrating to know that he was so close and yet so far away. It was like living in the same village as your best friend and being forbidden to visit his house.

But Grant would keep an eye on that old tanker, the *Evening Star*, and when he saw Jock again in Glasgow or some other place they would talk things over; and Jock would get drunk and want to fight the world, as he always did. He smiled to himself, remembering the times he had kept Dewar out of trouble.

★ ★ ★

It was the evil time for Jaggers. He slept badly and awoke unrefreshed. Jaggers had a premonition of disaster. He remembered how he had had just such a premonition on two former occasions, and each time the ship in which he had been sailing had been torpedoed and sunk. Jaggers had reason to be afraid; to his way of thinking, the *Rosa Dartle* was a doomed ship, and maybe he was doomed with her. A volatile cargo such as this ship carried was nasty stuff to have under your feet.

Rather unwarily he confided his premonition to Toresen. He felt that he had to tell someone, to let someone share his fear. As might have been expected, Toresen laughed.

'That's not a premonition. You're just plain scared.'

Such a reception of his confidence did not help to endear Toresen to Jaggers. There had been little love between them before; there was even less now. Jaggers could imagine Toresen relating the story to others: 'The bosun's got a premonition. The bosun's scared stiff.'

Jaggers hoped maliciously that Kline would settle Toresen. Perhaps a whisper in Kline's ear might help things along. What Jaggers managed to whisper in Kline's ear was that Toresen had called him a jumped-up Yankee bastard with the brains of a louse and a yellow liver. In fact, Toresen had said nothing of the sort; when Kline was out of sight he was out of mind as far as Toresen was concerned. But Jaggers's whisper served to blow the embers of Kline's hatred into a white heat, and the clash was inevitable.

It occurred in the crew's mess-room during a game of poker. Kline was playing with Jaggers and two or three others when Toresen walked in. Toresen rested his behind on the table and lit a cigarette. Kline's breathing quickened, the breath coming noisily through the half-blocked passages of his nose, but he said nothing. He won three hands in succession.

Toresen said: 'You're doing well, kiddo.'

Kline looked up at him then. 'So what?'

Toresen eased himself off the table. 'Mind if I cut in?'

Kline said: 'I wouldn't play with you under orders from Roosevelt himself.'

Toresen's voice was soft and gentle. 'How so, kiddo?' The question was just a question, but movement had stopped in the mess-room, and six men were looking from Kline to Toresen and back again at Kline, and those six men seemed to be holding their breath, waiting for something to happen.

Jaggers put in slyly: 'I expect he means there's enough in the game already. That's what you mean, ain't it, Joe? Not room for another.' He put his hands on his belly, lifting it and letting it go again. His head was lowered and he was looking up at Toresen with hooded eyes. 'Not room for Chippie, hey?'

Kline spoke slowly, enunciating each word in his hoarse, thick voice, as if to make sure that none were missed. 'There wouldn't be room for that son-of-a-bitch if there wasn't another card player in the ship.'

Toresen dropped a hand on Kline's shoulder. His voice was still gentle, but it had an edge to it, a fine edge of warning. 'How so — Yank?'

Kline's voice grated. 'Get your hand off me — Limey.'

Toresen left the hand where it was. 'You don't like me, do you?'

Kline laughed harshly, but without amusement. 'You're goddam right, I don't.'

'Well, well,' Toresen said. 'Don't let it get you down. I've seen people I liked better than you, if it comes to that.'

'I said take your hand off me.'

Toresen dropped the hand from Kline's shoulder. 'All right, kiddo. But don't get above yourself. You go around this ship looking for trouble and you'll find it. Plenty of trouble.'

Kline said: 'Maybe you'd like to make it for me.' His voice was sneering.

'Maybe.'

An idea seemed to occur suddenly to Kline; but, in fact, it had been in his mind for a long time. He had just been waiting for the right time and the right place. Now he could prick this Limey windbag once and for all.

'You think you're strong, hey? You think you're a tough guy?'

Toresen's face showed the flicker of a smile. He knew he was strong, but he took no credit for his strength; it was just something you had, something that was given to you, like a straight nose or black hair. He knew he was strong, but he never went around boasting about the fact.

'What do you think, kiddo?'

Kline said: 'I think you're just one big bladder of wind. I'll prove it.'

'How'll you do that, kiddo?'

Kline swept the cards to one end of the long, narrow table with a sweep of his arm.

43

'Any of you guys got a razor blade — two razor blades?'

It was Jaggers who answered quickly: 'I have. I'll fetch a couple. You wait here.'

He got up and went out of the mess-room, belly swaying, his hand holding it.

'What is this?' Toresen asked.

'You'll see. You'll see.'

Jaggers came back with the razor blades. 'Here you are, Joe — brand new, never been used.'

Kline took the wrapping off the blades and measured a distance on the table with his arm. He wedged the blades into the table, each with one sharp edge upward. The distance between them was equal to twice the length of a man's forearm from the elbow to the wrist.

Kline looked at Toresen, grinning maliciously. 'Now, you sit opposite me, and put your elbow on the table between them blades.'

Jaggers saw what was going to happen. He was rubbing his hands. He had even forgotten about his belly and was leaving it to look after itself.

'What's the idea?' Toresen asked.

'The idea,' Kline said, 'is a test of strength — your strength and mine. We see which one of us can press the other guy's wrist down on

44

to the razor blade. Best man wins. Other one gets himself cut. Understand?'

Toresen understood. It was easy enough to understand. 'That's a damn-fool idea.'

Kline sneered. 'Scared, big fella? I never see a big guy yet that wasn't all wind when it came to the pay-off. Scared?'

Nobody else said a word. Jaggers sniggered, nodding his pear-shaped head, enjoying it.

Toresen took off his jacket and rolled up the right sleeve of his shirt. Kline did the same. They sat down, facing each other across the narrow table, knowing that this was the showdown.

Kline's arm was like a piece of cable chopped off. He clenched his fist, and the sinews stood up in ridges. He opened his fist and the ridges collapsed. The forearm was covered with black hair, but higher up, where the bicep muscle stood out, big and lumpy, the skin was smooth and hairless. Kline rested his elbow on the table, clenching and unclenching his fist, making the sinews and muscles move under the skin, and grinning.

'Let's see who's tough. Let's see.'

He had no doubt in his own mind. He had always had abnormally strong arms, and that strength had been developed for boxing. It was years since he had been in the ring, but the iron had stayed in that good right arm. Kline could afford to grin.

Toresen put his elbow next to Kline's, the palm of his hand flat against Kline's palm. Toresen was the taller man by a head, but the two forearms were of equal length; Kline had a gorilla-like length of arm. The fingers of the two men interlaced, gripped, locked.

'OK, let's go,' Kline said, and put the pressure on, suddenly, fiercely.

Toresen was ready for that quick thrust; he had expected it from a man like Kline. The muscles bunched in his arm, the bicep hardening. Kline increased the pressure, and Toresen's hand went back a little way. Kline was strong, no doubt about that; he was no pushover. Let the arm go a bit farther, and there would be no hope of bringing it back to the vertical; it would be down on the razor blade.

He answered pressure for pressure, and the arms were upright again. But only upright; Kline held him there. Kline's mouth was tight, the breath hissing through his nostrils. A vein throbbed in his temple, twisted like a snake. Toresen felt the sweat forming on his forehead beginning to trickle; but there was sweat on Kline's face too. This was not so easy as he had expected.

Jaggers said softly: 'Look at them muscles.

46

Who's going to crack? Which one gets his wrist sliced?'

Toresen's arm ached. It was as if he had been supporting a heavy weight for an hour, a day, a lifetime. Much more of this and he would have to give way — any man would.

He was looking at Kline's face, the hard, battered face of the ex-pug, with the scar tissue above the eyes; he was watching for a sign of weakness and finding none. Some words spilled out of the side of Kline's mouth.

'OK, now let's really start.'

And the pressure was on again, real pressure. Toresen's hand went back.

'Let's hear you squeal — Limey!'

Through five degrees the arms moved, slowly, agonizingly, the muscles cracking. Ten degrees. Coming up to fifteen. There were six silent men in the mess-room and the other two breathing hard, the sweat pouring down their faces. But Kline's mouth was open, gaping, and Toresen saw it and knew suddenly that Kline was finished.

Toresen drew up a last reserve of strength, and the arms moved up again to the vertical. Kline knew too that he was finished. Something seemed to have snapped in his arm; the power had gone out of it. Toresen said nothing, but he was forcing Kline's wrist down towards the razor blade, slowly, inexorably. Kline's whole body moved over sideways and the tendons in his shoulder cracked.

There were two inches separating Kline's wrist from the blade. Toresen looked into his eyes.

'Enough, kiddo?'

'Damn you, you son-of-a-bitch, you Limey bastard! Damn you to hell!' Kline snarled, and spat in Toresen's face.

Toresen rammed Kline's wrist down on the steel blade, and the blood spurted.

'You asked for it. By God, you asked for it!'

★   ★   ★

When Carson saw Kline's bandaged wrist his dark Indian face moved into the semblance of a grin. Carson had heard all about the trial of strength; things like that travelled round the ship in a matter of minutes. On board ship the only secrets were those locked in the mind of one man.

'You injured yourself?' Carson asked.

Kline scowled, but made no answer. He knew that Carson knew. He knew that the whole ship knew, and the knowledge gave him no pleasure.

Carson was glad that Kline had been

slapped down. Maybe that would teach him his place. Maybe there would be less trouble from him in future.

He did not know Kline. Kline was a ferment of hatred, the defeat rankling like a barb in the flesh. 'I'll get him,' Kline told himself. 'I killed a man when I was fifteen. Maybe I'll kill another man. Maybe.'

'You ought to be more careful,' Carson said. 'You kid seamen, you want to watch out for yourselves.'

'I'll watch out for myself,' Kline said. 'I'll watch out all right.'

Mr Thouless mentioned the affair to Captain Henderson. Thouless was inclined to think that disciplinary action of some kind ought to be taken.

Henderson was less impressed by the urgency of doing so. 'Seems to me the carpenter has already taken all necessary action. Damned good thing he was the winner. We don't want our one competent man damaged. What was the argument?'

Thouless confessed ignorance on that point. 'This man Kline's a born troublemaker.'

'He picked the wrong one to make trouble with when he picked Toresen,' Henderson said.

★ ★ ★

49

They ran into the wolf pack in the Black Pit, the region of no air cover, and for four long days and nights of terror and disaster the pack hunted and harried them. By day great cauldrons of foaming water creamed above the rumbling depth-charges, and sometimes oil came up to lie like a dirty blanket on the sea, and with the oil perhaps men's bodies, lifeless, filthy, and discarded. By night the thunder of an explosion and the sudden glare of flame in the darkness came as the indications of another ship torpedoed.

And still the others pressed on eastward at the same slow rate of knots, while their escort fought an unceasing battle with the unseen enemy which came and withdrew and came again, striking first at one point and then at another until the men in the ships were weary from long watching and plagued by the constant fear of death, of the sudden bursting asunder of steel plates to allow the sea to gush in, the sea that would have no mercy.

Grant hated U-boats. He hated them more bitterly than enemy aircraft, for against the U-boat he felt helpless: he could not fight back as he could against an attacking plane. The invisible enemy was worse than the visible one; this was a sly killer who crept up on you and struck without warning. And once the pack had found you there was no way of shaking it off; the convoy did not have sufficient speed.

By the third night of combat they had lost five ships and thirty thousand tons of cargo. The men who had died were not yet numbered, but the rescue ships were packed with survivors, and many of these were to die from their wounds or their burns or the thick black oil that was clogging their lungs.

A corvette had taken a disabled merchantman in tow, a valuable ship loaded with aircraft. For a whole day the merchantman wallowed at the end of the tow-rope before a second torpedo put a finish to her struggles and she slipped down to her last resting-place on the bed of the sea, taking with her the aircraft that had never been used and ten doomed men who had had no time to escape from their iron coffin.

It was the evil time for every one. In the *Rosa Dartle* was the all-pervading sense of treading on the crater of a volcano that might at any moment belch fire and destruction. Men carried their lifejackets everywhere, yet they knew that no lifejacket could protect them from the flames of a burning cargo.

'What we need,' Toresen said, 'is asbestos lifejackets.'

'What we need is wings, so we could fly right away from this lot,' Tarbat said. 'Oh, for

51

the wings, for the wings of a dove.'

Toresen looked at Tarbat's fat bulk. 'Some dove you'd make. Some wings.'

Grant kept watch over the *Evening Star* because Jock Dewar was in that ship. Each morning as the dawn came grey out of the east he looked for the old tanker with the tall, thin funnel, waiting for the outline of bows and masts and superstructure to detach itself from the gloom and form into the solidity of a ship. Each morning as he saw the familiar shape ploughing through the steel-grey water he felt the release of tension, the sweet sense of relief in the knowledge that Jock was still alive. It was Jock he thought of, not the ship; but in his mind this friend was identified with the *Evening Star*, and while the ship survived Jock survived also.

'You seem pretty interested in that old tub,' Rankin said. 'Got shares in her or something?'

'More than shares. A friend.'

'Oh, yes, you told me. That makes a difference, doesn't it?'

'You're right. It makes all the difference.'

The *Evening Star* was the last ship to die. She died at daybreak, when the air was cold and damp and the sun was no more than a vague promise somewhere below the eastern rim of the sea, when men's eyes were tired from the long night watches, and a tongue passed across cracked lips discovered the taste of salt, when the white flicker of a wave-top appearing suddenly out of the darkness was like the ghost of former shipmates lost in this terrifying immensity of water, when cooks were everywhere busy in their galleys, and over all this great and moving company of ships lay the dull vision of the waking day.

She died suddenly in a wreath of flame, in a crimson bloom of fire, with tendrils of smoke writhing and twisting through it to spread and billow and be finally wrenched to tatters by the wind. She died as an island of blistering heat in a cold and bitter sea when men were beginning to breathe freely again after the ordeal of the night, and the promise of a new day was about to bring new hope and new resolve. She died giving light to the others, a baleful light of warning that smeared them all with bloody fingers, as though marking them with the red badge of Cain; and in her death they all saw the pattern of their own destruction.

Forty men died with the *Evening Star*; forty men were burnt at this drifting stake in the middle of the Atlantic, their flesh peeling away in charred and shrivelled fragments from hot bones. Their hair flamed as they ran like living torches, trying to escape where there was no escape. And the fire took them, some at one point, some at another, played cat and mouse with them in cabins, in the engine-room, in alleyways and deckhouses and storerooms; played with them and killed them, some quickly, some more slowly, but killed them all.

And Jock Dewar, Grant's friend, was one of the forty.

Grant watched the death of the *Evening Star* from the poop of the *Rosa Dartle*. He could hear the sullen roaring of the fire and the wind carried the smoke towards him, so that he could smell its harsh and acrid scent, bitter in his nostrils. He gripped the taffrail and stared at the fire, seeing with his mind's eye his friend burning in that inferno, hearing in imagination Dewar's screams of agony, until at last there were no more screams, no more flesh to burn, no more eyeballs to hiss and crackle and burst like roasted chestnuts — no more Jock Dewar.

He heard a voice behind him shouting excitedly: 'By God, that's some blaze. That's a fire you could warm your hands at.'

It was Petty Officer Rankin. He had come up beside Grant and now he too rested his hands on the taffrail and stared at the funeral pyre of the *Evening Star*.

'That's high octane, all right,' There was a tremor in Rankin's voice; he was frightened, but he went on talking to hide his fear.

'That's ten thousand tons gone sky high. That's about two million gallons; enough to run my old motorbike for two hundred million miles. Think of it. And all gone in one big flaming fire.' His voice dropped. 'All those poor bastards too — cooked — cooked like joints of meat — roasted like — '

Grant turned on him, snarling. 'Stow it. For Christ's sake, stow it, can't you?'

Rankin was taken aback. He stared at Grant with his mouth hanging open. Grant had never snarled at him like that before; he had never seen such an expression of mingled anguish and hatred on a man's face. At first he could not understand it; then he remembered that the sergeant had had a friend on board the *Evening Star*.

'I'm sorry,' he mumbled. 'Sorry.'

He did not look at Grant again because the light was getting stronger, and it embarrassed him to see tears in a man's eyes, and especially a man like Grant. He turned away and tried to forget that there had been any tears.

★   ★   ★

They lost no more ships after the *Evening Star*. After that the wind came, throwing the sea into a fury; and so for three days they had only the storm to contend with as they struggled eastward. And the storm was enough.

But they came through the storm also, and a Sunderland flying-boat of Coastal Command came out to meet them, and flashed a greeting and circled the wide pattern of the surviving ships. And there were no more U-boats.

So they came in through the Western Approaches and smelled the land, and saw the islands coming up out of the mist, and were glad. And the escort turned away and left the heavy merchant ships to go to their various destinations — to Liverpool, to Hull, to Avonmouth, to Cardiff, to Middlesbrough.

And the *Rosa Dartle* went into Loch Ewe and anchored under the snow-capped hills of Scotland.

4

Northward

Toresen was on the forecastle with Mr Thouless. Under Toresen's hand the windlass was rattling and thumping as the cable came up through the hawse-pipe. The anchor came out of the mud, and the *Rosa Dartle* was free to move out of the safety of the loch to the danger of the open sea.

'Away again,' Toresen muttered to himself. 'Joe Stalin, here I come.'

The rain dripped from Toresen's sou'wester, dripped down his oilskin coat, shone on his face and hands and gumboots, rattled on the windlass, glistened on the paint of the deck, dimpled the water of the anchorage, and shrouded the hills in a grey wash of murky cloud and drifting raindrops.

'Goodbye to all that,' Toresen said.

For five days they had lain at anchor while the convoy had gathered, chained to the bed of the loch like a dog chained to a kennel, and on each of the five days it had either rained or snowed. Other ships had come and gone, small craft had chugged back and forth, and

57

the gulls had been there always, diving for food or hovering effortlessly on the cold winds blowing in from the sea.

But now this brief interlude was over and the worst of the journey lay ahead, in the far North, beyond The Shetlands and The Faeroes and that line marked on the map but invisible to the human eye — the Arctic Circle.

They moved out slowly, with a Harrison boat ahead and astern of them, a ship with rust streaks down her sides and tanks on deck. They went out through the boom like cattle going out through a field gate, and turned northward, and began to roll and toss as the sea met them, and were away.

It was not a large convoy. There were fifteen merchant ships and a fleet oiler. The oiler, a dirty, drab-looking ship flying the Blue Ensign, was the only other tanker.

'Makes you feel conspicuous,' Henderson remarked to the second mate. 'Easy to pick out.'

To Jaggers it seemed ominous. 'They go for tankers first. We'll be number one on the list.'

'You ought to feel honoured,' Toresen said. 'Most important ship in the convoy. Should have a special ensign.'

Jaggers did not appreciate Toresen's humour. 'You can keep that sort of honour. I don't want none of it.'

For escort there were six destroyers, an anti-aircraft ship, three corvettes, and two armed trawlers. Toresen said it was a useful ring of steel, but Jaggers was not comforted. There were too many holes in the ring.

★　★　★

On the second day out from Loch Ewe the weather cleared, and there was a short period during which the sun was visible, rather pale and watery, but visible. It came like a busy guest at some gathering, who puts in a brief token appearance and then leaves again, having done all that duty demanded. They had passed between The Faeroes and The Shetlands and were heading almost due North, with the wind meeting them and the sea uneasy, the caps of the waves flicked white, and spray falling on the forecastle head, so that the iron gleamed wetly in the pale sunshine.

There were four columns, with four ships in each column. The *Rosa Dartle* was the third ship in the second column from starboard, and at the head of the column was the Commodore's ship, a six-thousand-ton tramp with crated deck-cargo and a long, thin funnel that puffed out sudden short spurts of black smoke like signals.

'There's an example for you,' Henderson said. 'The Commodore himself. Ought to know better.'

The other tanker, the fleet oiler, was at the tail of the second column from port, and the whole convoy was a compact, square little group, surrounded by the spaced-out escort vessels with their Asdic sets pinging and their radars scanning the sea for the enemy that would surely come.

Eight of the ships were American, and that was another source of complaint for Joseph Kline.

'Why couldn't we have travelled in one of them? All them good American ships, and they have to plant us in a Limey tanker. What sort of a game is that?'

Carson wondered about that also. It seemed a queer arrangement. But there were a lot of queer arrangements in the War, and you had to take things as they came; no use raising a howl. Carson was a philosophical man. He did not waste his energy kicking at brick walls; he accepted them and found a way round if he could. Kline was not like that; he kicked like mad and got his toes hurt and accomplished nothing.

There was one Russian ship, too, an old three-island steamer of about three thousand tons. It looked out of place in the company it was keeping, but it ploughed along gallantly at the tail of the starboard column, and by some means or other contrived to keep station while surrounded by foreigners who did not even speak the same language.

It was Muller, a music-lover, who named this ship 'The Little Russian'. Kline, who had never heard of Tchaikovsky or his symphonies, missed the allusion but thought the name was a good one. He used it, others repeated it, and soon the tail-ender on the starboard side, the bottom right-hand corner of the square, was never anything but 'The Little Russian', a term almost of endearment for a rusty old vessel that all would have been sorry to lose.

'If that little blighter can make it,' Toresen said, 'you bet your life we can.'

'Not so much of that one to hit,' Jaggers said. 'We're a big target — too big.'

'"The Little Russian' is on the outside. She'll keep the tin-fish away from us.'

'Some chance.'

Throughout the hours of daylight a Catalina flying-boat of Coastal Command stayed with them, patrolling in a wide circle, searching the water for the dark shape of a U-boat and exchanging signals with the escort.

'While it's that boy, I don't mind,' Tarbat said, coming out of his galley to survey the prospect. 'When it's a Jerry plane on the same stunt, not so good.'

Tarbat had been on the Russian run before, in a ship that had limped into the Kola Inlet with a fire burning in her after-hold and a thirty-degree list to port. Tarbat, under considerable difficulty, had managed to keep the galley stove alight and the meals cooking. He had put plugs of cottonwool in his ears, so that the noise of the guns should not disturb him in his work. He felt safer when not able to hear the racket of the explosions, and he had been able to concentrate on the fine art of keeping frying-pans and saucepans on an even keel while the top of the stove was sloping at an acute angle. Tarbat maintained that it was his feet that had seen him through. Big, firm foundations assured his equilibrium.

On the third day the wind freshened and backed a little, hitting them on the port bow. They were some four hundred miles east of Iceland, and the weather had become markedly colder. Grant noticed it when he did the round of the guns. He found Sime on the starboard-bridge Oerlikon so wrapped up in scarves and Balaclava helmets that it seemed a wonder he should be able to see or hear anything that was going on around him.

'What's up with you?' Grant said. 'You look like a damned cocoon.'

'Cold, Sarge, cold,' Sime muttered. His eyes, like stones in the depths of his woollen covering, turned on Grant, expressionless. The usual half-grin might have been hovering about his lips, but there was no means of telling; his mouth was covered, and his words came through the wool in a muffled undertone.

Grant felt an aversion to Sime. It was not simply a question of disliking his gluttony, his gross table manners, his inefficiency; there was something else that repelled him, some inner quality. Once he had touched Sime's hand. The hand was cold, slightly damp, as if it had sweated and the sweat had cooled, but it was not the coldness or the clamminess that had made Grant feel physically sick; it was another sensation altogether; it was as though he had touched with his finger-tips the very character of the man and had found it a thing of slime. After that he avoided touching Sime, as one might avoid touching a slug.

'It'll be colder than this,' Grant said harshly. 'I can promise you that.'

Sime turned away and appeared to be looking at the ship on the starboard bow, a ship of the Liberty type, a seven-thousand-tonner with flush decks. Grant wondered whether that ship too had problem boys like Sime and Bowie. He supposed so. You were lucky indeed if you had all good men. And yet, for a job like this, what you needed were not just good men but supermen.

A similar thought had occurred to Captain Henderson as he stood on the bridge, gripping the rail with his hands in order to ease the weight on his artificial leg. Driving ships through on the North Russia route was a job for heroes, for such men as had sailed with Jason, such men as Ajax and Achilles. And what did you have? Men like Jaggers.

Henderson felt the wind on his cheek like a breath of the North. It would not be long now before they crossed the Arctic Circle. That in itself would make no difference; it was an arbitrary line, and you could not tell by any obvious natural feature when you had passed from one side to the other. There would be no sudden marked fall in the temperature, no immediate appearance of ice, nothing. And yet, in a way, you would have moved from one world into another, into a sterner, harder, colder world that could discover the weakness in a man, that could separate the men of spirit from the worthless ones, the ones who could endure from the ones that would break at last.

★   ★   ★

The second clash between Kline and Toresen was more inevitable than the first. Kline was not the man to forget that Toresen had humbled him in front of the crew; he had a scar on his wrist to remind him, and that visible scar had its invisible counterpart in his mind. He had vowed to himself that he would settle that score with interest, and he waited only for an excuse, feeding in the meanwhile his anger and his hatred.

'I'm going to cut that big slob down to size,' he said to Muller. 'I'm going to make him eat dirt.'

Muller did not like to hear Kline talking in that way. He could not understand why Kline should go about looking for trouble when there would be trouble enough of another kind before many more days had passed. Toresen was the last man Muller would have wanted to pick a quarrel with, but Kline was different, and every time he saw Toresen the hatred boiled up in him afresh. A ship was too small a space to contain Kline's anger.

In the end it was Jaggers who brought the matter to a head — as he wished to do

— making Kline the instrument of his own spite.

Kline was in the crew's mess-room playing cards with three other men — and he was losing steadily. Kline hated to lose; he played games to win, and if he did not win there was no pleasure in the game for him.

Jaggers was in the mess-room too, but he was not playing; he was just watching and taking note. He could see the way the game was going, and he knew that Kline was becoming more and more of an angry, dangerous man. Jaggers liked to see that.

'You don't seem to have the luck tonight, Joe,' he said softly. And he grinned at Kline with a wolfish baring of the teeth. Jaggers's teeth were yellow with gold fillings that gleamed when he smiled, reflecting the lamplight.

Kline glowered, his brows ridged and lumpy. 'What in hell's it got to do with you?'

Jaggers rubbed one flat hand upon the other, so that they made a kind of hissing noise. 'Nothing, Joe, nothing. I just made the remark, that's all.'

'You keep your remarks to yourself,' Kline said. 'I don't need 'em, see?'

'I see,' Jaggers said; and he waited for Toresen to come into the mess-room, hoping that Toresen would not fail to come now that

Kline looked ripe for violence.

Toresen came sure enough; he came to make himself a mug of cocoa, and he looked at Kline and at the card game.

'Who's on the winning end tonight?' he asked.

Jaggers said with his wolf's grin: 'Not Joe. He's got all the bad luck.'

Toresen leaned over Kline's shoulder and looked at the American's cards.

'Too bad. Maybe you should change the game.'

Kline's neck turned red. He did not move his head to look at Toresen, but he knew just where Toresen was standing, and he did not like it.

'Don't crowd me, fella. I don't like bein' crowded.'

Toresen moved away to make his cocoa. 'It's a bad night,' he said. 'I think there's snow coming.'

'You a weather expert?' Kline sneered.

Toresen mixed the cocoa with sugar and condensed milk and ran hot water on to the mixture, stirring it.

'No need to be an expert to know when snow's coming in these waters. You can't go wrong.'

He moved along the table back towards where Kline was sitting, carrying the mug of cocoa in his right hand. Jaggers moved in the same direction just behind Toresen. When Toresen was level with Kline Jaggers brushed past, jogging Toresen's arm. He managed it just as he had intended. The hot cocoa slopped over on to Kline's thinning hair and ran down his face.

Kline came to his feet with a yell. He brought his hand up under the mug that Toresen was still holding, and the rest of the cocoa spurted over Toresen, half blinding him. Kline swung a punch at Toresen's jaw, and the carpenter, caught off balance, went down like a felled tree. Kline kicked him viciously in the ribs.

'Now, now,' Jaggers said. 'Careful now.' But he made no move to interfere. He was enjoying this; it was going just as he had hoped. He shifted away from Kline to the other end of the mess-room, his hands under his belly, his tongue roving over his thin lips, waiting for more trouble.

Toresen was an easygoing man. Except when drunk he did not go around looking for fights, but this savagery of Kline's brought savagery in return. When Toresen got up off the deck of the mess-room there was more anger in him than there had been for many months. It was not the blow on the chin that angered him — he could have accepted that with good humour. It was the boot in the ribs that he would not accept at any price.

The mess-room was an inconvenient place in which to fight; the table and the chairs got in the way. Toresen forced Kline back against the table edge, but Kline twisted away and sank his fist into Toresen's kidneys. It was no day for sticking to the rules. Toresen folded under the blow, and Kline brought up a wicked right to the jaw. It just missed the jaw and caught Toresen's nose. The nose gushed blood, and a stream of it ran down over Toresen's mouth and chin, dripping on to his shirt. He dashed the blood away with the back of his hand and went for Kline.

Toresen's rush drove Kline back against the end bulkhead of the long, narrow mess-room, slamming him hard against the iron.

'It's a fight,' Jaggers said delightedly, rubbing one hand upon the other and dodging round the table to keep out of the way of chance blows. 'Boys, you never saw a better fight than this. I take the Yankee to win.'

Kline lowered his head and butted Toresen in the stomach. The breath came out of Toresen like a rush of steam, and as he folded Kline's head came up sharp like a cannon-ball. The others could hear the crack of it on

Toresen's jaw. The carpenter went down again.

'Nice bit of head-work,' Jaggers said admiringly. 'With a head like that the boy should be good at figures.'

'Depends on the kind of figures,' a tubby, bald-headed seaman grinned. He was enjoying the fight too. 'I'd say that there Kline knew his way around. Good with his feet too. Might make a footballer.'

Nobody was helping Toresen now that he was down. He would not have expected any of this crew to do so, and he would certainly not have asked them to. He looked upon them all with contempt; he was as contemptuous of them as he was of Jaggers. They knew it, and the knowledge did not make them love him. They would have been glad to see him beaten up, and Kline looked like the boy to gratify them.

Kline rammed at Toresen's face with the heel of his boot; he was in the killer mood, savage as a man could be. There was a red mist in his brain, and he did not care if he maimed Toresen. Damn the consequences.

Toresen was dazed by the blow on the chin, but not too dazed to see Kline's boot coming. He rolled aside, and Kline's heel jarred on the steel deck. The red mist was thicker for that pain.

'I'll get you, you Limey bastard. If it's the last thing I do I'll get you.'

Toresen was up again, shaking the fog from his senses. He swung a long, looping right at Kline that announced its coming a mile off. Kline, the old campaigner, saw it and moved his head a fraction so that the fist went over his shoulder and Toresen's bloody face was close against his own. Kline butted with his head again, this time at Toresen's face, not worried about the blood smearing his hair.

But Toresen could be a dirty fighter too when there was need for dirt. He brought his knee up hard into Kline's stomach. Kline gasped and went back against the mess-room sink. Toresen slammed him with a left and a right, and stood back to get his breath.

Kline hung on to the sink, spitting blood; and his hand went into the sink and found an empty whisky bottle that had been used for disinfectant. He gripped the neck and smashed the bottle on the tap behind him. Glass clattered into the sink, and Kline went at Toresen with the jagged, broken bottle in his right hand, jabbing at Toresen's face.

'Now we'll spoil your pretty looks. We'll make you so your own mother wouldn't know you.'

Toresen backed away, keeping his eye on the bottle. Kline's right arm flickered out like the tongue of a snake, like the dancing devil of a pinewood flame, in and out, in and out.

'Watch it, Limey, watch it!'

Toresen watched it. He had not said a word. He let Kline do the talking. The blood ran down from his nose and dripped from his chin; his shirt was slimy with blood. And he watched the bottle, knowing how mean Kline was, knowing that Kline would delight to jab the jagged edge of glass into his face, maiming and perhaps blinding him. So he watched the bottle and retreated slowly down the length of the mess-room.

Finally he could retreat no farther. He had run out of room.

Kline laughed harshly, and the bottle flashed under the electric light like a cut jewel. It slashed Toresen's chin, laying it open to the bone.

'That's number one, Limey. Just a start.'

Jaggers had become scared. It was all very well seeing the carpenter take a beating, but this was something different; this might have consequences that would involve him, Jaggers. If Toresen had his face sliced up with a broken bottle there would be questions asked as to why certain people had stood by and let it happen.

He put a tentative hand on Kline's shoulder. 'Now, Joe, that's enough. You've marked him. Call it a day.'

Kline knocked the hand away and snarled at Jaggers: 'You keep out of this or you'll get yourself marked too. I haven't finished with this guy — not yet, by Christ!'

Jaggers hopped back out of harm's way. If Kline had suddenly turned into a cobra Jaggers could not have been in more haste to get away from him.

'Well, I've warned you,' he said. 'There'll be trouble.'

'You're damned right there'll be trouble. There'll be trouble right here and now, and I'll be the boy to make it. I been pushed around by this big bear long enough.'

He moved in again and struck at Toresen's face, but Toresen was too quick; he shifted his head and the bottle smashed against the bulkhead behind him. Kline found himself with only the neck of the bottle in his hand. He tried to jab it into Toresen's eye, but Toresen gripped his wrist in a big, enveloping hand and stopped him.

Kline was wearing a plaited leather belt. Toresen's right hand went under the belt and he heaved Kline up on to his shoulder. Kline was no light weight, but Toresen made the operation look easy.

'See that,' Jaggers whispered. 'Just see that.' But he was not happy about things any more;

he had not meant it to work out this way.

Kline had only a hazy idea of what happened next. The mess-room seemed to whirl around him; he seemed to be flying through the air; then there was a hellish blow on the head, a streak of crimson light, and blackness like a hood falling over him.

Toresen looked down at Kline's senseless body lying on the deck of the mess-room, and dabbed at his bleeding chin with a cotton rag.

'Damn swine!'

Jaggers looked down at Kline also and pulled at his lower lip. He looked up from Kline to Toresen.

'You think he's dead?'

'Not him,' Toresen said contemptuously. 'He's got a head like a rifle bullet. Pour a bucket of water over him and he'll wake up quick enough. But maybe one day I will kill him. Maybe.'

'If he don't kill you first,' Jaggers said softly. 'He ain't going to love you any more after this.'

'He tried to blind me,' Toresen said. He saw that Kline was beginning to stir; in a moment he would wake up. 'I knew he was a bastard, but I never thought he was that much of a bastard.'

Kline's eyes came open but failed to focus properly; he was still dazed.

'From now on,' Toresen said, his voice grating, 'you steer clear of me and I'll steer clear of you. Maybe that way we'll both keep our noses clean.'

Kline's gaze ceased wandering and came to rest on the vast bulk of Toresen standing over him. Kline said nothing, but his eyes were wicked.

★ ★ ★

''The Little Russian' is lagging,' Rankin said. 'And there's one of His Majesty's ships gone to give her a talking to.'

Rankin and Brennan were on the poop, taking a little exercise by walking back and forth across a six-yard strip of deck. They could see the Russian ship with a destroyer alongside, a lean, rakish craft with a single, squat funnel and wicked-looking guns.

'What's the Russian for 'Put a snap in it'?' Brennan asked.

'Perhaps they just show the whip.'

'They've finished with her, anyway.'

The destroyer curved away from the Russian ship, rolling heavily, bow-wave curling over in a cascade of foam. She came round in a wide half-circle and resumed her station astern of the convoy. A black billow of smoke began to pour from the funnel of the

Russian, carried away on the wind like a gradually disintegrating banner of mourning.

'She understood,' Brennan said. 'She's doing her best to put on speed.'

Rankin said: 'If that's her best we could do without her in the convoy. They'll see that smoke as far away as Norway.'

He looked at the black smoke cloud drifting away to the south-east, and wondered when the first questing aircraft would come sweeping out from the Norwegian bases, from Trondheim and Bodö and Bardufoss and Tromsö. The airfields were there, all along the route; you could never get far away from them. You were caught between them and the ice; they were an inner arc within the arc of your journey. Banak and Kirkenes and at last Petsamo, in Finland, from which they struck at you, even within the haven of Murmansk.

'We need jokers like him,' Rankin said. 'Probably show lights too. Nice work.'

But the Russian was closing with the convoy again, and the smoke thinned. A flicker of Morse came from the Catalina, and a flutter of signal flags broke out from the halyards of every ship. A mine floated down the middle of the convoy, bobbing up and down as the waves passed under it. The ships avoided it, leaving a wide gap between that black, ominous-looking sphere and them-selves. When they had all drawn clear a corvette exploded it at a safe distance with machine-gun fire. The crackle of gunfire and the answering blast of the explosion were the first warlike sounds that had touched the nerves of the convoy. They were a reminder — if any such reminder were needed — that here was no easy security, that the price of safety was unceasing vigilance.

'All right in daytime,' Rankin said, 'but one of those playthings in the dark wouldn't be half so funny. One of them could make a nasty mess of this ship.'

'Careless of someone, leaving them lying about,' Brennan said. 'Somebody ought to be told. We've got enough trouble on our plates without stray mines.'

'You'd better tell Hitler.'

'There's a few other things I'd tell him if I got the chance. The best years of my life being wasted — '

'Come off it,' Rankin said. 'Don't give me any of that sob-stuff. You never were so well off. Regular pay, good grub, a bed to sleep in, nice suit of clothes — you never had it like that in Ireland.'

'All I want now is a good stiff dose of nerve tonic.'

'Well, you said you could do it.'

Just before nightfall the convoy altered course a few points to starboard, following the approximate line of the Norwegian coast that lay some five hundred miles away to the east, a coast invisible to them, yet menacing them with the threat of its presence. The days were shortening as they moved north, and at night the aurora borealis came to give a weird, unearthly illumination that was not like the sun or the moon, but like a monstrous fire burning below the horizon and throwing great bands of coloured flame across the dome of the sky. The ships moving forward under those ice-cold flames were like so many black coffins floating on the surface of a sea of molten lead. In that strange light men's faces looked pale and ghastly, as though they had all been corpses dug up from those same black coffins. It was easy then to believe in trolls and ice-monsters, and at the changing of the watch men spoke in low voices, half fearful of breaking that spell of silence that lay upon the sea and upon the moving ships.

The wind had dropped, and with it the temperature. Grant, doing the round of his guns, could feel the frost in the air. It bit at the exposed tips of his ears as he crossed the catwalk, reminding him that every revolution of the ship's propeller, every pulsation of the diesel engine was bringing them so much closer to the barrier of ice that reached down from the Pole, stretching as far south as Bear Island, that bleak tower of rock that reared itself out of the sea midway between the shores of Norway and Spitsbergen.

Grant paused half-way across the catwalk to look up at the streamers of the aurora swirling and twisting overhead, and it was at that moment that the first depth-charges went down. He could hear the steel sides of the ship drumming to the vibration of the explosions, shock-waves travelling through the water to beat against the vessel's plates with an urgent warning thunder. The rail under Grant's hand trembled slightly, and the sergeant felt his own pulse race suddenly and briefly before returning to normal. He had heard a hundred, possibly a thousand, depth-charges explode, yet each time there would come this brief racing of the pulse, this moment of excitement as the shock touched the ship and the ship gave its answering drum-roll of defiance. But it was always the first depth-charge of a voyage that had a special quality about it. It was like the first service in a tennis match: it opened the game; the ones that followed were only repetitions of the first, some louder, some fainter, as the distance varied, but not essentially different.

Grant peered into the shadow of the night, and could detect no sign of activity. The black outlines of the ships seemed motionless. He could see only one escort vessel, and that, too, was like a black charcoal mark, fixed, immovable, unchanging. Truly, there was nothing to indicate that this was the sea, that these were ships all moving forward at a constant speed; they might have been lightless houses scattered over a vast plain, sleeping with barred and bolted doors. Yet someone, somewhere, had heard an echo and taken no chances, but had attacked the sender of that echo.

Grant waited for a repetition. There was none. There had been the one attack, then silence, nothing more. Perhaps the Asdic operator had imagined the echo; perhaps he had forgotten what an echo really sounded like; perhaps it had been a shark or a sea-monster or a piece of wreckage floating below the surface. Grant shrugged his shoulders and moved aft along the catwalk.

★   ★   ★

The depth-charges woke Muller, and he lay in his bunk, staring up into the darkness of the cabin, trying to stop his hand from trembling. He heard Kline shifting in the

80

bunk below, and then Kline's hoarse voice: 'You awake boy?'

'Yes,' Muller said. 'I'm awake.'

'You know what that was?'

'I think so.'

'You bet so. Ash-cans. That's the start of it. Hell! they pick a fine time to start. Waking a guy out of his beauty-sleep.'

Muller heard Kline moving about, rummaging for something. Then there was a flare of light, flickering up and down and throwing grotesque shadows on the white-painted sides of the cabin. Muller's nostrils detected the rich odour of cigar smoke. It drifted upward, enveloping him in an aromatic screen. He lay there, tensing himself for the next explosion, only gradually relaxing as none came.

'Now whad'ya think?' Kline said. 'Was that genuine or was it just somebody couldn't sleep good and didn't want others to neither?'

Muller said nothing.

'I been figuring things out,' Kline went on. 'Tomorrow or maybe the next day we'll be out of range of them Cats. That's when we get another kind of follower — one with swastikas on the tail. Are you with me, boy?'

Muller did not answer.

'Hell,' Kline said. 'You passed out again already? The way some guys can sleep.'

Muller lay in his bunk, staring up into the darkness and waiting for the next explosion.

* * *

The depth-charges woke Jaggers also. Sweat came out on Jaggers's forehead, and there was sweat on the palms of his hands. He sat up, head a little on one side, listening. After a while he got out of his bunk and began to dress by the light of a blue-shaded bulb that he left burning all night in case of emergency. When he had finished dressing he lit a cigarette and sat on the edge of the bunk, smoking, trying to make up his mind. It would have to be done now while the sea was calm. That was if it were to be done at all. It took two cigarettes to bring Jaggers to a decision. Then he pulled on a coat and left the cabin.

Jaggers had expected it to be dark on deck, but when he had pushed his way through the stiff canvas black-out curtains he saw that the aurora was shedding its eerie luminosity over the ship. Jaggers cursed softly. It would have to wait.

* * *

At two o'clock in the morning Brennan stepped out of the poop deckhouse into a pitch-black night. The Northern Lights had faded, clouds had come up, thick and heavy, to blot out the stars, and there was no moon. It was the middle of Brennan's four-hour watch, and he had been into the mess-room for a cup of hot cocoa and a few swift drags at the charred butt of a cigarette which he had found in the pocket of his duffle-coat. Now he felt able to face the second half of his watch with renewed vigour, though it was the devil of a watch, this one from twelve to four; it found you at your lowest ebb and robbed you of the best period of sleep.

'Indeed it's a dark night,' Brennan muttered to himself as he hesitated by the poop rail, trying to get his bearings. 'If I was to take the wrong turning now, as the saying is, I might find myself well and truly in the drink. And that wouldn't be half the unpleasant experience, I'm thinking, with the weather turning as cold as a shoulder of frozen mutton. Now, where would that blessed catwalk be getting itself to?'

Brennan moved along the rail and heard a sound below him. He stopped and listened, peering down over the rail. It had sounded like the clank of a bucket, but who would be moving around with buckets at this time of a dark, cold, miserable night? Brennan, his eyes gradually becoming accustomed to the darkness, could just make out two shadowy figures moving on the deck below him.

'Who the devil's that?' he called.

The figures stopped moving, as though Brennan's voice had petrified them. Behind him Brennan could hear the *tonk-tonk-tonk* of the diesel exhaust coming from the funnel; he could hear the faint hiss of water running along the ship's side, and the low whine of a breeze that might grow to a wind and even into a gale, but was at present no more than a cold breath flowing over the ship. Apart from these sounds, Brennan could hear nothing. It was a quiet night. Hours had passed since the depth-charges had shaken men from sleep and set the blood racing, and there had been no more. Now there was only the darkness and the cold flowing out of the night. And where were the other ships? Brennan could not see them. How did you keep station now? By instinct perhaps, by a sixth sense developed by ship's officers to cope with just such situations as this.

Brennan leaned over the rail and called again to the shadows below him. 'Who's that? What are you doing down there?'

There was no answer, and Brennan's curiosity was aroused. 'I'll find out just what's going on,' he said. 'I'll come down and see for meself.'

It was the bosun's voice that came suddenly out of the shadows below. Brennan, deceived by the darkness, had not realized that the man was so near.

'Just a little job that me and one of the hands is seeing to. No need to worry yourself, Paddy. It is Paddy, ain't it?'

'A fine time to be doing a job of work,' Brennan said. 'Time to have your head down, I'd say. What kind of a job is it that won't wait till the morning?'

'Just a matter of tightening up, as you might say. Have to see to these things when they need doing, dark or no dark. No rest for the wicked.'

Brennan thought he heard the other man give a snigger at that, but he could not be certain. It was a funny business. What could need tightening up at two o'clock in the morning? It was not as if there had been any rough weather to work things loose. The sea was pretty smooth; if it had not been so that part of the deck where Jaggers was standing, would have been slopping with sea-water. It was a funny business altogether, but it was nothing to do with Michael Brennan. He had his own job to do. He thought he heard a bucket clink again, but that also might have been imagination. He could just make out the pale oval of the bosun's face staring up at him. He and the other man seemed to be waiting for Brennan to go away before they went on with their work.

Jaggers said: 'You be getting along to your gun now, Paddy. And keep a sharp look-out for those Jerry planes, there's the boy.'

'There won't be any tonight,' Brennan said. 'Too dark.'

But he was getting cold standing there, and it was no business of his, none at all, so he left them to it and groped his way along the after catwalk and along a dark alleyway, and up a ladder and then another ladder, until he came at last into a dark gun-box; and there he settled himself for two more long, slow hours of watch-keeping.

And by the time the watch was over he had forgotten all about the bosun and jobs that had to be seen to in the middle of the night.

5

First Blood

The clash between Kline and Toresen might have had more repercussions if it had not been for the fact that everyone, from Captain Henderson downward, had more important matters to think about. For they were five days out from Loch Ewe, and the Catalina, that last brittle link with home, had left them.

Now they were alone and must fight their own fight without air cover of any kind, relying only on their guns and their resolution to see them through.

The cloud had thickened, pressing down upon them; and the grey ships moved forward at their slow, regular speed, their progress indicated only by the white break of water at the bows, and the ripple astern. 'The Little Russian' lagged and was spurred on by a destroyer, and poured out black smoke and struggled back into position; and the convoy went on in its compact, geometrical pattern, with the outriding warships searching the cold depths for echoes and the horizon for enemy planes.

But the day passed without incident, without even the tremor of a depth-charge. They went on unmolested over a gently heaving sea, and a thin, hard snow fell on the decks and lay there, not melting. From horizon to horizon there was nothing but the sea and the ships that appeared to be scarcely moving, as though the chess game in which they were the pieces had been abandoned on the board just as it had been at the last move, as though this were a nightmare journey in which they could make no progress but must remain just as they were until the last day of eternity.

'Too good to last,' Kline said to Muller. 'They're lying doggo till we're properly in the trap. Then — wham! You'll see.'

Muller feared so too. Everyone feared so. There seemed to be a thread of tension running through the ship, an expectation of something building up, unseen, unheard, but there, just below the surface of the sea, just beyond the rim of the horizon, something.

'Damned if I don't wish they'd come,' Rankin said. 'So we could get shooting.'

'They'll come soon enough,' Grant said. 'Don't worry.'

'I'm not worrying.'

'You must be bloody well unique then,' Grant said.

Mr Thouless was tense. Henderson could see it in him, and he wondered just how long a man could go on at such a fever pitch.

'Why don't you relax, Tom — just for a minute or two now and then? You'll wear yourself out.'

'Me?' Thouless appeared genuinely astonished. 'I'm not likely to be worn out. Got to keep on your toes.'

Henderson felt that Thouless kept too much on his toes, never seemed able to keep still, jerking about from one place to another. He seemed to have an electric charge inside him. Henderson wondered how much sleep Thouless was getting. About one thing there could be no doubt; the mate's appetite was good; he never missed a meal and never failed to do justice to one. Perhaps that was because his nervous energy burned up the calories. Certainly, no amount of food ever seemed to make him any less lean and hungry-looking.

'If I didn't keep on the tail of that bosun,' Thouless said, digging up the regular grouse, 'God knows what work would ever get done on board this ship.'

'We'll get rid of him next trip.'

'It's not the next trip I'm worrying about,' Thouless said.

It seemed to him that Jaggers was getting worse; you had to watch him the whole time. Thouless felt that fate was dealing with him unkindly. With a crew such as the *Rosa Dartle* was carrying you needed a bosun like that American, Carson; there was a proper man. But instead of a proper man he was stuck with Jaggers, a lazy, good-for-nothing belly-acher, if ever there was one. And Thouless believed Jaggers was getting liquor from somewhere — perhaps he had smuggled some on board in Glasgow. Twice he had noticed a bloodshot look in Jaggers's eyes, a slight slurring of the speech; twice he had seen Jaggers stumble on the deck when there had been no reason to stumble. Thouless himself was an abstemious man and he despised drunkards. If Jaggers had any liquor on board and Thouless got his hands on it it would not be long before it was over the side.

'I'll keep my eye on him,' Thouless muttered. 'I'll certainly keep my eye on that pot-bellied swine.'

Jaggers felt Thouless's eye on him as though it were a needle sticking into his back. There seemed to be no getting away from the mate.

And Jaggers was afraid. When he passed along the catwalk he would peer nervously down at the grey-painted deck below him and think of the explosion there would be if a torpedo struck the ship. And then Jaggers would hurry off the catwalk to the poop or the forecastle or the bridge deck, where perhaps it might be a little safer. Perhaps.

'Damn them all!' he cursed. 'Damn them all to hell!'

★ ★ ★

On the sixth day they altered course again and headed east-north-east, and on that day the flying-boat found them. It found them soon after daybreak, coming with the cold grey light that filtered through the cloud cover, not closing with the convoy but staying just beyond the range of the guns, looking them over as a butcher might look over a herd of cattle destined for the slaughterhouse.

Sergeant Grant was in his cabin smoking a cigarette when the insistent clamour of the alarm-bell began drumming in his ears. Grant did several things in very rapid succession: he stubbed out the cigarette, flung an Arctic coat over his battle-dress, seized a steel helmet and a lifejacket, and dashed out of the cabin.

His action station was on the starboard-bridge Oerlikon, and it was to that point that he was moving with all the speed at his command. Racing across the catwalk, he had no time to observe where the enemy aircraft might be; his one object was to get to the gun. He had a hazy impression of other men running; he bumped into someone at the end of the catwalk, and saw that it was Toresen. 'Now's your chance,' Toresen said, and stepped aside to let him pass. He climbed one ladder, then another, and came to the bridge, saw Captain Henderson was already there, and went out on to the wing and into the gun-box with Michael Brennan.

He was panting with the sudden exertion, and he gasped out the important question: 'Where are they?'

Brennan pointed to the black outline of the aircraft, low down, away on the starboard bow. 'There she is.'

Grant leaned against the side of the gun-box, getting his breath back. 'Only one?' He had expected a mass onslaught, the sky dark with aircraft, and there was only this one, far off, out of range. It was an anti-climax. 'Only one?'

'There'll be some more,' Brennan said. 'Now they've found us there'll be some more all right.'

Grant began to complete his dressing. He pulled a Balaclava helmet out of the pocket of his coat and put it on; he found a scarf in the same place and wound this round his neck.

He put the steel helmet over the Balaclava and the lifejacket over the coat; he slipped his hands into a pair of wool-lined gloves. There was no telling how long it would be before he would be able to leave the gun, and the wind had ice in it.

'I'd like to be able to think you're wrong, Paddy. But, by God, I think you're right.'

He took the binoculars from Brennan and examined the plane through them. It was unmistakably a Blohm and Voss Ha 138, the outline of the engines visible above the high wing, three Junkers Jumo diesel engines, the slab of the hull below, and the tail-plane supported high on twin booms, so that it would clear the water when the flying-boat landed. This aircraft, with its long range, was well suited to the job of convoy shadowing; it could stay in the air for hours without refuelling. It could keep them in sight and send out its radio messages with clockwork regularity, while the ships, lacking fighter cover, could do nothing to harm it.

Grant had seen this sort of thing before. You stood to your guns and watched the plane going round and round and round, just outside the range of gunfire. And all the time you knew that the radio signals were going out, giving your position to bomber aircraft, to submarines, to surface raiders. The flying-boat was a marker you could not shake off.

'He'll keep in touch,' Brennan said. 'I think he likes the company.'

Grant nodded. 'But it's a one-sided liking.'

★   ★   ★

Petty Officer Rankin had his crew closed up on the twelve-pounder, and the gun cleared away. And there they waited, gradually becoming cold and bored, shuffling their feet on the packed snow, beating their hands, longing for a smoke. Rankin had difficulty in keeping them alert, ready. They had all come running fast enough at the sound of the alarm bells, but now, as the time crept away — half an hour, one hour, two hours — and nothing happened, they became increasingly impatient, grumbling, cursing the circling aircraft and the men inside it.

'Come nearer. Just a little nearer. We'll let you have it then.'

But the Ha 138 knew a trick worth two of that. It went round in a wide circle, now at the head of the convoy, now at the tail; now on the starboard side, now on the port; and the beat of the Jumo engines came faintly across the steel-grey water, rising and falling, as though mocking the watchers in the slow grey ships.

One of the men took a piece of chalk out of his pocket and marked on the base of a shell: 'To Adolf, with love and kisses.'

'Weak-minded bastard,' Rankin said. 'Do you think Hitler is coming out here to be shot at? He'll be safe in Berchtes-bloody-garden.'

But he left the inscription on the shell. Perhaps it was a boost to morale, like those slogans chalked on troop trains: 'Berlin or Bust,' 'Adolf Hitler, Here I Come,' and 'Jerry, We're on the Way'; like that song about hanging out the washing on the Siegfried Line. Only that one had misfired — pretty badly.

Rankin swung his arms in an attempt to warm himself. The wind was not strong, but it was bitterly cold. Spray was freezing on the rigging, giving it a white, ghostly look. Before long the destroyers and corvettes would be having trouble with ice. Too much collecting on their decks and upperworks could make them top-heavy, liable to turn turtle in a heavy sea. The ice had to be chopped off, and that was no pleasant job. With the merchant ships an upper coating of ice was no danger; it would take more than that to make them top-heavy. But the ice was treacherous underfoot; it could cause the breaking of a limb.

Rankin swung his arms rhythmically, their movement hampered by the thick clothes and the bulky lifejacket he was wearing. He had heavy leather sea-boots on his feet, with two pairs of knitted sea-boot stockings, but his feet were cold nevertheless. Yet he knew that it would be colder than this. He moved his toes inside the boots, trying to get the circulation into them. He stopped swinging his arms and went to the gun. He tested the traversing and elevating gear. The gun-barrel moved with a glutinous sound, like half-set glue giving way reluctantly.

'Stiff,' Rankin said. 'Too stiff.'

He wondered whether he ought to put some paraffin in the gears. The gun would be a useless bit of iron if it became frozen into immovability. Perhaps he would consult Sergeant Grant on that point. Rankin had complete faith in Grant's judgement; he was glad that Grant was in charge of the armament, and not that fellow Wilfer, who had been killed in Philadelphia. In some ways, Rankin thought, that accident had been a stroke of luck. He would not have wished such a thing on Wilfer, but for a tight corner Grant was his man. And this looked very much like a tight corner.

He swung the gun in the complete arc of its fire, and the grease gave way gummily. Maybe it had better have some paraffin.

* * *

The American seamen stood in a little huddle on the poop of the *Rosa Dartle* and watched the plane performing its leisurely circuit. There was no likelihood of their being needed to fire the four-inch gun, since the only purpose of that ancient weapon was to engage attackers floating upon the surface of the water. It could be elevated only far enough to give trajectory to a long shot, and an aircraft would have had to be flying very low and very slowly for such a shot to stand any chance of hitting it. In fact, the odds against such a hit were probably several millions to one.

Therefore, strictly speaking, there was no point in the Americans going to their action station, since they would not be called upon to use the gun; but they had gone there because they could think of nothing better to do. The poop was as good a place as any from which to observe what was going on. Nobody felt like staying in his cabin when the ship was likely to be attacked at any moment, and though, as the hours passed, they became gradually colder and the attack appeared less and less imminent, they still could not drag themselves away from that circular steel platform where the four-inch stood on its pedestal, pointing a thick finger at the ship astern.

Kline said hoarsely: 'Why don't they get after that kite? For God's sake, why don't they?'

'What with?' Carson asked. 'You think they got wings?'

Kline kicked the packed snow with the toe of his boot, expending his venom on the inanimate substance under his feet.

'Hell, I don't know. They oughta do sumpin'. They just let him fly round like he owned the place.'

'Maybe he does. Maybe he won it in a game of poker.'

'You bein' funny?'

'You bring out the clown in me,' Carson said. 'Maybe it's the face.'

Kline stared at Carson and his hands swung loose at his sides. He had a lump like a door-knob on the back of his head and he was bitter as gall. He gave another vicious kick at the snow.

'I don't go for that kind of clowning.'

'Okay,' Carson said. 'So you don't go for it.'

He stared back at Kline, his eyes hard. He

was glad Toresen had slammed this man down. Perhaps he would have to slam Kline too, slam him good and hard, just to teach him, once and for all, who was the boss. But not now, not just now. There were other things at this moment. He shrugged his shoulders and looked away at the circling plane.

Muller said: 'I have to go below. I'll be right back.'

'That kid,' Kline said contemptuously. 'That's the third time he had to go for a leak. He's scared.'

'Who ain't?' Carson said. 'And maybe it's the cold at that. Damn near froze myself. Could be the cold.'

'Could be, but it ain't. He's scared.'

'So am I,' Carson said. 'If I had me a hole to dive into, I'd be in it right now. There just don't happen to be no hole, that's all.'

Muller wished he could stop shivering. He wished he had something to do, something to occupy his hands and his mind so that he did not have to keep thinking of that black plane circling round and round, and of the other planes that must surely come — soon, very soon now. Perhaps when it started it would not be so bad; perhaps it was the waiting that was the worst part. But he did not really believe that. And he went on shivering.

The eerie thing about it all was the quietness. Apart from the diesel exhaust and the faint whining of the wind, there was no sound except the variable drone of the Jumo engines. All those other ships were moving quietly forward as if the threat were not there, as if by ignoring that threat they could make it fade away into nothing. Yet they must all know that somewhere to the south on frost-bound airfields men had been busy preparing the planes. Somewhere the pilots and navigators and bomb-aimers had received their briefing, the engines had roared into life, and the great wings had carried them up and away, out over the cold grey sea from which no fallen flyer was likely to be drawn alive. Even now, Muller thought, just below the rim of the horizon, those planes might be approaching. How many? Ten — twenty — fifty — a hundred? Muller shivered again and went back to the four-inch gun.

★ ★ ★

They came just at the moment when Tarbat was about to dish up the dinner. Tarbat swore very luridly, clapped a steel helmet on his head, shrugged himself into a lifejacket, and padded to the door of the galley with a carving-fork in one hand and a ladle in the other, as if with these weapons he thought he might either spear the soft under-bellies of the attackers or beat them over the head until they fell, stunned, into the sea.

'Just what you'd expect,' Tarbat grumbled. 'Coming at meal-times. No manners.'

The galley-boy, a pale, stringy youth with hair like tow, followed Tarbat, peering between him and the doorpost, using the heavy, bulky figure of the cook as a shield. The galley-boy's teeth were chattering; he put his right fist in his mouth to stop the castanet-work of his jaws. He did not realize he was biting his hand until he tasted the blood on his tongue. He took the fist out of his mouth and stared at the blood stupidly.

Tarbat said: 'God Almighty! There's some of 'em!' And he prodded the galley-boy with the carving-fork to draw his attention to the German planes.

The boy gave a howl and ran back into the galley and hid under a bench.

'That won't do you any good,' Tarbat said. 'You can't hide yourself from this lot.'

They came in two waves, with fifteen in each wave. The Heinkels came in first and the Junkers followed. They came in low with a resolute purpose, and the gunfire maimed but did not deflect them. They came in from the starboard side, from the south, fast, hoping to surprise the defence; but they found the ships ready, the guns ready. They came in on a broad path of fire and steel, in through the glitter of the shellbursts and the puffs of white smoke that hung like heads of thistledown under the leaden roof of the clouds.

One faltered and fell, spinning like a sycamore leaf. Another exploded suddenly, burst into fragments, into a black gush of smoke and a red blossom of flame, out of which the bodies of men hurtled on their last journey, men who would need no coffin.

But the others pressed on, on and over the convoy and away on the port side, climbing and separating, each now a unit independent of the others, each a target to draw the fire of the guns, to fly in and away, and wait and come in again.

And 'The Little Russian' was hit, straddled by bombs and hit in the forward hold. Billows of smoke hid the bridge, but for a while even so she held on, held her place at the corner of the square, in the compact defensive formation of the ships, out of which the glittering, bursting steel and the fire and the tracer came hissing and whining up into the sky. But another bomb struck her abaft the funnel, and the funnel toppled like an old tree in a storm, and 'The Little Russian' drifted away to starboard, away out of line with her speed slackening and the smoke coming thicker and blacker, with crimson streaks of fire and a flickering cascade of sparks, a column of smoke reaching up to touch the low roof of clouds, joining the clouds and the sea like a prop between the earth and the heavens.

And 'The Little Russian' lay over on her starboard side and was almost hidden by the smoke: and she went in a sudden burst of glory, in a flaming, racketing splitting apart of decks and hull and engines, a dissolution of what had been a composite machine, dreamed, designed, and constructed, into nothing but fragments of churned-up metal and glass and timber, of wire and rope and canvas and the slime and pulp and ultimate degradation of men's bodies. So 'The Little Russian' was lost to them, was the first to go; and she went completely and finally, went in thunder and lightning as a god might go, leaving no trace and no survivor.

★ ★ ★

Sergeant Grant had got his sights on to a Heinkel 111 coming in obliquely across his line of fire. He lay back on the harness of the Oerlikon and moved the barrel smoothly,

103

without jerking, stepping with sure feet on the floor of the gun-box and waiting for the exact moment when the plane would be close enough and yet not too close. The Heinkel was a black silhouette crawling on the wires of his cartwheel sight, a black spider in a metal web, caught there by the skill of the man behind the gun, the man with his eye to the rubber eyepiece and his fingers on the firing-lever, waiting for the moment.

All around him Grant could hear the dreadful cacophony of the struggle — the thunder of aircraft engines, the fierce crackle of machine-gun fire, the intermittent blast of the twelve-pounder, the steady, regular beat of a Bofors, the hideous music of a Vickers pom-pom from one of the warships, and the thin, distracting shriek of falling bombs; he heard all these sounds blending into one conglomeration of sound that was an assault upon the eardrums; yet his mind was closed to it all, so that for him there might have been no sound, might have been nothing but himself and the Oerlikon and the Heinkel, the man, the gun, and the aircraft, a trio enclosed in a small, exclusive world of their own, into which nothing else could enter, beyond which nothing was of any importance.

Grant watched the silhouette on the radial wires of the sight and kept it flying towards the centre of the circle, always towards the centre. He judged the moment and pressed the firing-lever, and the sight jumped and vibrated, and a spurt of flame came out of the muzzle of the Oerlikon. The breech mass was thrust back by the force of the explosion and the empty shell-case was flung into the bag under the gun and another round went into the chamber and was fired. And all this happened in the space of one-eighth of a second and went on happening.

The rests of the gun shuddered against Grant's shoulders and the sight vibrated like a plucked wire and became useless; and through the smoke Grant watched the Heinkel, and saw his tracers mounting towards it in a stream of glowing points of white fire, a dotted line printed upon the dark page of the sky.

And suddenly the gun stopped firing; suddenly it failed to respond to the pressure on the firing-lever, and was silent: dead, useless metal in the hands of the gunner.

Grant cursed the gun. He was certain that the magazine could not yet be empty; therefore there must be a stoppage, and this just at the critical moment. The Heinkel was away, had escaped, would hide in the clouds and come in again. And the gun had a stoppage.

Grant went through the stoppage drill, and the gun remained stopped. Something inside it must have broken, some piece of mechanism made in an English factory had let him down at the moment of stress a thousand miles away in the Arctic.

He began to strip the gun, keeping his gloves on at first, but when he was unable to manipulate the intricate parts with gloved hands he pulled them off, ignoring the agonizing cold.

The noise around him went on, and he ignored that too, crouching down in the gun-box and searching for the one weak part of the gun that had let him down when he most needed not to be let down.

He worked swiftly and methodically, with Brennan to help him, and the gun disintegrated under his hands, breaking down into its components. He laid the components out neatly on a sheet of canvas so that they could be gathered up easily when the time came for reassembly.

And then Mr Thouless interfered.

Thouless, busy with other things, had not noticed at first that the starboard Oerlikon had ceased firing. When he did notice it, the gun was already lying spread out in large and small pieces on the sheet of canvas. With so much going on in the way of gunning and bombing and general frightfulness, it seemed to Mr Thouless's orderly mind that this was about the most inappropriate moment that could possibly have been chosen to strip down an anti-aircraft gun.

He moved to the wing of the bridge with his springy stride and the intention of telling Grant so. Grant did not see the mate approaching; he was crouched down with his back to the opening in the gun-box, and he was very busy and his fingers were frosted. If Thouless had known anything of the state of Grant's mind he would have realized that this was not the time to offer any kind of interference in the sergeant's particular department.

But Thouless did not know. He said: 'What in God's name, man, do you think you're doing?'

Grant did not answer, did not so much as turn his head. Thouless came closer, resting his hands on the side of the gun-box and looking down at the bewildering array of Oerlikon parts laid out at his feet. It looked to Thouless like a jigsaw puzzle that might take days to fit together; goodness knew how long that gun would be out of action, and the planes still coming in and the ship with her thousands of tons of volatile cargo waiting for the spark that should send them off in a rushing volcano of destruction. Here was the gun in pieces, and this man ignored him, crouched down there with his back turned, working methodically at the job, as methodically and calmly as if this had been an ordnance shop and not the high, windswept bridge of a ship at sea.

Mr Thouless said, his voice rising: 'Don't you know better than to take a gun out of action at a time like this?'

Sergeant Grant had found the trouble; it was a broken rocker, a little piece of dull-grey metal no bigger than a man's thumb, yet essential to the working of that intricate mechanism. It was a clean break across some flaw in the steel; the two pieces lay in the palm of Grant's hand, and he could see the striations on the face of the broken metal. Mr Thouless's voice was a jarring note, breaking in upon his thoughts, angering him with its irrelevance. He turned his head, staring at the mate, the two small pieces of metal still lying in his hand.

He said in a voice as frosty as his icy fingers: 'Get to hell out of it, and for God's sake don't ask stupid questions.' Then he turned his back on the mate again and snapped at Brennan: 'Get the box of spares. Get me a new rocker. Move.'

Mr Thouless's mouth opened to reply to

Grant's words. The colour had flared up in his pale face. The nerve of this man, speaking to him like that!

But then Thouless's mouth clamped shut and he stood back, watching Grant reassembling the gun. Grant, having made that one bitter remark, ignored Thouless. The gun seemed to grow under his hands, as if the parts were moving into place of their own volition.

The gun began to fire.

Mr Thouless walked away along the bridge. Perhaps he had been over-hasty; perhaps he ought not to have interfered. Nevertheless, the sergeant should not have spoken to him like that. It was rude — too damn rude. But the man knew his job. Mr Thouless could not help marvelling at the way that gun had seemed to grow together.

* * *

Rankin's ears were ringing from the blast of the twelve-pounder. The gun, with its thick, stubby barrel, made a phenomenal crack of an explosion. But it was a reassuring sound; it took the mind off the threatening roar of aircraft engines and the shrill whistle of bombs, of other unidentifiable noises that might be the presage of disaster.

Rankin kept his team going, ramming shells into the breech, firing, reloading, firing again. Smoke curled away from the muzzle of the gun, and the fumes of burnt cordite caught at Rankin's nostrils. He had no time to feel scared; there was too much to do. He chose his target and sent up his barrage. With the twelve-pounder there was not much chance of scoring a direct hit; you set all your fuses at a certain range, flung up as many shells as you could in front of the plane, and hoped that it would fly into the line of fire. It was a haphazard method, but it made a most heartening din. In the sky the shells burst with a sudden brief glitter, like the glint of sunlight on a fragment of tinsel; after that came the smoke, a greyish-white puff, swelling out into an ever-increasing ball until the wind caught it and tore it into shreds and tatters.

Rankin was so intent on throwing up his barrage on the starboard side that he did not see the Junkers 88 away to port tilting into its long dive on the ship. It was one of the ammunition supply numbers who saw it and hauled at Rankin's arm, yelling: 'Look! On this side. Look!'

When Rankin looked the plane had released its bomb and was pulling out of the dive, up and away. He could see the almost symmetrical wings and the long, forward-thrusting Jumo engines that made a line with the glass nose of the fuselage; he could see the dive brakes and the four bomb racks under the wings. And all this he saw in that swift moment before the bomb struck the water, before the *Rosa Dartle* shuddered at the explosion, and before a great fountain of sea-water cascaded down upon the twelve-pounder, drenching Rankin and the rest of the gun-crew in an icy shower.

The shudder ran through the ship as though she had been a dog shaking itself after a swim. She heeled over a few degrees to starboard and came back again slowly.

In the engine-room the noise was like thunder rolling along the steel plates, along the lines of rivets; it was louder than the sound of the engines, louder and far more ominous. The engineers looked at one another, looked up at the shining steel ladders that led away out of their metal dungeon to the freedom of the open deck above, looked at their lifejackets hanging ready, listened to the gradually decreasing thunder of the hull, then shrugged their shoulders and went on with their work. You had to forget about such things as the side of the ship bursting open and ice-cold water flooding in. If you had ever seen a rat in a wire trap dropped into a tank to drown, if you had ever watched its desperate struggles to break out of the cage, if you had seen the bubbles coming up from its jaws and the eyes bulging and the weakening spasms of the limbs until finally it lay in the cage without movement and without life, you had to forget all that too. If you could forget. You had to concentrate on the job in hand and forget all else, forget that above your head the guns were firing and the bombs were dropping, that this iron coffin of a ship was loaded with ten thousand tons of volatile alcohol, and that you were down in the bottom of the ship, caught there, trapped like a rat. You had to forget about the rat.

Henderson, on the bridge, his hands gripping the rail, was late in seeing the Junkers too. Only Bowie on the port Oerlikon saw it and fired at it and cursed it. But Henderson turned quickly as the bomb fell, twisting suddenly on his artificial leg so that the pain went up into the stump; and he saw the water spout and felt the shudder that was an ague in the bones of the ship; and he felt the ship heel over to starboard and right itself. And Henderson, who knew more about this ship than anyone else, who had gained much knowledge of ships in many long years at sea, wondered just how much damage that

112

bomb had done, that near miss which might so easily have been a direct hit if there had not been some slight miscalculation, perhaps some final moment of panic in the mind of a German pilot that had made him pull out too soon. And though the *Rosa Dartle* righted herself and went on without apparent harm, Captain Henderson still wondered; for that bomb had been very close, and there might be some damage that was not apparent to the eye, something that might manifest itself later at some critical moment, like the flaw in a small steel component of an Oerlikon gun.

'That was a nasty piece of work.'

Henderson turned and saw Thouless standing there, and Thouless's face was tense, the skin drawn tight over the nose; even the beard seemed to be electrified, each separate bristle standing out like a wire. Henderson almost expected to see sparks flickering at the ends of the beard.

'Just as you say, Tom. Very nasty.'

'You think it did any damage, sir?'

'Difficult to tell. Nothing apparently wrong. We must hope for the best.'

'It was close.'

'Too damned close. I should say we were rather lucky.'

'Don't know about luck. Too soon to talk about that.'

Thouless, like Henderson, was wondering what had happened below the waterline. The ship had taken an almighty wallop. Even if she had not been holed, she had had a beating. That bomb had rattled her plates more than any depth-charge — and depth-charges could do the devil of a lot of damage if they were too close. Thouless was concerned about it. He began to impart his concern to Captain Henderson. 'I'm wondering, sir — ' Then he stopped. Where was the use? Henderson did not appear to be worried; his big, weatherbeaten face above the coiled scarf was placid as ever. Not that you could ever tell what the Old Man was thinking; sometimes the eyes would twinkle, sometimes the mouth would twitch, but he did not give much away, not Frank Henderson.

Henderson's head was turned to him, slightly on one side, shoulders massive under the thick coat.

'Yes, Tom? You were saying — '

'Nothing,' Thouless said. 'It was nothing.'

★ ★ ★

The American seamen gathered round the four-inch on the poop had the best view when the second ship caught it. It was the ship immediately astern of the *Rosa Dartle*,

114

the ship with a deck-cargo of tanks. The bomb slanted down from a Heinkel and struck her aft of the bridge and just below the waterline. It went into number three hold and exploded in the cargo. It blew the covers off number three hatch and sent the heavy boards flying. It severed the wires holding some of the tanks to the deck and it burst open the bulkheads separating number three hold from the engine-room and from number four. It let the sea in, and icy water gushed over the hot engines and the firemen and the engineers. There was a blast of steam and shrieking, and a mad clawing for ladders, and some escaped to the deck, but others were caught in the stokehold or thrown against the moving shafts and pistons of the engines by the tide of water; and they did not get away.

The Americans did not know all this; they would not have desired to know. They knew only what they saw, and that was enough. They saw the ship lose speed and list to port and drift away to starboard as if out of control. They saw the list increase, so that soon the ship was showing the whole expanse of her decks sloping down to the water, and the gaping jagged hole that was number three hatch. They saw men running, clinging to handholds. They saw the tanks which had been released by the severing of their retaining wires slide down to the port side, to smash against the other tanks and build up a weight of iron against the bulwarks. The port rails went under; the masts and samson's-posts and funnel lay flat upon the water, and the entire starboard side became visible for a moment. Then the ship gave a heave and a roll, and the masts and samson's-posts and funnel had gone, and there was the keel showing above the surface like the black curved back of a whale, and round it a few dots that might have been men.

A destroyer came up fast with scrambling nets, and they saw three men or perhaps four go up those nets. And then the monstrous, almost obscene, bottom of the ship had gone, and there were only the floating pieces of wreckage remaining on the surface, the flotsam, the baulks of timber, smashed rafts, an oil drum, men's bodies.

The men watching from the *Rosa Dartle* reacted in different ways, according to their differing characters. Kline swore — obscenely, vividly, the foul words dropping from the side of his mouth in a continuous stream of blasphemy. Muller prayed, his lips moving almost soundlessly. He prayed as a frightened child might have done: 'Oh, God, don't let it happen to us. Oh, God, please don't let them get this ship. Oh, God, help us, help us.'

Carson muttered: 'Those poor devils!' And his jaw tightened and his face and eyes were bleak, but there was anger deep inside him that was not allowed to break out in words or action. Only his hands were knotted into fists and his cheekbones were like high mountains on the relief map of his face. The rest of the men were dumb, watching like cattle and saying nothing. For this that they saw might have been the pattern of their own fate, and those men whose frozen bodies lay in their useless kapok jackets, bobbing like dummies upon the surface of the waves, and those other men who had gone down in their iron coffin to the slime and the darkness that was never broken by the light of day, might be only the first, to be followed by others — tomorrow, or the next day, or the day after. And what man could tell who these others might be?

★   ★   ★

They were gone. Suddenly it was very quiet, a graveyard quiet. A stillness settled on the convoy, a hush like the hush of death. But the planes had gone, disappearing beyond the southern rim of the horizon. The entire action had taken less than half an hour and had seemed like a year. It had lasted less than half an hour, yet two ships had been sunk and five planes had been shot down; seventy-four men had died and a million pounds worth of cargo had gone drifting down to the bottom of the sea. It was not a negligible result for so brief an action.

But now the planes had gone, and the men in the ships were cleaning their guns, clearing away the empty shell-cases, reloading magazines, filling up the ready-use lockers, and making ribald jokes to keep their spirits up. For they knew that this was only the beginning; that there would be more to follow: more planes, more bombing, more ships sunk. And as they filled the magazines and greased the ammunition and fixed the Bofors shells in their clips of four, they wondered when the next visit would come, and how many there would be, and which ship was the next on the list. They snatched their food with the oil of the guns still on their hands and their faces, their cracked lips black with grime and their eyes bloodshot. They drank sweet, hot cocoa from thick mugs and counted the days still to be got through, and whichever way they counted, the path ahead looked long and dark and hazardous.

But on this day there were no more attacks. Only the Ha 138 continued to circle them, keeping watch. But as night fell this plane also left them, and they were alone on the dark sea, pressing forward, leaving the sunken ships and the wreckage of the fallen aircraft and the dead men, carrying with them only the memory like a drawing etched on the mind, fadeless.

Under cover of darkness the convoy altered course, heading farther north, farther from the coast of Norway and the aircraft bases, hoping thus to outwit the questing reconnaissance plane, hoping to slip through without further molestation.

But the men going on watch at midnight under the cold flames of the aurora had little hope that any such manoeuvre would succeed in throwing the enemy off the scent. Shivering in the Arctic night, they watched the swirling banners of green and rose and purple, waiting with gloomy foreboding for the new day.

6

Icarus

Morning found them moving through the ice. Sergeant Grant, doing his round of the guns, could see the ice stretching like an expanse of crazy paving around and between the ships, so that it seemed as though you could have walked from one to another. And, as always, there was that impression of motionlessness, the impression that none of these ships was moving, that they were all fixed in position on a board, pinned there like dead moths on a collector's card, and as incapable as the moths of altering their positions.

It was silent. There was no wind. The sea was calm; only an occasional undulation causing the ice to heave gently, as if something serpentine and monstrous lurked beneath that broken, greyish covering.

Brennan was on the starboard-bridge Oerlikon, huddled in a mass of clothing. He had been singing very softly *La Donna e Mobile*, but with different, rather obscene words. He had sung almost two verses before he realized what he was doing and pulled himself up with a jerk. 'There's words to be having on your lips, Michael, and you maybe due for the long journey. Sure, it's praying you ought to be, asking the blessed saints to be putting in a good word for you. You'll need the good words, Michael, you'll need them.'

Brennan heard Grant come into the box, and he shifted his head to look at the sergeant. Brennan's opinion of Grant had gone up several degrees since he had heard him tell the mate to get to hell out of it and not ask stupid questions. The mate, of all people. He did not know that Grant had apologized to Mr Thouless, that he had gone to Mr Thouless immediately they had been able to stand down from the guns, and had asked pardon for on overhasty remark.

Mr Thouless had looked surprised. He had not expected an apology, and he found difficulty in accepting it with good grace.

He said gruffly: 'Doesn't matter.'

'But it does matter, sir,' Grant said. 'I lost my temper. I shouldn't have done that.'

'Enough provocation,' Thouless said. 'Forget it.'

But Thouless himself did not forget it. He said to Captain Henderson: 'That sergeant's a good man.'

Henderson's mouth twitched at the corners as he looked at Thouless. 'Have you only just found that out, Tom? I could have told you as much weeks ago.'

Grant released the stop that held the Oerlikon gun in an upright position, and moved it up and down and from left to right. It moved a little stiffly, but not stiffly enough to affect the aiming. It would do. In such cold it was a wonder that everything did not freeze solid.

'Any news, Sarge?'

'Now what news would I have, Paddy?'

'Thought you might have heard when we're due to arrive in Archangel.'

'Not tomorrow.'

It was Grant's belief that they never would get to Archangel. Russian icebreakers were supposed to make a way for you through the White Sea, but would they? Grant had little faith in anything Russian. He believed that if they got to any port it would be Murmansk. They would be lucky to get there.

Brennan said: 'It's quiet. I never knew it so quiet.'

The only sounds were the tonking of the diesel exhaust coming faintly from aft and the mutter and tinkle of the ice as it slid past the sides of the ship. The bows opened a way through like a ploughshare going through earth; astern was a channel of clear water that gradually became covered again as the evidence of the vessel's passage was rubbed out. There was an eerie quality about that vast sea of ice, so still, so silent, with the apparently motionless ships spaced out over its surface. You could imagine that it would remain like this for ever, that there would be no escape; only this silent, petrified journey going on and on and on across the frozen wastelands of eternity.

One of the destroyers was refuelling from the fleet oiler, the two ships joined by a flexible pipe through which was flowing the oil that was the life-blood of the engines, without which the destroyer would be no better than a helpless hulk, a derelict moving only at the whim of wind and tide.

'Tricky job, that,' Brennan said. 'Looks easy from a distance, but you get close to and it's not so good.'

'It'd be a tough job in a storm.'

'Wouldn't be a job at all. It'd be an impossibility.'

Brennan swung his arms, slapping his gloved hands against his sides. 'Those trawlers are the boys now. Give 'em a shovelful of coal and they'll steam half-way round the world and cook with it as well. Don't get them singing out for oil as soon as they lose sight of land.'

'It's a wonder they stick it. In rough

weather you'd think they'd be swamped.'

'Not them,' Brennan said. 'These are home waters for them, as you might say. Come up here in peace-time, fishing. One boyo told me this convoy job was a cakewalk compared to the old trawling game. Easy, he said, easy.'

'Trawling must be fun,' Grant said.

It was cold. It was so cold you could almost sense the iron of the ship contracting, pressing in upon you, trapping you in a tiny, frozen cell from which there would be no release. A pale streak of sunlight glittered on a row of icicles hanging from the roof of the wheelhouse. Grant looked at the sky and made a mental note: four-tenths cloud, eight thousand feet. The sky between the clouds was a pale blue; it looked cold also, and pitiless. The clouds sailed past like great ships, galleons with billowing canvas. Must be some wind up there, Grant thought. It would be a cold wind too. And maybe there was snow coming, a nice thick blizzard. Perhaps you could hide in a blizzard.

'We gave them the slip,' Brennan said. 'We fooled them.'

'That's what you think. I wouldn't lay a bad shilling on the chance of your being right.'

'They won't find us up here,' Brennan said.

'It's just a stone's throw from the North Pole. Look at that ice.'

'Don't kid yourself, Paddy.'

Grant had just reached the end of the catwalk when the reconnaissance plane came up over the horizon. It came from the east; it had been searching in a wide arc, covering that area in which the convoy had to be because, though it could alter course, it could travel at no greater speed than the ten knots of the slowest ships, and that speed limited the range of manoeuvre. On such a clear, still day the aircraft's task had been simple. For the convoy there had been no way out.

In a series of short, urgent rings the alarm-bells were sounding. The crews ran to the guns, and it was the same as on the previous day, except that now there was the ice around them and some patches of blue sky, and now and then the pale glint of sunlight that had no power to warm their chilled and sleep-robbed bodies.

'Our dear friend,' Henderson said. 'Just couldn't keep away.'

'No friend of ours,' Thouless muttered. 'Why don't they give us a carrier? One fighter plane could deal with that damned follower in half a minute.'

'That, Tom, is a question for higher authority, for My Lords of the Admiralty.

Perhaps there are no carriers.'

'Damn bad management. Ought to have built more. Fault of the Navy. Never believed planes could sink ships till they saw it done. Hide-bound — always were.'

It was a relief to the feelings to put the blame on someone. The Admiralty was a good target, impersonal, a long way off. You could curse the Admiralty as much as you liked if it made you feel any better to do so, but it made no difference to the Ha 138 flying so leisurely beyond the range of the guns; it did not stop the flying-boat from sending out its signals to the bases in Norway, calling the vultures to the feast.

'They'll come just when I've got the dinner up,' Tarbat said. 'You'll see. Just like they done yesterday, the bastards.'

And Tarbat lit a new cigarette from the butt of the old one, and spilled tobacco ash in the dough, and swore at the galley-boy to keep the galley-boy's spirits up. 'They do it out of spite,' Tarbat said.

The galley-boy was shivering as if he had malaria. 'What's up with you?' Tarbat said. 'You ill or something?'

The boy sniffed and wiped his nose on his sleeve.

'Why don't you get a handkerchief?' Tarbat said severely. 'Unhygienic, that's what it is.'

Tarbat, with the cigarette dangling from his lips, and his stained and greasy trousers, was a great advocate of hygiene.

'I wish I was home,' the galley-boy whined, and he began to sniff again.

Tarbat blew smoke into the stew to give it flavour. 'You'll be home, son, one of these days. Keep your pecker up. We ain't dead yet.'

'I had a dream las' night,' the galley-boy said. 'I dreamt I was drownded. It was awful.'

'It don't do to take any notice of dreams. Look at Pharaoh's baker; see what happened to him. And all on account of believing in dreams. You ain't drowned, are you?'

'I might be — soon.'

'Get away with you,' Tarbat said. 'You'll never drown. The sea wouldn't take you. It'd spew you up again like a piece of bad meat. You'll hang one day, but you won't never drown — never.'

The galley-boy seemed unconvinced. 'It was ever so clear, that dream. There was waves as high as mountains, and wind too. But underneath it was calm, all green-coloured and cold. It went down for miles, and at the bottom it was black mud, and when you touched the mud it came up like smoke all round you. And there were the dead men with their eyes like white stones, and the mud going in and out of their mouths like they was smoking. And one of 'em said in a kind of hollow voice: 'Here he is. Here's the one we was waiting for'. And then he put his hand out and touched my arm, and there wasn't any flesh on the fingers, just bone, and cold as icicles.'

Tarbat planted himself in front of the galley-boy and laid a heavy hand on the galley-boy's shoulder and stared into his eyes.

'Cut it out, see?' Tarbat said. 'You forget all about that stuff. We don't want to hear no more about it. Nobody's going to get drowned — nobody.'

★   ★   ★

The convoy had moved clear of the ice when the attack came. It was a torpedo attack by float-planes, Heinkel 115's, and they came in in successive waves with three in each wave. They came in at less than a hundred feet, levelling off for the torpedo-dropping run, and when they had dropped the torpedoes they turned and climbed, their engines roaring in the attempt to draw clear of the deadly fire of the guns. Because of their low altitude and the necessity of levelling out and steadying themselves for the run-in, they were very vulnerable aircraft. But the torpedoes were killers.

128

It was one of the American ships at the head of the starboard column that took the first hit, but the ship did not die easily. She slackened speed and moved out of line as if suddenly tired of it all, and as the other ships went past her they could see the smoke writhing upward from her after-hatch and a fire-party with hoses pouring water into the hold.

Carson said: 'That's one of our boys.' And he watched the ship slide astern. He watched her for a long time, with the smoke coming from her and the gunfire, and he saw the second torpedo go into her, the one that was to finish the job. And Carson's jaw hardened, and he clenched his fists tightly, for this was an American ship with American seamen on board, and that made things different. It was one of his own.

Kline was moving about on the four-inch-gun platform, beating his hands and swearing. 'Jeeze, this is it again! This is it!'

And then Toresen appeared on the poop and yelled up at Carson: 'Hey, Steve, come down here a minute, will you?'

Carson went down, and Toresen said: 'The mate wants you to get some of your men into a fire party with me. Okay?'

'That's okay,' Carson said. 'But what's the idea? I thought the bosun was head of your fire-fighters.'

Toresen said: 'Jaggers isn't quite in the condition to fight any fires. Not at this moment.'

The fact was that when Mr Thouless looked for the fire party that should have been standing by, neither Jaggers nor any of the others were at their action stations. Only Toresen was there.

'Where's that bosun?' Thouless asked.

Toresen said: 'I think you'd better come and see for yourself, sir.'

Thouless looked sharply at Toresen. 'What d'you mean by that?'

But Toresen was not to be drawn. He shrugged his shoulders and repeated: 'Come and see for yourself.'

Mr Thouless went down aft, with the carpenter following him along the catwalk. Thouless felt like running; it was very exposed on the catwalk; but with Toresen at his back it would have been undignified to run. He walked rapidly, but with a strong effort of will avoided breaking into a gallop or even ducking his head.

The guns were making the very devil of a racket, and a fragment of metal dropped, whining, out of the air, hit the rail two feet ahead of Thouless's hand, and fell with a clang to the deck below.

'Nasty bit of shrapnel,' Toresen said; but

130

the mate simply grunted. He was in no mood for carpenter's small talk. Toresen grinned at Thouless's back, wondering how the mate would react to the sight of Jaggers.

They went into the after accommodation, and Toresen for one was not sorry to have cover over his head. There was altogether too much waste metal flying about for his taste, and even a splinter of spent shell falling out of the sky could give you a nasty jolt.

Thouless went straight to Jaggers's cabin and flung the door open. Jaggers was there right enough, lying at full length on his bunk, lying on his back with his stomach rising and falling rhythmically as he breathed. The breathing was noisy, stertorous, the breath hissing in and out of his slack mouth.

Mr Thouless's nostrils twitched. The cabin reeked. He stepped over to the bunk and slapped Jaggers's face. The snoring skipped a beat and then went on as before, but on a slightly different note.

'This man's drunk,' Thouless said, stating the obvious. 'Dead drunk.'

'That's what I meant, sir.' Toresen had come into the cabin behind the mate. He, too, was looking down at Jaggers. The expression on Toresen's face was one of contempt. Here was a fine way to sneak out of things: drink yourself unconscious and leave the work to others. That was the sort of way a louse like Jaggers would take.

Thouless gripped the bosun's tousled hair and jerked the head up. Jaggers had not shaved for several days and there was an embryonic beard sprouting from his heavy chin. The head came up under the pull of Thouless's hand, but the eyes remained closed.

'You won't wake him, sir,' Toresen said. 'He wouldn't wake for the trumpets of the Day of Judgement.'

Thouless let the head fall back on to the pillow and wiped his fingers fastidiously. 'Where'd he get the stuff? Did he bring it aboard in Glasgow?'

Toresen gave a grin. 'There's ten thousand tons of it under your feet, sir. Who'd notice a gallon or two out of that lot?'

Thouless's head came round and he stared at the carpenter. 'So that's the way of it. By God, I might have guessed as much. But when did he get it?'

'That's more than I know, sir. He didn't let me in on the secret; but there's been some dark, calm nights. Plenty of opportunity.'

Thouless's gaze was moving round the cabin. There was an enamelled mug lying at the foot of the bunk; it had obviously rolled there from Jaggers's nerveless hand. Near the bunk, standing on the floor and within easy reach, was a gallon can that had once contained turpentine. Thouless picked up the can; it was about half-full. He pulled the cork out and sniffed. There was a strong odour, but it was not turpentine. Thouless tipped the can and let the half-gallon of pale liquid run over Jaggers's face and body. Jaggers slept peacefully on.

'If I had my way,' Thouless said angrily, 'I'd drop him in one of the tanks and let him have a proper bellyful of the stuff. How many more of our lovely crew are like this?'

'I don't know, sir. You'd better look.'

'I intend to do so,' Thouless said.

He found two more men in the same condition as Jaggers and three others who were too far gone to be of any use. There was no more to be done at that moment except take the alcohol and pour it over the drunken men.

'Damn pigs. Let 'em wallow in it. But I'll make sure they get no more.'

It was Toresen who suggested enlisting Carson and some of his men for the fire party.

'Get him,' Thouless said. 'He's my man.'

★ ★ ★

The Heinkel came in from the starboard side, and Grant brought his hot gun to bear on it. The Heinkel was ahead of the *Rosa Dartle* and a long way off. Grant could not be certain at first that it was aiming at his own ship; it might have been going for the one in the outer column, a ship that should have been level with the *Rosa Dartle*, but for one reason or another had fallen back. When the Heinkel levelled out at little more than mast-height Grant was suddenly certain. This is it, he thought; this is our boy all right. And Brennan thought so too.

'You'd better get him, Sarge,' Brennan said. 'He's after our blood, and no mistake.'

Grant pushed up on the shoulder pieces of the Oerlikon, and the barrel went down, and the Heinkel drifted into the cartwheel, the massive floats hanging beneath it and the long 'greenhouse' on top. He gave a short burst at a thousand yards and was ahead of target. He brought the gun on again and gave a long burst at seven hundred, and saw the torpedo drop from the belly of the plane. It splashed white as it hit the water and came on, driving towards the path of the ship.

The Heinkel dipped its starboard wing and tried to climb, and a Bofors shell hit it below the port engine. There was a burst of flame and a banner of black smoke, and the port

134

wing sagged; the plane dropped and came round, dragged by the starboard engine. It came towards the *Rosa Dartle*, rapidly losing speed and height, with the smoke and flame tearing out of the port engine and the wing flapping.

Suddenly Grant knew that it was going to hit the *Rosa Dartle* and that nothing could stop it; against this threat the gun was useless.

Brennan knew it also. Watching the plane, fascinated by impending disaster, he forgot about the torpedo and failed to see it go past the bows in a flurry of foam, missing the ship by no more than the breadth of a man's hand.

But the Heinkel did not miss. For a moment it seemed as though it might do so; for a moment the nose came up as the plane struggled to gain height, and then both engines were dead and there was no more traction, no more power to pull clear.

The floats tripped on the starboard rails of the forecastle and were ripped off. They dropped into the sea and the fuselage of the aircraft ploughed on across the deck. The nose crashed into a ventilator pipe, turning it into a piece of crumpled iron, and the nose itself was crumpled like an eggshell beaten by a spoon. The tail of the machine tilted; it lifted high with the rudder flapping, and one wing swung round in a quarter circle until it was hanging over the foredeck like a monstrous diving-board. The tortured metal screeched once, and then was silent as the whole mass slid to a halt. Then there was nothing but the mutter of the flames eating at the port engine and a black cloud of smoke that half-obscured the wreckage.

The aircraft and the tanker were one now. The Heinkel had come to sink the ship and had fallen like a shot bird out of the frosty sky. Now it lay on the forecastle of the *Rosa Dartle* with broken wings and a fire eating into it. It had come to the end of its last flight and henceforth could move onward only at the slow ship's speed, dipping and rising with the unhurried dip and rise of the tanker's bows.

The Heinkel was dead, but even in death it could be lethal. The fire might spread, would most certainly spread if nothing were done to quell it. And a spreading fire in a loaded tanker could be the prelude to destruction.

Henderson was aware only too clearly of this fact as he looked down from the bridge. He turned to look for Mr Thouless. The mate must summon his fire-fighters; they must get on to the job at once; there was no time to lose if the ship were to be saved.

He need not have worried. When he looked

down again Mr Thouless was already on the catwalk; he was running towards the fire with a red, cylindrical canister in his hands. And behind him were Toresen, Carson, Kline, and Muller.

Mr Thouless did not care for the look of things. As he approached the forecastle the sound of the flames became louder; there was a savage, menacing quality about that sound. The flames were crimson against the black background of smoke, and the heat was melting some of the snow on the forecastle. A stream of water flowed towards the scuppers and froze before it could get there. As Mr Thouless came to the end of the catwalk he caught a glimpse of something inside the crumpled glass nose of the plane, then the smoke obscured it once more. Mr Thouless was not sorry to have that vision removed; it had not been a pleasant sight.

He tilted the fire extinguisher to set off the reaction, and pointed the nozzle at the heart of the flame. A jet of foam hissed at the fire.

Thouless yelled over his shoulder at Toresen: 'Get some more stuff on that engine. Hurry now before the whole damn lot goes sky-high.'

Toresen and the others needed no urging. More jets of smothering foam flowed over the engine of the Heinkel until it could not breathe. The fire sank and died, suffocated under the layer of foam. The smoke cleared, and the snow that had briefly melted in the heat hardened again to ice. The rudder of the plane flapped lazily as the ship rolled.

Then Mr Thouless noticed for the first time that there were two men standing on the other side of the wreckage, close to the angle of the bows where they had taken refuge from the flames. They were in thick flying-suits and their faces were blackened. They stood there staring at the plane, and then their eyes moved and came to rest on Thouless.

'Survivors. Goddam survivors,' Kline said disgustedly. 'Goddam Nazis!'

Mr Thouless stared back at the two airmen, hating them. Then he looked again at the nose of the Heinkel, and what he saw was no better the second time. He jerked his head in the direction of that crumpled wreck and said harshly: 'See what you can do about that, Chips.'

'That man's dead,' Toresen said.

Thouless swung round on him. 'I know that. I'm not expecting you to try artificial respiration.'

Toresen and Kline went to work with axes, and the man who had been an air gunner came out in pieces. Toresen had a strong stomach, but he felt queasy. Kline seemed unmoved.

'He had brains, that guy,' Kline said. 'You just take a look, you can see that. He had brains.' Kline put emphasis on the 'had', making a grim joke of it.

Muller stared at the scarlet splashes on the glass of the Heinkel's nose, and the grey pulp, and a hand severed at the wrist. And Kline could joke about things like that!

Muller turned away. He looked at the two men who had crawled alive out of the wreckage, and he felt dazed. It occurred to him suddenly that there was no longer any noise, no roar of aircraft engines, no gunfire. He looked up at the sky, and there were only the clouds drifting past; he looked at the sea, and there was only the gentle heaving of the water; he looked up at the bridge, and saw Sergeant Grant and Brennan cleaning the Oerlikon. His gaze came back to the wreckage, to the two men in the bows, to the obscenity that Toresen and Kline were dealing with, and he realized that for the moment it was over, that the ship had escaped.

But there seemed no reality in it: it was a dream, a nightmare; you could not escape; you were held prisoner in a web stretching from horizon to horizon; it was a nightmare from which there was no awakening. As if drawn by an attraction he could not resist, his eyes returned again to that mangled object that had been a man. He turned suddenly, stumbled to the starboard rails, and was sick.

Mr Thouless approached the two men in the bows. One of them, with an effort that was painfully obvious, drew himself to attention, heels together, chin up.

'Lieutenant Mohr.' His voice was sharp, nervous, with a certain overtone of hysteria. There was so much black oil on his face under the leather flying-helmet that it was difficult to tell how old he was. But the voice was boyish. It seemed strange to Thouless to be so close to these men. Aircraft were impersonal things; you seldom thought about the men inside them. You shot down the plane, not the men; you endowed the machine with the qualities of a human being and you thought of it as someone old and cunning and infinitely wicked. And then a boy stepped out of it.

'You speak English?' Thouless said.

Lieutenant Mohr shook his head, but the other man said: 'I do. My name is Fehler.'

'You are lucky to be alive,' Thouless said.

Fehler smiled. Thouless could see the white line of the teeth. 'Lucky? A matter of opinion, perhaps.' He looked aft along the deck of the tanker, along the steel pipes and the girders. 'A reprieve, but for how long?'

Mr Thouless said: 'For a long time, we hope. Were there any others in the plane?'

'None. Only what you see.' He nodded towards the dipped nose of the Heinkel, the twisted framework, and the mystery of life that had changed to the mystery of death. His mouth twitched and his eyes clouded. 'Only what you see.'

The other man who had given his name as Mohr turned suddenly and spoke to Fehler in German. To Thouless it seemed that there was a peremptoriness about the words. It was as though Mohr were in the habit of giving orders and in the habit of being obeyed.

Fehler said with an almost imperceptible lift of the shoulders and an almost imperceptible note of mockery in his tired voice: 'Lieutenant Mohr demands to see your captain. At once.'

'Tell him,' Thouless said, 'that he will see Captain Henderson when Captain Henderson chooses to see him.'

7

Graveyard Watch

Henderson did not choose to see Mohr and Fehler until night had fallen on the convoy. Until then there were too many other matters requiring his attention. From his position on the bridge he could see the tail of the Heinkel sticking up from the forecastle with the evil badge of the swastika painted on it.

'There's a fine flag to be sailing under,' Henderson muttered. 'If I was superstitious I might be inclined to think no good would come of it. But of course I'm not superstitious any more than Tom Thouless is.'

Superstition or no superstition, there was bad weather coming. It had been calm for two days, but Henderson had seen the glass falling and had felt the wind freshening on his face, and knew that the calm was past. Henderson knew the kind of weather that could hit you in these latitudes, and he did not like the signs. He had not forgotten the shock of that bomb which had fallen so close. There was nothing apparently wrong with the ship, but when you ran into a gale weaknesses had a way of showing themselves — in ships as well as in men.

There had been signals between the *Rosa Dartle* and the escort commander, Aldis lamps flickering across the intervening stretch of water.

'Congratulations on catching one alive.'

'Two in fact.'

'Look after them.'

'I will keep them on ice.'

When Mohr and Fehler came to his cabin Henderson saw that they had shed their flying-suits and had cleaned themselves. They now appeared as two very young men, having about them none of that evil aura that seemed to belong to the aircraft in which they flew. The mask had been taken away, and in losing it they seemed to have shrunk, to have been reduced to human proportions. Their youthfulness produced in Henderson a momentary stab of envy. They were no more than boys. How was it possible that such as these could cause so great a fear?

Perhaps it was the recollection of that fear which put the harshness into Henderson's voice as he sat behind his desk staring at the two Germans.

'Which of you is the one who speaks English?'

Fehler said: 'I am. I studied at Oxford for a time.'

'You did, eh?' Henderson gave his full attention to Fehler. He saw a slim, dark-haired boy with a rather prominent nose and velvety eyes. Might have supposed him to be a Jew, Henderson thought, if that had not been out of the question; no Jew would be flying in a Nazi plane, at least, one would not have supposed so. There was a good-humoured twist to Fehler's mouth; he looked friendly; he had none of the sullen resent-ment that was so obvious in the other man's face. Henderson felt that he could have liked Fehler; but all the while he could sense Thouless's presence behind him; Thouless hating both the Germans, hating everything that they stood for, unable to make any allowances. I was never much good at hating, Henderson thought; never seemed worth while. But Tom hates their guts.

Mohr especially had roused that hatred in the mate. It was his arrogance that did it. One might have supposed the ship was being honoured by his presence, that the officers and crew were hotel lackeys whose duty it was to wait on Mohr and obey him. He had marched into Henderson's cabin with his shoulders back, his head up, and a faint sneer of disdain tugging down the corners of his

144

mouth. He had come to attention with as much of a click of the heels as one could manage in flying-boots, had shot out his right arm in the Nazi salute, and had barked: 'Heil Hitler!'

Henderson had to look down at his desk to hide the smile on his face; it was as much as he could do to avoid laughing outright. So they really did act like that. He would never have believed it if he had not seen it. And it was so comic, laughable — and yet, sinister.

But it was only Mohr. Fehler, coming behind Mohr into the cabin, simply raised his hand slightly. It could have been any kind of salute; it could have been merely a friendly gesture exchanged between acquaintances. Fehler did not say 'Heil Hitler!' He left that part of the ceremony to Mohr.

Mohr was a thick-set, athletic-looking man with very blond hair, tightly curled. A handsome enough devil, Henderson mused; would have been more so if he had not looked so sulky. He was what the Nazis would call pure Aryan — as if there was such a beast. This was the type they would have liked to turn the whole nation into. A handsome face, certainly, but the sulky arrogance spoiled it, gave it a bad-tempered childish look.

'Heil Hitler!' Mohr barked, and dropped

the right arm stiffly at his side.

'Of course,' Henderson said, the smile hovering about his mouth. 'A very noble sentiment — very noble indeed. I trust the Austrian is well.'

Fehler, a little way behind Mohr, grinned suddenly. He had detected the irony in Henderson's voice; it did not seem to offend him.

Mohr, not understanding, stood at attention until the ship rolled and flung him off balance. He looked angrily at Henderson and Thouless, as though he believed that they had been responsible.

Henderson said: 'You had better stand at ease. We're running into bad weather.'

Mohr looked at Fehler, and Fehler translated. Fehler's left wrist was in splints; he had damaged it when the Heinkel crashed. The chief steward, who had seen to the dressing, suspected a fracture. Both men had strips of sticking-plaster on their faces, but it was a miracle that their injuries were no worse. It was a miracle, indeed, that they were alive.

'It is hardly necessary for me to point out to you,' Henderson said, 'that you are now prisoners-of-war.'

Mohr, through Fehler, answered: 'We are German officers. We demand the treatment

146

that is due to our rank.'

Henderson's mouth twitched again. 'You will be treated according to the book. You may rest assured of that. Accommodation may be cramped; that cannot be avoided. We did not expect you to drop in on us.'

He heard Thouless give an exclamation of impatience. Thouless had been looking over Henderson's shoulder and had seen that the captain's right hand was manipulating a pencil. On the pad on the desk a sketch of the two Germans was taking shape, almost, it seemed, without any conscious attention from Henderson. Thouless's lips tightened. Here was a fine time to be drawing. Could the Old Man never keep away from his sketch-book?

Henderson, ignoring the mate's disapproval, went on with his two occupations.

'I don't know how long you will be with us,' he said. 'It is possible that you may be transferred to one of His Majesty's ships. On the other hand, it may be decided to put you ashore in Russia and let our allies take charge of you.'

He saw Fehler's expression alter. Fear came into the velvet eyes. He paused while Fehler translated to Mohr, and the colour drained out of Mohr's face. Mohr's voice rose indignantly and a spout of words came out of

147

his mouth. Henderson waited patiently until they ceased.

'What does he say?'

'He says you cannot do that.' Fehler's voice sounded brittle. 'He says we are your prisoners — prisoners of the British. You cannot hand us over to those — those barbarians.'

'It is a question,' Henderson said, 'whether Russians are more barbaric than Nazis, but we will not discuss the point. However, it is not for me to decide what shall happen to you; that is a decision for the naval commander. For the present, at least, you must remain on board this ship.' He paused, observing their reactions, then continued, his mouth twitching again. 'I hardly need to point out to you that there is a certain degree of doubt as to whether we shall remain on the surface. Attempts have been made to sink us, and more attempts may be made. Perhaps you know as much about that as I do. I trust, more for my own sake than for yours, that any such attempts will prove unsuccessful.'

He saw Mohr's eyes dilate a little; he seemed to have lost some of his confidence. Perhaps the fact that he was now standing on the other side of the fence had not fully come home to him until this moment. These men had courage; that was certain. No man who was not possessed of courage could bring a vulnerable aircraft across hundreds of miles of Arctic sea and press home a low-level attack on a heavily armed convoy. Henderson himself would not have cared to do it. But a man might be courageous in the position he knew, and yet lose that courage when transferred to a situation of which he had had no experience. Henderson preferred a ship to a submarine or an aeroplane, but he was aware that submariners and airmen might not share his preference.

He said in his deep, rather tired voice: 'There are interesting points to this situation; it has its ironical aspect. You have been hunting with the hounds; now you will have to run with the hare. The question is: which side do you support now? I think your loyalty must now be divided — between your country and your own lives.'

Mr Thouless coughed. It was an impatient cough. Once let the Old Man start talking and you never knew when he would stop. He was still sketching too, filling in the details. You might almost have supposed this to be a pleasant social occasion, a little informal chat, a get-together between the nations.

Henderson heard Thouless's cough and knew the meaning of it. He brought the interview to a close.

'I don't think there is anything else. It will be necessary to keep you under supervision. There might be a good opportunity for sabotage. We cannot afford to take chances. I am sure that you will understand.'

'We understand,' Fehler said.

As they were going out of the cabin the ship rolled to starboard. It was a heavier roll than any previous one, heavy and sudden. Mohr staggered, lost his footing, and fell down, half in the cabin, half in the alleyway. The colour surged up in his neck and face, and he scrambled quickly back on to his feet and stood for a moment in the doorway, breathing hard, his mouth working angrily. It was obvious that he wished to vent his rage on someone and could think of no excuse for doing so. He controlled himself with an effort, said something curtly to Fehler, and went off down the alleyway with Fehler following him. A seaman went with them.

Henderson shaded in some portions of his sketch, and said to Thouless without looking up: 'The dark boy is all right. I wouldn't trust the other one an inch.'

'I wouldn't trust either of them,' Thouless said.

'Because they're Germans?'

'Because they're Nazis.'

'But we don't know that, do we? Not all

Germans are Nazis.'

'They're all the same to me,' Thouless said.

'They shouldn't be, Tom. Because, you know, it's the non-Nazis that we shall have to deal with in the end.' He held up the sketch he had made. 'Look here, upon this picture, and on this. That's from *Hamlet*. Do you remember the speech, Tom?'

'I don't read Shakespeare.'

'You ought to. He has some very interesting views on warfare, and one quite remarkable example of seamanship in *The Tempest*, which I commend to your notice. I confess I have never fully understood it myself. However, as I was saying, look at these two pictures.' He touched with his finger-tip the sketch of Fehler. 'That man will give us no trouble. He has a sense of humour.' He touched the other sketch. 'That one will need watching. He is, if I am not much mistaken, an ideological maniac; and that is a very dangerous beast indeed.'

The ship rolled again, timbers creaked, an oilskin coat swung out away from the bulkhead on which it was hanging, swung quite a long way before swinging back and slapping stiffly against the bulkhead.

Henderson watched the oilskin.

Thouless said: 'The weather's getting bad.'

'It'll be a lot worse before we've done with it,' Henderson replied.

* * *

Tarbat said: 'Two more mouths to feed. League of Nations, that's what this ship is. You know, boys, what I'd do if I was Captain. I'd drop those two flaming Nasties overboard, that's what I'd do. Let 'em swim home. That'd cool their ardour.'

Tarbat, taking his ease in the gunners' mess-room, his feet up, a cigarette stuck to his lower lip, was talking over the events of the day.

'I thought we'd had it, boys. When I see that flaming Jerry plane coming straight for us I says to meself, Reginald, I says, this here's curtains for you. You better say your prayers now.'

'Did you?' Rankin asked.

'Did I what?'

'Say your prayers.'

'What d'you think? There was a miracle, wasn't there? That was all on my account; all because of me saying my prayers. You can thank your Uncle Reg that you're still alive and kicking.'

'You better keep on praying,' Bowie said. 'We ain't through yet.'

There was a constant rattle of dishes in the mess-room as the ship rolled, plates shaking in their racks, knives and forks sliding about inside their drawer. Tarbat's fat body was wedged between a chair and the table, both of which were bolted firmly to the deck; first the chair took Tarbat's weight, then the table edge. The deadlights were clamped down over the portholes, and on the inside of the iron a coating of ice had formed. They could hear the wind howling outside, and now and then the vessel would shudder as a wave struck her.

'It's getting proper nasty,' Tarbat said. 'Hark at that wind.'

Bowie said peevishly: 'It's all right for you. You can climb into your bunk and stay there all night. You don't have to go out in it like we do.'

Bowie had the graveyard watch, from twelve to four, and he was not looking forward to it with any expectation of pleasure. It was going to be freezing cold up on the exposed wing of the bridge, and with this wind blowing, the cold would go through any thickness of clothing.

Sime had cut himself a sandwich, a slab of cheese between two half-inch slices of Tarbat's bread. He was chewing stolidly.

'You stoking up the fires, Sharkgut?'

Rankin asked. 'You thinking about hibernation?'

Sime grinned at him, but said nothing. His jaws went on working. Now and then Rankin could see the churned-up food inside. It was like looking into the works of a concrete mixer.

'That Sharkgut,' Bowie said. 'One of these days he'll bust hisself. And what a mess that'll be.'

Sime went on chewing. He never paid any attention to remarks about his eating powers.

Bowie took a pack of cards out of a drawer and sat down at the table and began to shuffle them.

'Anybody want a game — pontoon, nap, poker?'

Nobody rushed forward to accept the invitation.

'I'm going to get my head down,' Rankin said. 'Best to pack in as much sleep as you can when you can.'

'You'll die sleeping,' Bowie said.

'I hope I do. I just hope I do. But not tonight.'

'You never know. Well, if nobody wants a game I'll play by meself.' He began to lay out the greasy, dog-eared cards for a game of patience.

Tarbat let smoke drift through his nose.

Sime drank cocoa and belched loudly, dragging out the operation as if he enjoyed it. Bowie wiped his nose on the back of his hand and laid a red six on a black seven.

Rankin said: 'I wonder where we've got to. How many more days?'

Tarbat answered with the voice of authority: 'We're two hundred miles due east of Bear Island. Three more days. Maybe four.'

'Galley navigation,' Bowie said contemptuously.

Tarbat blew a smoke ring and watched it admiringly as it floated away. 'You don't have to believe me,' he said magnanimously. 'But I know.' He shifted his feet and leaned his body against the roll of the ship. He put his head on one side, listening to all the noises that were making themselves audible in the mess-room; particularly he listened to the mournful sound of the wind. 'Of course,' he added, 'this weather may hold us up. If you ask me it's going to be worse before it's better. Proper sea for storms, this is.'

Sergeant Grant came into the mess-room, pushing back the hood of his coat and shedding snow. He pulled off his Balaclava helmet and began to rub his cheeks, trying to bring the warmth back into them. The snow melted slowly, forming a dirty puddle on the bare, painted floor of the mess-room.

'What's it like outside?' Rankin asked.

Grant began to unclip the fastenings of his coat. It was a coat of stiff waterproof cloth with a fleece lining and elastic inside the cuffs to prevent the wind blowing up the sleeves. Under it Grant was wearing a leather jerkin and two or three pullovers.

'It's the hell of a night,' he said. 'You can't see an inch in front of you. Snowing fit to crease itself, and as cold as a meat-storage plant.'

He moved across to the radiator and leaned back against it. The coat was dark with melted snow; a little thin steam rose from it. His lips and cheeks felt stiff, frozen. He lit a cigarette and could hardly feel the tip of it in his mouth.

'One good thing about bad weather,' Tarbat said. 'They can't find you so easily. You don't get torpedoed in a sea like this.'

'You just sink from natural causes,' Grant said. 'That's a consoling thought.'

★   ★   ★

When Bowie went on watch at midnight the snow had stopped falling, but in all other respects conditions had worsened. It seemed to Bowie when he came out of the blacked-out alleyway that he had stepped into

156

a kind of waking nightmare. He had not moved two paces when the wind struck him, slamming him back against the side of the deck-house with a shock that jarred his ribs. He took in a breath, and it was a breath of ice, ice cutting at his lips, his throat, his lungs. The wind was a shaft of ice, piercing with sharp, bitter probes the clothing that Bowie had wrapped about his stunted body. It wrenched at his coat with invisible fingers, and the skirt of the coat flapped against his legs, fluttering wildly.

He could see nothing. The world around him was a world of darkness; and out of that darkness came the noise — the noise that put fear into Bowie's heart. For it was not simply the rising and falling shriek of the wind that he heard, not simply the vibration of metal, the clangour of iron striking iron; it was the sound of water, of water foaming, thundering, rushing headlong; water that he could not see, but could hear only too well.

The deck rose under his feet, tilted sideways, shuddered, fell away from him. Bowie found a rail and clung to it. He could feel the snow on the deck, and he stood there, waiting for some small degree of sight to come to him. And after a while he could make out the faint white glimmer of the snow and the foam of the breaking seas.

He groped his way along the rail, gripping it with his gloved hands, until he came to the gap where the catwalk began. He moved out on to the catwalk, on to that slender flying-bridge linking the high parts of the ship, and below him he could hear the wild rushing of the seas as they swept across the after-deck. Looking down, he could make out the pale drift of foam showing like phosphorescence through the darkness; and now he felt the bitter whiplash of freezing spray slashing at his cheeks, and the rail under his hand was slippery with ice, and the boards of the catwalk as treacherous as the frozen surface of a pond.

He wondered where the other ships of the convoy could be. In the howling darkness all around the *Rosa Dartle* there was no sign of them. She might have been alone, abandoned to the fury of the storm. And yet those other ships must surely be not far away; even at this moment one of them might be bearing down upon the *Rosa Dartle*, might be about to ram her, perhaps to cut her in two; and how could such a disaster be avoided when there was no vision, nothing but a black tunnel of darkness out of which the wind came blustering and roaring like some dragon breathing, not fire and brimstone, but snow and ice and imminent annihilation?

Bowie, clinging to the rail and peering fearfully to left and right as the ship staggered under the buffeting of the sea, imagined that he saw black shapes advancing out of the heart of the night, towering castles that might be the upperworks of great ships. He felt like yelling out in terror; and if he had done so, no one would have heard him; no man's voice could have prevailed over the tumult of the storm.

But he made no sound, save perhaps a soft whimper; and though imagination showed him nameless horrors in the darkness, his mind yet told him that they were only imagined. So he went on across the catwalk with the rush and gurgle of the sea below him, and came to the deeper blackness of the bridge-deck, and groped from handhold to handhold until he found the ladders and the bridge and finally the tiny sanctuary of the gunbox, swaying out into the night, dipping and rising as the port side dipped and rose, and taking the wind and the spray and the whole invisible onslaught of the Arctic gale.

A voice suddenly grumbled hoarsely in Bowie's ear: 'About time too. Thought you was never coming. It's gone eight bells five minutes ago. Where you been?'

'Couldn't find my way,' Bowie said. 'Can't see a blame thing. What a night!'

'You oughta started earlier. You think I wanta do half your watch for you?'

'Forget it,' Bowie said. He moved farther into the gunbox, brushing past the upright, snow-coated Oerlikon cover. 'What we supposed to watch for on a night like this? Need a searchlight to see anything. By God, it's cold. You ever know it as cold as this?'

He realized suddenly that he was talking to himself. The other man had had four hours of it, and even the charm of Gunner Bowie's enlightened conversation was not sufficient attraction to hold him any longer.

'Him and his five minutes,' Bowie mumbled, trying to extract the maximum protection from the flapping canvas of the gun cover. 'You'd think I'd robbed him of a hundred quid.'

There was no real shelter in the gun-box. The wind whirled round inside it in a spiral, finding out every corner. Bowie hunched his shoulders, pulled the hood of his coat lower, plunged his hands into the pockets, shuffled his feet in the snow, and became progressively colder and more self-pitying.

'What a life; what a blooming life,' he muttered. 'All them people in nice warm beds safe on land, and me stuck up here like a ruddy weathercock. Flaming politicians starting wars. I'd like to have my MP up here now.

That'd give him something to think about.'

But then he tried to remember who his MP was, and had to admit to himself that he had not the least idea.

'Don't matter anyway. They're all alike: a shower of bastards, the whole lot of 'em. Wouldn't be no loss if they was all dropped in the Thames with concrete overcoats and lead shoes.'

He stared into the darkness on the port side, and the darkness seemed to press upon him like a solid thing. Once he thought he saw a light flicker, but when he looked again there was nothing. Perhaps the light had been only in his own head, something at the back of the eyeballs. His head ached with the cold.

Now and then he peered over the edge of the gun-box and tried to see the foredeck and bows of the ship, but there too he could detect no more than an occasional faint glimmer that might have been the foam rushing from one side to the other. There was something particularly frightening in this sightlessness. He could hear the thunder of the seas falling on the deck below, and yet he could see nothing. He might have been standing on a high rock surrounded by a restless ocean, but that a rock would not have moved so alarmingly.

He began to wonder how securely this box

was fixed to the wing of the bridge. Was there not a possibility that it might break away under the strain? The idea having come into his head, he could not get it out again. Each time the ship heeled over to port he waited for that moment when the gun and its surroundings, and he with them, would be wrenched away from the ship and cast into the dark ocean that hissed and bubbled below him. He listened for the first tell-tale cracking of metal, and thought he heard it a dozen times; he thought he could feel the box moving independently of the bridge to which it was joined, and he felt sure that it was gradually shaking itself free.

He had worked himself up into such a state of nervousness that when something touched him on the shoulder he gave a yelp of terror. But it was only the third mate's hand.

Bowie heard the third mate's voice: 'What's wrong, gunner? Something bite you?'

He turned then, and could just make out a whiteness that might have been the man's face and the bulk of him blocking the opening into the gun-box.

'You give me a scare, sir. You give me a proper scare.'

'Guilty conscience, hey? Well, come into the wheelhouse for a spell. There's a mug of

162

cocoa. It'll warm the cockles of your heart.'

'They can do with some warming,' Bowie said.

He followed the third mate along the rocking bridge and into the shelter of the wheelhouse. Out of the wind it seemed immediately several degrees warmer, but even with the doors closed, there was scarcely less noise inside than out. Bowie could see the helmsman as a dark silhouette, his arms stretched out on the wheel as though he had been crucified, but the man paid no attention to Bowie; he kept his gaze fixed on the faint red glow of the compass bowl, seeing in that card and needle the course that the ship must take.

The third mate pushed a mug of steaming cocoa into Bowie's hands, and Bowie let the thick, sweet, slightly oily liquid warm his lips.

'Have a sandwich.'

He took the sandwich also and bit into the bread and the corned beef, swallowing big lumps of them and washing them down with hot cocoa.

'Devil of a night,' the third mate said. He was a very young man, younger than Bowie; but he sounded cheerful, as though the gale were a challenge that he was glad to meet.

'I can't see a thing,' Bowie said.

'Neither can I.'

'But the rest of the convoy, sir. Where are they?'

'God only knows,' the third mate said, and laughed, as though it were the best joke in the world.

'But in that case, mightn't one of them run into us? In the dark. I mean — '

'Nothing more likely,' the third mate said, and he laughed again. 'Better drink that cocoa before it happens.'

Bowie could not understand the third mate's attitude. He did not seem to appreciate the seriousness of the situation, took it as no more than a joke. It did not seem a joke to Bowie. Here was this great ship plunging on into the darkness with fifty-seven men on board and ten thousand tons of inflammable cargo, and here was this boy of a third mate, the officer of the watch, not apparently giving a damn. It was wrong, all wrong.

The third mate disappeared into the chart-room, and Bowie, steadying himself against the side of the wheelhouse, ate his sandwich and drank his cocoa and felt even more alarmed than he had felt in the gun-box. The helmsman coughed, but made no other sound; he might have been unaware of Bowie's presence. Bowie listened to the wind beating against the windows and the agonized creaking of the wheelhouse timbers. Blind, he thought, going ahead as blind as a mole in a tunnel. God Almighty, anything might happen.

The third mate came out of the chart-room again and said: 'You'd better get back to your post now, gunner. And keep a smart look-out.'

Bowie said: 'I don't think it's safe.'

The third mate stared at him. 'How d'you mean — not safe?'

'That gun-box. I think it's coming adrift.'

'Not likely,' the third mate said; but he went with Bowie to look at it.

The box was still there. 'Not come adrift yet,' the third mate said. He put his hands on the side and wrenched at it. He jumped up and down to demonstrate to Bowie the strength of the fixture. 'Not going to either.' He was amused at Bowie's fears but ready to humour him. 'I'll guarantee it, gunner. If anything happens you can come to me for compensation.'

He went away then, leaving Bowie to himself and his thoughts. Reassured at first, Bowie gradually became less confident. The box seemed to tremble with every lurch of the ship; even the gun rattled on its mounting. Suppose this unnatural shaking were to set the ammunition off. That was another

165

possibility that plagued Bowie's mind. He groped towards the ready-use locker and listened. When the ship rolled again he thought he could hear the sound of movement inside the locker, metal grating on metal. It would take no more than a sharp blow at the critical point to start a chain reaction that might end in the whole lot going up and he with it. He shifted away from the locker and took refuge on the other side of the gun. As if that would be any protection!

To add to his misery, it began to snow again — fine, hard snow which the gale blew into the exposed parts of his face, stinging like the pricking of innumerable needles. He felt sure that the sharpest of the pricks must have penetrated the skin, that his face was bleeding from a hundred tiny cuts. His resentment, searching for a target, settled on the third mate, despite the fact that that young man had given him cocoa and a sandwich.

'All right for him inside the wheelhouse. Out of the wind, out of the snow. All right for him to say this box is safe enough. He won't be in it when it breaks adrift. Only Joe Muggins.'

Bowie decided not to be Joe Muggins any longer. Where was the sense in it? He could see nothing in the darkness, especially now that it was snowing; he could hear nothing above the clamour of the storm. He would be just as much use to the ship taking his ease in the warmth and comparative comfort of the mess-room as he was getting himself frozen stiff in this hazardous position on the exposed wing of the bridge. He would go below.

But having come to this decision, he hesitated a moment before putting it into practice, and in that moment he saw a glimmer where there should have been no glimmer, where there should have been nothing but the dark void of the night. It was on the port beam, and close. It was like a ghost suddenly appearing — a faint, dim paleness that came and was gone again.

Bowie gripped the outer edge of the gun-box and stared blindly; and the box went down as the ship rolled, dipping towards the broken surface of the water. And Bowie saw the glimmer again, saw the ghost again, and knew in a sudden flash of terror what that glimmering ghost must be, the only thing it could be.

He turned then and ran out of the gun-box, ran along the bridge to the wheelhouse, struggled with the door, got it open, and burst in upon the third mate, yelling: 'A ship! A ship! Close on the port side. A ship!'

And then they heard it — he and the third mate and the helmsman — heard the grinding crash of steel on steel, of timber splintering, cracking, breaking.

The bridge trembled, and it was like no ordinary trembling caused by the wind and the rolling of the ship; this was more vicious; it was as though the deck under their feet had been shaken by an earthquake.

Bowie was taken off balance and fell at the third mate's feet, and even in that moment of imminent disaster he was able to notice and record on his senses the peculiarly pungent odour of damp leather that came from the third mate's seaboots. Something fell heavily across the back of Bowie's legs, and in the darkness he kicked out wildly, seized by a panic that he made no attempt to control. He scrabbled with his fingers at the caulked boards on which he was lying. The third mate staggered away, and the smell of damp leather went with him. There was a sound of glass splintering, and some sharp object slashed Bowie's left cheek as he turned his head. He felt the warm, salt taste of blood in his mouth, and he was sure that this was the end of him, that the whole structure of the bridge was giving way and taking the wheelhouse with it.

He began to scream then. He lay there and

screamed in panic, with the blood running down his cheek and all around him the noise of destruction and the darkness, and mile upon mile of icy, wind-lashed ocean. He went on screaming until a rough hand caught him by the hood of his coat and hauled him to his feet. He heard the third mate shouting in his ear: 'Stop that bloody noise! You're not dead.'

He realized suddenly that the wheelhouse was still intact, that the helmsman was still at the wheel, and that there was no longer any sound of rending metal or cracking timber; only the constant thunder of the sea and the shrieking of the wind that had become the normal background music of the night.

He stopped screaming. There seemed to be no point in it any longer. He stood there, shivering, half ashamed of himself for having given way to panic.

'You are all right, aren't you?'

'Yes,' he said. 'I'm all right.' He could feel the blood trickling down his face, but he would not say anything about that now. It was nothing. He had expected death and death had not come. What was a slashed cheek compared with that?

'Now,' the third mate said, 'we'll have a look at the damage that bastard did to us.'

The wheelhouse door was jammed. They

had to force it open. It gave way suddenly and they stumbled out on to the bridge, into the snow and the wind that tore at them icily.

The third mate moved ahead and Bowie followed him. He was following very closely, and when the third mate halted suddenly Bowie thudded into him.

He heard the third mate's voice, anxious, excited, awed. 'Keep back. For God's sake, keep back. There's nothing here — nothing — nothing at all.'

The gun-box had gone; the Oerlikon had gone; the ammunition had gone. The third mate's foot, moving cautiously forward in the darkness, had come to a point where there should have been solidity, and had found only empty space. If his hand had not been gripping the rail, if he had been less cautious, or if the ship had chosen that moment to lurch to port, then he would most surely never have saved himself. As it was, he halted on the brink and drew back, his heart leaping.

'That ship,' he said. 'It took our wing. And we're damn lucky it did nothing worse.'

Bowie was thinking: Lord, if I'd been in that gun-box I'd be a goner now. And the thought of this narrow escape made him tremble. A near thing; oh, not half a near thing!

He said plaintively: 'I told you that box wasn't safe. I told you, didn't I?'

Indignation made his voice rise, shrill and accusing above the bass rumble of the storm. 'I told you!'

8

Gale Force

When dawn came they were alone. They looked across the troubled waters and could see no other ship. Only the advancing armies of the waves; great waves that flung themselves at the low grey roof above and from whose peaks the spray was blown like smoke. As the light came slowly, seeping gradually through the thickness of the clouds, they searched with anxious eyes the hills and valleys of the sea around them. But still there was no other ship. The convoy was gone. It was as though each vessel had melted like a ghost, or had sunk for ever below the ravaged surface of the ocean.

The broken end of the bridge was like a jagged wound. The torn steel supports that had held the gun-box in place pointed outboard like accusing fingers. But the culprit, the ship that had caused this damage, was gone like the others, where there was no telling. They did not even know which ship it had been, appearing so suddenly out of the darkness, its ghostly outline glimpsed for a

172

moment by Gunner Bowie, and then vanishing again, leaving only the shattered timbers and twisted iron as a legacy of its coming.

Bowie's cut face was a subject of interest to the other gunners. There was a nasty slash, stretching from the cheekbone to the corner of the mouth; but it was not deep, and the steward had mended it with sticking-plaster. Bowie was inclined to swagger, his memory conveniently ejecting all recollection of the abject terror he had exhibited in the gloom of the wheelhouse.

'How'd you get that cut?' Rankin asked. 'Did somebody come at you with a knife?'

'Glass out of the wheelhouse window,' Bowie said. 'Fell in when that other ship hit us. Splinter sliced my face. Half an inch more and it'd have had my eye out.' He recalled the narrowness of his escape with relish. It made him a kind of hero. 'And if I hadn't got away from that gun in double quick time I wouldn't be talking to you now, and that's the truth.'

Bowie had been luckier than his opposite number on board the unknown ship. Daylight revealed what the darkness had hidden — splashes of blood on the splintered end of the bridge.

'Somebody caught it,' Mr Thouless said.

He stood on the see-saw of the bridge with Captain Henderson beside him, and surveyed the damage. On the woodwork were the dark stains of the blood and nothing else. 'Somebody caught it,' he repeated.

Henderson said: 'Better have that gap closed up. Don't want anybody falling overboard. Enough trouble without that.'

'I'll get Jaggers on to it,' Thouless said.

'If he's sober.'

'He'll be sober when I've finished with him.'

Henderson put his hands on the bridge rail and looked down at the fore part of the ship. It had a ghostly appearance, the rails, the catwalk, the rigging, all coated with ice, as though everything had grown old and white and bearded. Seas were coming over the forecastle, and the Heinkel was in a bad way. It had been washed up against the after-rail of the forecastle head and it was shifting spasmodically as the ship bucked and rolled. Henderson did not care for the look of it.

'You'd better have that Jerry plane secured too,' he said; and he had to raise his voice and speak into Thouless's ear to make himself heard above the noise of the wind and the sea. 'Don't want it to explode or anything like that. Don't know whether it's likely. Best not to take chances.'

'I'll see to it,' Thouless said.

174

★ ★ ★

Jaggers came out of his drunken slumber to discover the avenging figure of Mr Thouless bending over him. Thouless's beard was very close to Jaggers's face, and Thouless's hand was clamped on to his shoulder, the fingers biting into it like steel claws.

'Get up, you damned drunken swine! Get up!'

Jaggers's mouth felt as though it had been scrubbed out with salt. He tried to moisten his lips with a tongue that might have been a strip of old shoe leather. Inside his head somebody was beating a gong. It was a big gong, one of the kind that sends out vibrations capable of breaking tumblers at a distance of ten feet. Jaggers put a hand on each side of his head, holding it together, and groaned. The cabin was swaying about him; nothing was still. He was not sure whether this was genuine movement or simply the hallucination of his hangover. He had the father and mother of all hangovers.

'I'm sick. Oh, God, I'm sick.'

'You'll be sicker yet. Get up. And look sharp about it.'

Mr Thouless's voice grated on Jaggers's nerves. His nerve ends were all sticking out, ready to be grated on; they sent spasms of pain shooting through his body. He closed his eyes to shut out the evil sight of the mate's beard, but when he opened them again the beard was still there.

'You heard me,' Thouless growled.

Jaggers groaned again. There was no escape.

'I heard you, sir.'

He began to crawl out of the bunk, and it was like rolling a corpse out of a coffin. Mr Thouless looked on without pity, even with a certain amount of bitter pleasure. The bosun was a wretched-looking object with his tousled hair, his heavy, unshaven jaw, and eyes like dull pebbles stuck in blobs of mud. When he had struggled out of the bunk he still clung to it, his stomach sagging. He put his hand to the stomach and took it away from there and put it to his head. The pebble eyes looked at Thouless appealingly.

Mr Thouless ignored the appeal. There was no way to his heart for Jaggers.

'I've got a job for you and your fine alcoholics. A nice, pleasant job. It'll clear your heads.'

★ ★ ★

They went along the forward catwalk with the mate leading, the bosun second, and three seamen following. They went with their hands gripping the ice-covered rails, with the deck below them awash, and the wind beating the spray in their faces. Jaggers felt like death. He wished he had died in his bunk, just so long as he was out of it all.

The ship was staggering. It seemed to be wriggling its way through the sea like a snake. Jaggers saw the forecastle lift high, lift until the catwalk was a steep uphill path, then twist and fall, with salt water foaming inboard like the rushing torrent of some mountain river. It made Jaggers ill to look at the lift and fall of the ship's bows, to watch the white-streaked seas sweeping past and the tide that frothed and gurgled across the deck below the catwalk. Nor did he like the look of that German plane sliding about on the forecastle. It looked to him as if a man could get himself badly hurt tackling that job. But when he hung back Mr Thouless's voice lashed him into motion again.

'Get a move on there. D'you think we've got all day?'

As far as Jaggers was concerned they had as many days as you cared to mention. It was only Thouless who was in a hurry, and Thouless was a human dynamo, generating enough electricity to shock even Jaggers into motion.

They came out on to the forecastle head, and the tail of the Heinkel whipped at them viciously.

'Get a rope round it,' Thouless yelled. 'Don't just stand there like a set of dummies.'

'What's he think we are — cowboys?' Jaggers muttered. But he unslung a coil of rope from his shoulder and flung the end of it over the fuselage of the plane. He made a move to draw the rope through under the belly of the fuselage, but the wind came in a gust and the tail and rudder struck at Jaggers. He jumped back, skidding on the wet ice, and the nerves jangled in his head.

Thouless jeered at him. 'What's the trouble? Did it bite you!'

'I'll bite you, you bastard,' Jaggers snarled, but the snarl was not loud enough for the mate to hear. He flung the rope at one of the seamen, and this man succeeded in looping it round the fuselage. They held on to it then and passed it round a stanchion and drew it tight. The tail of the plane tried to get away, the rudder flapped angrily, but it was tamed. They made the wings fast to the deck, and the Heinkel was as helpless as a roped steer; it could not shift.

Thouless was not satisfied. Heavy seas breaking over the bows could smash the aircraft to pieces. But there was nothing more they could do. He would have liked to drop the Heinkel over the side, but there was no way of doing so, not with the deck leaping under your feet and spray coming over and freezing on your clothes, and the wind blowing in gusts that must be close on sixty miles an hour, and maybe even more. Now that the job was done, it was best to get off the forecastle and back amidships without wasting any more time. Even the Spartan Mr Thouless was not enjoying this exposure to a freezing wind and freezing sea-water.

'All right,' he shouted. 'That'll do. Get back aft.'

The three seamen went first. Jaggers hesitated, waiting for the mate.

'Get moving,' Thouless said.

Jaggers started towards the catwalk, and a sea came over and caught him. It caught him as he should never have allowed himself to be caught — without a handhold. He went down flat, and the salt water poured over him, choking him. He slid along the ice and his head came up against the iron of the windlass with a crash that knocked him out as thoroughly as the alcohol had done. Then he slid away again as the ship rolled, senseless, unable to aid himself. He went like a corpse, slithering on the wet ice, with his arms and legs spreadeagled and the icy water splashing over him, until the rails stopped his progress. And there he lay. He was out — cold — very cold indeed.

'My God!' Thouless grumbled. 'What tools they give you!'

He yelled at the three seamen to come back and carry Jaggers because Jaggers was incapable of carrying himself.

'If he's killed himself,' Thouless muttered, 'it'll be no loss; damned if it will.'

★ ★ ★

Captain Henderson did not like the look of things. They had lost contact with the convoy, that was certain; and the weather showed no sign of improving. If anything, it was becoming worse. True, there was no great fear of attack either from aircraft or from U-boats while the gale lasted, but if, when the wind and the sea died down, they should still be separated from the escort, and if then they should be located by the enemy, there would be little chance of escape.

But that was looking ahead. Meanwhile there was the more immediate danger, the threat of the storm itself. The *Rosa Dartle* was pushing along at half speed, but she was labouring heavily. The strain upon her structure in these short, steep seas must be very severe indeed. She was taking a hammering, no doubt about that, and Henderson was still not at all easy in his mind concerning that near miss on the port side. He looked at the sea and he felt the wind tearing at him, and he reckoned it must be up to force ten on the Beaufort Scale. When you got up into the double figures you could look out for trouble. The *Rosa Dartle* had trouble already; Henderson would be surprised if she did not have more before another day had passed.

He was feeling the effects of the gale in his own body also. A man with one good leg and one artificial one, however skilfully he might move from handhold to handhold, was at a disadvantage. And the stump was sore; by God, it was sore. Henderson felt tired, but it was no time to feel tired; there was the very devil of a lot of work to be got through yet.

And during the morning Thouless brought a disquieting piece of information.

Mr Thouless, moving restlessly about the ship, conscientiously poking his nose into everything, noticed something in the port bulwark just aft of the bridge-deck. And that something was nothing less than a thin crack in the metal.

Mr Thouless was standing on the catwalk. He hoped that he had been mistaken; at that

181

distance it was difficult to be sure. Therefore, he went closer; he went back to the bridge-deck and along the port rails. He leaned over the rails and looked down at the bulwark just below him. It was a crack, sure enough. As Mr Thouless watched it, it opened slightly, showing as a dark line; then, as the strain was relieved, it closed again and became almost invisible.

Thouless stood there for some minutes, watching the crack opening and closing; and as he watched, his hands gripped the rail tightly and his mind played with several possibilities, none of them at all pleasant. Then he went to tell Henderson.

'I'll have a look,' Henderson said; and he went back with Thouless, holding on to the rails with his big, gloved hands, and feeling the jar whenever the weight of his body was thrown on to the artificial leg.

When they came to the after end of the bridge-deck Thouless pointed downward at the bulwark where it sloped up to join the superstructure. He put his mouth close to Henderson's ear.

'There! Do you see it? There!'

'I see it,' Henderson said. And, as Thouless had done, he stood there for some minutes, watching the crack and thinking of unpleasant possibilities. Then he turned away. 'Let's go, Tom. Nothing we can do here except get ourselves a lot of publicity.'

He did not wish to have the story of that crack noised around the ship. It could do no good for everyone to know; it could only cause apprehension. The officers would have to be told, but they could keep it to themselves.

'Maybe it was that bomb,' he said, giving voice to his thoughts.

'Maybe it was,' Thouless said.

'Not that it makes any difference what it was. It's there, and that's the important thing.'

He wondered how deep the crack went. Perhaps it was only on the bulwark, superficial. Perhaps the storm had found a fault there. Perhaps it was nothing to worry about. But Henderson was not the man to try fooling himself. The crack was something to worry about, and he knew it. Nevertheless, there was no need for the crew to know.

But despite Henderson's plans for secrecy, it was no more than an hour before everyone on board from the galley-boy to the chief engineer knew that there was a crack in the ship's port bulwark, and everyone was conjecturing just what the effect of that crack would be.

It was Bowie who had noticed the captain

and the mate standing by the after-rail of the bridge-deck. He had seen Mr Thouless pointing at the bulwark, and then he had seen the two men put their heads together, and both of them had looked grave. Bowie was an inquisitive man, and when Henderson and Thouless had gone away, he went to where they had been standing and looked down at the bulwark also. And the crack opened for his benefit, and he knew then what the other two had been looking at.

Bowie was not the man to keep information like that locked up in his own head. He believed in spreading bad news just as fast as possible, and on board ship any kind of news travels like a forest fire. Soon everyone knew about the crack, and soon everyone had been along to take a look at it, to pause for a while gazing down at that thin, ominous line, and then drift away again, thinking. And their thoughts were not happy thoughts.

Even Tarbat went to view the already famous — or infamous — crack. Tarbat's bulky figure was an unusual sight on the catwalk; swathed in a duffle-coat that he had won in a game of poker, and with a blue, knitted cap pulled down over his ears, he seemed to fill the whole space between the rails on either side. But Tarbat was unimpressed — or professed to be.

'Ain't nothing. Just a little crack like that. Nothing to worry about. Me, I've been in ships with cracks you could get your head into, and I'm still alive. Some people get easy scared.'

The galley-boy for one. 'It's like my dream, see?'

'What's like your dream?' Tarbat asked.

'This storm just like I dreamt it that night — like I told you. I bet we're going to sink too. I bet it'll all come true.'

'Get away with you,' Tarbat said. 'You got water on the brain.'

★ ★ ★

Only the German flyers, Mohr and Fehler, had not heard about the crack. Shut away in a small cabin amidships, they knew only that a gale was shaking the vessel and that the cabin groaned with the stresses that were being laid upon it. Mohr had never before been on board a ship, and Fehler had only been across the North Sea in good weather. Now they had dived, as it were, head-first into the middle of a nightmare, a gale such as the Arctic Ocean was adept at whipping up to plague and harass all who ventured over the boundaries of its domain.

There was a porthole in the cabin, and

through the circle of plate glass they could watch the white-capped seas that alternately towered above them or dropped away as the ship rolled first one way and then the other. They could see nothing but the sea and the clouded sky, and now and then a flurry of snow. No other ship was visible; nothing else floated upon the churned-up surface of the ocean.

'Where are the others?' Mohr said. 'Have we lost them? Are they sunk?'

Fehler could give no answer. 'It is a bad storm.' He grabbed the post of his bunk as the sudden tilting of the deck threatened to fling him off his feet. 'I think it must be a very bad storm indeed.'

'You think this ship is going to sink?' Mohr spoke carelessly. He would not have confessed to any feeling of uneasiness, much less of fear. But the carelessness was a little overdone, a little too studied. Fehler had been with Mohr for nearly six months, and he was not deceived. Mohr was uneasy. This was something that was beyond his experience; he had no memory of other similar occurrences to reassure him. He had faced many hazardous moments in the air and he had not flinched from them, but then he had been to a certain degree the master of his own fate; he had been an active participant. Now his role was a passive one, and that made all the difference. He had to take whatever might come to him, and there was nothing he could do to alter the issue one way or another. Fehler realized all this, and that was why he knew that the carelessness with which Mohr had asked the question was not altogether genuine. Mohr believed that there was some danger of the ship's sinking. Ships did sink, did they not? To be quite honest, Fehler was none too confident either.

But he said: 'No, I don't think so. The British know how to build ships.'

Mohr's head swung round quickly; the blue eyes stared coldly at Fehler. There was no smile on the handsome face. Fehler knew that the remark had annoyed Mohr; he had known that it would do so even before he had made it. And he did not care.

'You admire the British, don't you?' Mohr said. 'Perhaps you are glad to have fallen into their hands.'

Fehler knew that Mohr despised him. He did not care about that either. If it came to the point he despised Mohr also, so in that respect they were even.

In Mohr's eyes Fehler was decadent; he was not even a member of the Nazi Party. That to Mohr seemed inexplicable. He himself had joined the Hitler Youth at the first opportunity. Those had been grand times, marching along in the sunshine — the sun had always shone on the Hitler Youth, perhaps by order of the Führer himself — the brown shirts open at the throat, the shorts supported by leather belts, iron-shod boots beating out the rhythm of the march on the hard roads. And the songs they had sung — the patriotic, marching songs that told of the Fatherland and the old Germanic heroes, Siegfried and Sigurd and the rest of them; they had been fine too. And each one in his heart had believed himself a new Siegfried who would make Germany great, all-conquering, a leader of the whole world.

Mohr had once confided all this to Fehler, and Fehler had said: 'Wagnerian intoxication. Mass hysteria.'

Mohr had not understood just what Fehler meant, but in Fehler he had thought to detect a man who did not conform, who was outside the party, outside Nazism, a man to be despised and watched and suspected.

Mohr remembered the parades, the rallies, the massed uniforms, the rows of banners, the forests of arms raised in the Nazi salute, the great shouts bursting from thousands of throats: 'Heil, heil, heil! Sieg Heil!' And the Führer haranguing them, lashing them into a frenzy with his words, so that they were ready to follow him into the very fires of Hell if necessary, ready to die for the Führer and the Fatherland and all those glittering dreams of a race of supermen, of blond Aryan heroes.

But Fehler had taken no part in this, and had not wanted to. Therefore, Fehler was not to be trusted.

Fehler said: 'You should wish for the ship to sink. That was the object of our mission, was it not?'

Mohr sensed the mockery in the question, and he resented it. 'What I wish makes no difference.'

'Perhaps you could drop a lighted match into the cargo.'

'That would be easy, I suppose? They would allow us to do that.'

'For a man of your ability it should present no insuperable difficulty.'

Mohr said coldly: 'Do not forget yourself. Remember that you are speaking to your superior officer.'

He turned his blond head away from Fehler and stared moodily out of the porthole. Fehler lit a cigarette, an English cigarette supplied by the ship. He studied Mohr through the smoke. He was certainly the type beloved by the Nazis, the pure Germanic type.

Mohr said without turning: 'Do you have

to fill the room in with smoke?'

He had denied himself the relaxation of smoking because he would not accept English cigarettes. Now he was being tormented by a craving for tobacco, and the torment was being aggravated by Fehler's weakness. But Mohr would not give in.

'I will not accept their charity,' he had said. 'I will not lower myself to do so.'

'Are you going to refuse food also?' Fehler asked.

'That is different. I have a duty to maintain my body, to keep it fit to serve the Führer. But I will not accept their charity.'

'Can it make any difference? There will be little enough charity if they hand us over to the Russians.'

That was their abiding fear — the fear of being sent to some slave camp behind the Russian lines, perhaps to Siberia. A swift death by drowning might be preferable to that.

Fehler made no answer to Mohr's petulant question, but he went on smoking. His damaged wrist was paining him rather a lot now. It worried him. There was no doctor on board this ship, and that seemed strange. He would have supposed that all ocean-going ships carried doctors, especially in war. What happened if a man was wounded? Did they just patch him up as best they could? He supposed so. But it seemed all wrong.

'There's a ship out there now,' Mohr said. 'A little one.'

★ ★ ★

Captain Henderson was glad to see the trawler. It established a link with the convoy, if only a tenuous one. He could not tell whether the trawler had lost contact also, or whether it had been detached to search for the *Rosa Dartle*. Bearing in mind the trawler's speed, he did not think that likely, so perhaps after all this was only a chance meeting. One way or the other, Henderson was glad.

'A little one is better than nothing,' he said to Thouless.

Thouless grunted. A trawler was too little. In weather like this it would have its work cut out to save itself. But he was glad to see it too; it made the sea less lonely.

The trawler appeared first as a dark speck tossed up by a wave miles away on the starboard quarter. It closed the gap slowly, visible on the wave crests, disappearing into the troughs. So small a ship in so large a sea. But a tough ship with tough men in her, not easily beaten. As she came nearer she no longer looked black, but white, for the ice was all over her, and the seas were spouting over her too, the wind flinging spray above the bridge to fall on the decks like freezing rain.

'My God, I don't envy them,' Henderson said. 'I'll wager there's not a dry spot in the whole ship.'

Thouless grunted again. Henderson was probably right, but this was no time to worry about the discomforts of a trawler; there was enough trouble in the *Rosa Dartle* to keep anybody's mind occupied.

The trawler had a gun-platform on a steel column, just forward of the mast, with a twelve-pounder gun on it, and the platform and the gun were caked with ice. There was an anti-aircraft gun abaft the smokestack, and a rack of depth-charges at the stern.

'Baby warship,' Thouless muttered. But they had quite a sting in them, those babies.

An Aldis lamp flashed a message from the trawler. 'Glad to have found you.'

Henderson sent a signal back. 'We are glad too.'

'Stay with me and no harm will come to you.'

'That's what he thinks,' Henderson said. But perhaps he, whoever he might be, did not really think so. These signals exchanged by ships were always cheerful. They had to be.

No hint of alarm must be allowed to creep into them, no suggestion that everything would not turn out all right in the end.

'It's laughable,' Henderson said, 'when you come to think about it.'

Thouless could see nothing very laughable in the situation.

'What is?' he asked.

'That little blighter telling us no harm will come to us now he's here. Like a kid with a peashooter promising to protect his grandfather from footpads.'

'Wonder where the rest of them are?'

'God knows. Scattered like lost sheep. There'll be some rounding up to do when this gale blows itself out.'

* * *

Kline did not believe there would be any rounding up to do as far as the *Rosa Dartle* was concerned. He had been along to inspect the crack in the bulwark and had come back to vent his bitterness and his fear on Muller. Kline was a man who had to find some object on which to lay the blame for anything that affected his own well-being. In this case that object was the British shipbuilder.

'A fine way to make ships. There's Limey

workmanship for you. That's us finished sure enough.'

He shook a cigarette out of a packet and stuck it in the side of his mouth. His hand trembled slightly when he held the match to it, but whether from fear or from anger Muller could not tell. Kline was in a mood of resentment, and the erratic movement of the ship did nothing to abate it.

'Roll, you bastard, roll!'

He flung himself on to his bunk and the smoke came out of him in a cloud.

'If this storm don't ease up pretty damn quick, we're goners, every last one of us. With that crack.'

'It may not be as bad as that,' Muller said. 'It may be just superficial.' But there was no confidence in his voice. Kline might be scared; Muller could not tell, because all Kline's emotions seemed to explode in anger, but he knew that he himself was scared, scared right down to the bones. He had been in some storms before, but never one like this, never in the Arctic, never in a tanker with a crack in the port bulwark.

'Superficial be damned!' Kline said. 'About as superficial as a slit throat.'

The cabin was in a mess. Kline dropped tobacco ash and cigar butts just anywhere, and he never made any attempt at clearing up. It was Muller who did the chores; he even polished the brass thumbscrews on the porthole. Kline would watch him with a sardonic grin on his battered face. If Muller liked to waste his time on that sort of thing, let him. But the gale had beaten even Muller's attempts at tidying up, and the cabin was a litter of shoes and sea-boots and old magazines, and anything else that could not be secured.

Muller had taken to watching a gas-mask hanging against one of the bulkheads. The gas-mask swung like a pendulum, and by noting the extent of its movement Muller could gauge the angle through which the ship was rolling. It looked a pretty big angle, and Muller wondered just how far a ship could roll without going completely over. Thirty degrees? Forty-five? Sixty? He had no idea. He supposed it would depend on the ship and the way she was loaded. The *Rosa Dartle*, deep in the water, with all her cargo below decks, ought to be able to stand a fairly heavy roll. By the evidence of the gas-mask she was doing just that.

But it was not so much the rolling that worried Muller: it was the other movement, the see-saw movement of the ship's length about the fulcrum of her centre. Seas were lifting the *Rosa Dartle* as if the ten thousand

195

tons of cargo in her tanks were as buoyant as a hollow drum. She slid up on the high backs of the waves, pivoted at the crests, and slipped down into the troughs that followed. And each time she pivoted Muller thought of the terrible strain upon her structure, and of the crack opening in the bulwark; and in his imagination the crack widened, opened out into a great gulf in whose depths they all must perish.

He began to pull on his coat and his rubber sea-boots.

'Where in hell are you going?' Kline asked.

'I'm going to look at that crack. See if it's any bigger.'

'Lot of good that'll do. You thinking of putting some stitches in it?'

Muller knew there was nothing he could do about it, but just the same, he had to go.

'I'll just have a look.'

'Have one for me while you're at it,' Kline said, and he sucked smoke into his lungs and let it come up slowly, like a sulky fire. 'Spit on the bastard.'

The wind hit Muller when he stepped out of the shelter of the deck-house. He had never imagined that wind could be like this, like a solid ram striking him; and the icy breath of it took his own breath away, as if it had been a hand gripping his lungs and not allowing them to expand. For several moments he could do nothing but cling to a handrail and gasp for breath, with the spray rattling against the side of the deck-house like the chatter of machine-gun fire.

When he had recovered sufficiently to be able to move he went slowly, hand over hand, with his feet slipping on the wet ice and the wind piercing all the layers of clothing to strike at his shoulder blades and the vulnerable small of his back.

He found a man already at the after-rail of the bridgedeck, and the man was Carson. He, too, had come to look at the crack. Certainly there was no lack of interest in that thin, dark line.

Muller said: 'You think it's any worse, bosun?' And he had to repeat the question in a shout to make himself heard.

Carson shouted back: 'Could be.' He did not look worried. But with Carson it was a question whether he ever looked worried. There was not much information to be gleaned from an examination of that lean, leathery face with the beaked nose and the bright black, deep-set eyes. The expression of Carson's face altered about as much as the expression of a totem-pole.

Muller thought the crack was opening wider when the ship did its see-saw act. He thought it was opening wider and not closing so tightly afterwards. But perhaps he was simply imagining it.

'You think anything's going to happen, bosun?'

'Sure. Lots of things. Always things happening.'

You got a lot of information out of Carson.

'You know what I mean.'

Carson put a hand on Muller's shoulder and peered into Muller's eyes.

Carson's hand was a reassurance; it was strong, it did not tremble.

'We'll see this through, son. We'll see it through. I got business in the States — unfinished business. We'll see this job through.'

★   ★   ★

Jaggers woke up in the ship's hospital with a throbbing headache and a bandage to hold it in. The head felt as if somebody had been beating it with a hammer and had only recently left off. Jaggers tried to remember what had happened, and gradually memory came back to him. That damned Jerry plane on the fo'c'sle.

Jaggers was still not at all clear in his mind as to how the plane had got there. It had all happened while he had been under the anaesthetic of alcohol, and it had not appeared necessary to the mate to bring Jaggers up to date with the news. All that Jaggers knew, therefore, was that the plane was there, and that in helping to secure it he had sustained a very nasty smack on the head that had put him back into the state of unconsciousness from which Thouless had so recently roused him. At least, that was what he supposed had happened.

Jaggers turned the head slowly and very carefully, and his gaze met that of the second steward who was looking down at him with a superior sort of grin on his face. The second steward had a face like a suet pudding that had been left too long in the saucepan; it was round and pallid and flabby. The steward himself was round and pallid and flabby, and somehow damp-looking, as if his surface were so cold that it condensed the moisture in the air around him. His name was Stebbing.

'You've come round, then,' Stebbing said, and then he sucked in his breath with a loud hissing noise that sounded like steam escaping from a safety-valve.

Jaggers made no answer. He felt no desire for small talk with second stewards, not with his head in its present state.

Stebbing said: 'That's a nasty cut you got

in your noggin. You ought to be more careful. Lucky you got people like me and the chief to bandage it up for you.' He stared at Jaggers ghoulishly. 'Don't know whether it's cracked the skull though. Might be chips of bone, work their way down to the brain cells. We might have to do an operation.' He grinned, thinking perhaps with relish of a nice bit of trepanning. It would be exciting work with the ship rolling, especially when you had never done anything of the kind before.

Jaggers could not be sure whether Stebbing was joking, or whether he really meant what he said. But whatever happened, he had no intention of allowing a couple of ham-handed stewards to probe about inside his skull.

He said: 'You can forget all about that. I don't want no bloody operation.' And even the effort of speaking was enough to send fresh spasms of pain shooting up inside his head. It felt as if the top were coming off.

Stebbing plucked at his pendulous lower lip. 'Well, it might be necessary. How do you feel?'

'Awful,' Jaggers said. 'I feel like death warmed up.'

'In a cold oven at that,' Stebbing said. 'The skull, now, it's a delicate structure, very delicate. You get a splinter going in, pressing on the brain, and before you know where you are you're stark, staring mad. Wouldn't want that, would you?'

'I'll be mad all right if you don't shut your trap. And I might bite you.' He put a hand to his head and fingered it gently. There seemed to be nothing but bandage.

'Not that it makes the hell of a lot of difference,' Stebbing added. 'This ship's in a bad way if you ask me.'

'What's wrong? Just a bit smashed off the end of the bridge. That's nothing.'

'Not that,' Stebbing said. 'I wasn't referring to that. Being unconscious, you won't have heard the worst.'

Jaggers spoke impatiently, and then regretted it because it sent fresh waves of pain surging through his head. 'What worst? What you blabbing about?'

'There's a crack in the hull just aft of the bridge. Anything might happen.'

'Don't feed me that stuff,' Jaggers said. 'You trying to scare me or something?'

'Why should I want to do that? I don't get any bonus out of scaring people. I'm just telling you the plain, honest fact. Everybody knows it.'

Jaggers stared at the second steward's pallid face, and there was no grin on it now. For a moment Stebbing himself had forgotten about the crack. Remembering it now, he felt the seeds of fear growing again in his own mind. And the fear was there in his face for Jaggers to see.

'God!' Jaggers said. 'It just wanted that. A thing like that makes everything complete.'

'I thought I'd tell you,' Stebbing said, and went away on soft, rubber-cushioned feet.

Jaggers lay with his head on the pillow, staring into vacancy and listening to the creaking of the ship. And in every creak he thought to hear the vicious rending of metal.

★　★　★

The trawler stayed with them all day, keeping watch over them. Sometimes they lost sight of her, for the trawler was a small ship and the troughs were deep. But always she came bobbing up again with the water sliding off her and the wind folding her in a curtain of spray. Twice they lost contact in a blizzard, but when the snow cleared the trawler was still there, still keeping guard.

Captain Henderson sent a signal: 'Where are the others?'

Flashing across the gap of wind-lashed sea came the answer: 'Have no idea.' And then, as an afterthought: 'Who wants a crowd?'

Henderson wondered what type of man had command of the trawler. Some Wavy

Navy stockbroker, perhaps. Some amateur yachtsman with a job in the City and a boat at Burnham-on-Crouch. But, by God, the fellow was a seaman.

He wondered whether to make a signal about the crack in the *Rosa Dartle*'s bulwark, but decided not to. There was nothing the trawler could do about that. She would stay with them anyway — if she could. If she could not then it was just too bad. Perhaps tomorrow the gale would have spent itself and they would be able to rejoin the convoy; tomorrow, perhaps, destroyers would be rounding up the flock.

But there was a long night to be endured, a very long, bleak night. And Henderson was not looking forward to it with any expectation of enjoyment.

He made a last signal to the trawler: 'I am afraid of the dark.'

He might have guessed what the answer to that one would be.

'Do not worry. I will hold your hand.'

After that the night came, and the sea was around them; and they staggered blindly on into the darkness, into the black and freezing darkness of the Arctic gale.

9

Brief Candle

Tarbat rolled into his bunk early. He had had a long day, and the strain of cooking in a galley that was never still for a single moment had tired him out. He decided to have a good night's sleep so that he should awake refreshed for more labours on the following day. But having climbed into his bunk, smoked a final cigarette, laid his head on the pillow, and closed his eyes, he discovered that sleep was not to be snared so easily.

He lay awake, listening to the clamour that was going on all around him: the sound of the wind, the sound of the seas buffeting the ship, the sound of the engines, and the rattle of things in the cabin. Now and then he would feel a shudder pass through the *Rosa Dartle*, as though she had suddenly come face to face with some hideous spectre of the night. And then Tarbat would begin thinking about the crack, and he would wonder whether it had opened wider. In daylight he had delivered himself of several contemptuous remarks concerning that weakness in the iron body of the ship, but now, in the darkness, with nothing else to occupy his mind, with no sleep bringing oblivion, he began to have doubts. Perhaps after all there was some cause for alarm.

After a while he gave up the idea of sleeping. He reached for a cigarette and lit it, letting the smoke drift up to the bunk above, where the second cook was snoring like a hog. Nothing could keep him awake.

Tarbat smoked out his cigarette and lit another from the butt and went on smoking and thinking. And the more he thought, the more uneasy he felt. Finally, he could stand it no longer; there was nothing for it but to go and inspect the crack. Even if in the darkness he could see nothing, he had to go and look and listen, and perhaps learn something that could not be learned by lying in a bunk and smoking.

'It's no good,' he muttered. 'I'll never sleep like this, never.'

He got out of the bunk, and the ship flung him down in a corner, and he sat there for a time with his knees up to his chin and pain throbbing in his back. He looked up at the electric bulb in the white-painted deckhead above him, and the deckhead seemed to be performing queer evolutions. The bulb went out and then came on again. A drawer under

Tarbat's bunk suddenly shot out, tipped over, and emptied half its contents at Tarbat's feet. The second cook rolled from side to side and snored loudly, but did not wake.

'I never knew anything like this,' Tarbat muttered. 'And I been in some storms.' And he thought of the crack again, and doubts rose more strongly in his mind. He hauled himself up and began to put on his thick clothes.

When he stepped out into the open he was in two minds whether to go straight back again to his cabin. For it was certainly no night to tempt out anyone who did not have to be out. It was snowing, and the snow blew under the hood of Tarbat's dufflecoat, laying a frosty hand on his plump cheeks. He turned his back to the wind and edged his way along the rails until he came to the catwalk.

He did not like the sound of the sea roaring across the deck below him; it was a confident, threatening sound. It was as if the sea knew its power, knew that it had the ship at its mercy.

'I don't like it,' Tarbat mumbled. 'I don't like it one tiny little bit.'

But he went along the catwalk with the snow devils coming at him and the spume whipped up by the wind. He went with his shoulders hunched and his hands gripping the rails, wondering whether these shudders that he could feel passing through the ship and up into his body were simply the ordinary, normal vibrations that were to be expected in such a storm, or whether they were something disastrously, tragically, more. But he could not tell, and he came to the end of the catwalk and clawed his way to the port side and looked down at the point where the bulwark and the crack must be; and he could see nothing in the darkness but the glimmer of foam, and he could hear nothing but the wild howling of the wind and the thunder of the seas.

★　★　★

Captain Henderson had insisted on staying on the bridge. Thouless had tried to persuade him to go below and get some sleep, but without success. He might have known that this would be so. Despite the pain in his leg, despite weariness of mind and body, Henderson would not relax until the gale had blown itself out. His only concession to human weakness was a brief rest now and then on the settee in the chart-room. From there he was still in touch with all that went on, ready in a moment to take control.

For some hours after darkness had fallen

they had kept in touch with the trawler by occasional signals on the Aldis lamp; but as it came up to four bells in the first watch and the snow began to fall thickly, they lost contact and felt once again the solitude of the great ocean, the sense of a vast wall of darkness closing in around them and leaving no loophole of escape.

The broken window in the wheeluse had been patched up temporarily with canvas, but the wind found a way through, bringing with it a fine dust of snow. Snow crept through the strained door frame also, and collected in little ridges. It was very cold in the wheelhouse, and the helmsman was thinking that his feet had turned to ice; there was no sensation in them except a dull, nagging pain, and the pain was in his fingers also. He stared at the compass bowl and longed for his trick to end.

Henderson could feel the ship trembling, and the trembling seemed to go up through his body, as though he were an integral part of the ship, feeling the buffeting of the sea as a belabouring of his own limbs. The ship's agony was his agony, adding a mental strain to the physical one that was making his whole frame ache. He was glad of Thouless's presence then; nothing seemed able to sap Thouless's energy; he never showed the smallest sign of being tired; it was as though his limbs were in fact made of steel, steel springs that no amount of work could affect. Thouless gave the impression that, if need be, he could go on for a week without sleep, without rest, and with only the barest minimum of nourishment. Henderson envied him. At Thouless's age he could have done the same; at Thouless's age and with two good legs instead of one leg and a stump with a piece of insensible, creaking machinery stuck on the end of it.

He said: 'I wonder whether that plane is going to stand much more of this?'

'We made it as secure as we could,' Thouless said, 'but aircraft aren't made to stand a lot of pounding, even seaplanes.'

'How is the bosun getting on?'

Thouless said sourly: 'He'll be all right. Just a crack on the head. Maybe knock some sense into him.'

'In my experience,' Henderson said, 'it never works that way. More often the reverse.'

*　　*　　*

Jaggers was entertaining visitors in the hospital — Toresen and Carson. It had been Toresen's idea. He bore no love for Jaggers, but nevertheless felt that it would be an act of

209

charity to go along and see the invalid, to find out how he was progressing. He asked Carson to go with him, and Carson made no objection.

'Okay. Let's go and gloat.'

Jaggers, with his bandaged head and unshaven chin and the blood all drained out of his face, looked a pretty sick man. The pain was still throbbing, but not quite so vehemently as it had done when he first awakened. The throbbing had become muted, as though the gong-beater were using a smaller gong.

Toresen said: 'How's it going, kiddo? You don't look too perky.'

'I don't feel too perky neither,' Jaggers said. 'I don't feel worth two penn'orth of old rope.'

'You'll pull through though. I've seen worse cases than you get well in a couple of minutes when somebody mentioned shore leave.'

Toresen laughed, and the laugh seemed to beat back off the sides of the hospital. Jaggers closed his eyes, wincing.

'I got enough to put up with,' he said, 'without you making that noise.'

'You don't know when you're well off. Nice comfortable bunk, no work to do, away from it all, away from all the bad weather and such. You're doing fine. You ought to see what it's like up on deck.'

210

Jaggers's eyes opened again. Toresen could see the panic in them. 'I heard there was something wrong. Stebbing was telling me — '

Toresen was contemptuous. 'Now, what would that dishwasher know about the ship? What did he tell you?'

'He said there was a crack.'

'He said right,' Carson chipped in. 'There is a crack.'

'Bad?'

'Bad as all hell,' Carson said. He did not like Jaggers well enough to trouble about reassuring him. 'You got your lifejacket handy?'

'He can do without that,' Toresen said. 'No lifejacket is going to do anybody any good in these waters.'

Jaggers's scared gaze flickered from one big man to the other. They did not look nervous; they talked about these things as if they were matters that did not really concern them. Jaggers could not do that. Even in the insulated hospital in the middle of the ship the gale was a living presence, making itself apparent in every movement, every vibration, every agonized whimper of timber and metal.

'For God's sake,' Jaggers said, 'give me a smoke.'

Toresen felt in the depths of his clothing

and hauled up a flat tin. 'Here you are, kiddo.'

Carson refused Toresen's offer of a cigarette, but lit a thin, evil-looking cigar. The hospital began to fill with smoke.

'I been thinking — ' Carson began, and stopped suddenly. And then they heard it — a kind of ringing noise, the kind of noise that might be made by a sledgehammer striking an iron girder. It grew louder, became more highpitched, and stopped as abruptly as it had started. It was succeeded immediately by a sound like thunder, incredibly, frighteningly close. It was as though a storm were breaking — there, inside the ship — right at the very heart of the vessel.

The hospital shook; the light flickered and went out. Jaggers screamed and Toresen swore. Then the thunder stopped also; and as it stopped the ship gave a lurch to port, so violent and so sudden that Jaggers was thrown out of his bunk to fall in the darkness upon the reeling bodies of the other men. In a moment all three of them were lying in a heap, struggling to get to their feet, with the ship staggering wildly as if all control of it had been lost.

Jaggers heard Carson's voice. 'That crack! That Goddamn crack!'

He knew then that the disaster had come.

That which he had dreaded was upon them. Suddenly he became as uncontrolled as the ship, lashing out with arms and legs and screaming in a wild, scarcely human voice, the voice of utter panic.

A blow on the jaw silenced him. He did not know who had hit him — Carson or Toresen — but it was Carson who snarled savagely: 'Stow that! Stow that damn noise! That won't help.'

A match scraped and flared. Jaggers looked up and saw that the others were both standing. The light flickered on the white sides of the hospital, flickered and went out.

'We better get out of here,' Carson said. 'We better get out quick.'

Toresen groped to the door and tried to open it, but the door was jammed tight; it would not budge.

He steadied himself against the bucking motion of the deck under his feet, and said to Carson: 'Strike another match, Steve.'

The match flared. Toresen held on to the door knob with one hand, raised his foot and kicked out the lower panels of the door.

From the alleyway outside they heard the ominous gurgle of water.

★ ★ ★

213

It had been snowing for some time when Grant started out on his round of the gun positions. The snow flicked at his eyes as he went sliding and groping across the after catwalk, and he was a blind man feeling for familiar objects, but seeing nothing. He could feel the snow caking on the wool of his Balaclava helmet; he could feel some of it going through, penetrating to his neck and even to his back; he could feel a trickle of ice-cold water moving between his shoulder blades, moving down towards his waist.

He was about half-way across when the catwalk began to whip. He could feel the vibration of it through his gloves and through his boots. It was not like the normal shudder that came and was gone; this continued, increased, until the catwalk was like the plucked string of a violin.

Grant began to run then. He ran as in a nightmare, with a deep horror that was not fully understood, yet which pressed upon him, urging him forward. He ran clumsily, stumblingly, his heavy leather jack-boots sliding on the snow-coated boards of the catwalk and his heavy clothes hampering him. His heart hammered and his breath came like a sob, and once he fell and could feel the boards drumming under him; and then he was up again and rushing forward across the last yard of the way and on to the firmer footing of the midships section.

He heard the scream of rending metal rising even above the clamour of the storm, and the deck beneath him jerked upward, flinging him against the steel wall of the accommodation, so that all the bones in his body were jarred by the shock. A fount of seawater came up out of the darkness and fell upon him, drenching him under its icy impact. And then the deck went down again with the sickening speed of a scenic railway car rushing down a slope, and he was thrown against the rails with all the breath knocked out of him.

He clung to the rails desperately, staring into a dark gulf below him and wondering whether it could really be as he feared. He went down on his hands and knees and crawled to the gap in the rails where the catwalk began. He stretched out a hand through the gap and felt for the catwalk, and found nothing. There was nothing there but the jagged ends of steel, and below him the surging, boiling surface of the sea.

He drew back from the gap and, still on his hands and knees, fearful of standing up, he crawled away to the port side. And there his groping hand touched a man's leg, and he heard Tarbat's voice coming hoarsely out of the darkness.

'Who's that?'

'Me,' he said. 'Sergeant Grant.' And he stood up then, but still holding to the rails, not letting the stout feel of the iron go out of his hands.

'By God!' Tarbat shouted. 'By God, she's broke in two!'

'I know,' Grant answered. 'I know.'

They knew the answer now. There was no longer any doubt about the crack. It had opened into a great breach that had split the ship in halves. It was no longer one ship, but two — two helpless, wallowing derelicts at the mercy of the sea and the storm. For a while these two half-ships might stay afloat, since the whole vessel was a honeycomb of watertight compartments and there was buoyancy in each part. But in a storm such as this the end could surely not be long delayed.

'My kit's back there,' Grant said. 'All of it. Lost.'

And back there were Brennan and Rankin, the galley-boy and the crew, and all the men at work in the engine-room. They were all gone, all swallowed up in the night and the blizzard.

★ ★ ★

Captain Henderson had just sat down on the settee in the chartroom when the *Rosa Dartle* began to shudder, and he knew the meaning of that shudder. He got up from the settee and could feel the vibration coming up through the chartroom table on which his hand was resting.

He went into the wheelhouse, and Thouless moved towards him and said close in his ear: 'I think this is it, sir.'

He put his hand on Thouless's arm and gripped it hard. He knew that Thouless was right. This was what they had both been fearing ever since Thouless had discovered that crack in the ship's structure.

Several alternative courses of action passed through his mind and came to nothing because there was no time left. He made a move to ring through to the engine-room half the ship's length away, but at that moment the wheelhouse seemed to leap upward and jerk sideways all in the same swift movement, and Henderson was sent sprawling, with the pain jabbing like a needle in the stump of his leg and stars whirling in front of his eyes.

And then there was just the darkness; that and the noise of seas breaking over the ship and the high, wild screaming of the wind; and out of the darkness and the tumult he heard Thouless's voice.

'I'll go and see what's happened.'

He heard the door of the wheelhouse open and bang shut again, and he struggled to get up, but the artificial leg hampered his movements, so that he had to be content with a sitting posture, his back to the port wall of the wheelhouse and his legs stretched out in front of him.

He heard another voice, the helmsman's, fearful, uncertain, begging for reassurance.

'What's happened, sir? I can't see nothing, and the wheel's gone kind of dead.'

Dead! A dead wheel and a rudderless ship. Perhaps they were all dead, all murdered by the sea and the treacherous weakness of metal.

He said harshly: 'Come here. Lift me up.'

He heard the man shuffling towards him in the darkness.

'Where are you, sir? I can't see — '

'Here, man, here.'

A foot struck the stump of his leg and pain surged up again; pain and anger.

'Don't kick me, you fool. Give me your hand.'

The two hands found each other and gripped. Henderson was on his feet, and the ship tried to throw him down again, and failed.

'Has she broken her back, sir?' The voice

coming out of the darkness was like a whimper.

'How do I know?' Henderson said. 'She's nearly broken mine.'

The door of the wheelhouse crashed open and a whirl of snow came in with a gust of freezing wind. Thouless came with it also.

'Right enough,' Thouless said. 'Chopped in half. That was a crack all right.'

The helmsman gave a queer, bubbling cry of terror. It sounded more like an animal than a man.

'A pleasant situation,' Henderson said. 'I wonder where that trawler is?'

★ ★ ★

The trawler was two miles away, and the officer in command of her, who was not, as Henderson had conjectured, a stockbroker but had until the outbreak of the War earned a none too lucrative living on the stage, was worried about the *Rosa Dartle*. Having found the tanker, he took a fatherly interest in her and would have looked upon the loss of that ship as a personal bereavement. He had tried to stay within reach, but in the darkness and the storm and the blizzard it had been impossible to maintain contact. He was reluctant to use radio communication

219

because of the danger of such signals being picked up by the enemy and giving away the position. Radio would be used only as a last resort.

It was at 2028 hours when a look-out noticed a glow of light showing through the snow on the trawler's starboard beam. The light grew so rapidly that soon there could be no doubt that it must be a fire, and a fire in that position at that time was likely to be nothing else but the *Rosa Dartle*, a tanker with ten thousand tons of highly inflammable cargo on board.

The trawler altered course immediately and made all the speed that was possible in such conditions towards the beacon of the burning ship. As they struggled forward, butting through the icy seas and riding high on the crests of mountainous waves, the fire grew; and once, for a few minutes, the curtain of snow was drawn aside and they could see under the column of flame and smoke the stark outline of the burning tanker with her stern towards them.

Then the snow came again, and there was only the glow of the fire showing, a signal of distress that could not be mistaken.

The man who had been an actor and now was in command of an armed trawler felt a bitter disappointment. In spite of all his care, the tanker had come to grief; now there would be no possibility of leading it back in triumph to the convoy; now the best that he could hope for would be to pick up survivors. And with the sea that was running at this moment, that was a very slender hope.

He was turning these thoughts over in his mind when the glow of the fire suddenly seemed to burst apart, flinging out bright spears of flame in all directions. His brain had recorded the fact of the explosion even before the sound of it came rolling towards the trawler. The sound was merely a confirmation of the fact.

'That finishes it,' he muttered. 'Oh, the poor devils!'

The trawler stayed in the vicinity until morning, searching for survivors and finding none. Finally, she abandoned the search and went about her business. She carried with her the information that the tanker *Rosa Dartle* had exploded and sunk with all hands.

It was the kind of information that was not at all uncommon at that period.

10

The Day

Towards morning the gale abated. In fact, it seemed that the peak of severity had been reached at the time when the *Rosa Dartle* broke in two. It was as if this had been the object of the storm, and that having achieved its object it had ceased to have any further ambition. From that moment it had begun to die.

Not that it died quickly. The wind still blew strongly for hours, and before daylight came in drab colours to reveal the emptiness of the sea, the forward half of the *Rosa Dartle* had drifted many miles from the position in which the after half had caught fire and exploded in a furious burst of smoke and flame.

There had been nothing that those on board the still floating half ship could do. Indeed, it was fortunate for them that a gap had opened between the two halves, for the fire might have leapt the space dividing them and both might have gone up in one great conflagration. As it was, the forward half, the half without engines and without rudder,

222

drifted away into the night, hiding itself in the snow and the darkness from the searching trawler that had come too late to help.

The night passed slowly for the men on board, expecting that at any moment the ship might be overwhelmed by the seas beating upon her open wounds and threatening to capsize this drifting, helpless mass of steel and timber that still enclosed her thousands of tons of liquid cargo. The movements of the hulk were not like the movements of a ship with steerage way, a ship that could in the last resort put her head to the sea and ride out the storm in that manner. This ungainly mass shifted erratically, capriciously, now turning her starboard side to the wind, so that she heeled over to port, dipping her rails under, now floundering with her head to the wind and her bows ploughing deep into the advancing seas until all the foredeck was submerged and only the bridge structure stood up like a rocky island in the midst of the storm. Sometimes the bulkhead that was now the stern would take the full force of the attack, and then the spray would leap high over the superstructure and the ship would tremble as it had trembled in the final break-up.

There was no sleep for those on board. They waited in darkness for the inevitable, the moment when this floating island would continue to float no longer and they would be, not living men, but explorers on an uncharted sea. For, if the ship sank now, death was certain. In this sea there was no smallest possibility of launching a boat. A raft might get away, but what hope of life was there for a man on a raft with the temperature down below zero? The raft might float on for weeks, for months, but the men lying on it would be dead men, stiff and frozen. You could forget about rafts.

But the night passed away, and in the morning the ship was still afloat. Looking down from the bridge, Henderson could see that the Heinkel on the forecastle had taken a beating. The tail-plane was gone, the fuselage was twisted into a tangle of metal, and the port wing had broken off and had become wedged in the rails of the ship, with the engine hanging half over the side and threatening at any moment to plunge into the sea. The cockpit looked as if a steam-hammer had been at work on it; it was crushed and shapeless. It was hard to believe that this mass of broken and twisted metal had ever been a machine capable of lifting itself and its crew high above the clouds. There was no life in it any longer. It was a dead thing lying upon the deck of a dying ship.

Henderson noticed that the bows were lower than they should have been. The wind had died away to no more than a stiff breeze, and the seas that broke over the ship did so now almost gently in comparison with their earlier fury. The sea was like a man ashamed of his raging, trying to forget that he had so recently lost all control of himself and had lashed out wildly at everything falling in his way. Now it wished to forget; it wished everyone to forget. But there was the evidence still — the broken ship, the broken aircraft, the battered but unbroken men.

Thouless came up on to the bridge and stood beside Henderson, looking at the situation in the dull light of morning and weighing up the chances.

'Looks bad,' he said.

The ship was not only down by the head, unmistakably so; she was also listing to port. That might make it difficult to launch the starboard lifeboat. But one lifeboat might well be enough. A lot of men had gone with the after part of the ship. They would need no boat — ever.

'We shall have to call a muster,' Henderson said.

He looked at the sea, thinking about the chances of a boat, the risks of exposure, balancing those risks against the risks of staying on board this derelict. The sea, no longer raging, had not lost its power to harm them. They were still at the mercy of this great monster. They had not escaped.

'I wonder where that trawler went?' Thouless said.

He put the binoculars to his hot, weary eyes and searched the grey waste of the sea. There was nothing; no ship, no boat, no piece of floating wreckage that might have remained from the half of the ship that had gone down in a last blaze of glory, no raft supporting a man's dead body; nothing.

Henderson said quietly: 'The trawler may have sunk too.'

He felt tired, agonizingly tired. His whole body ached; it was a mass of strains and bruises, and the stump of his leg was sore where the living tissue joined the dead material of the artificial limb. Yet there could be no rest; there was so much to do, so many decisions to make. And it was he who had to make them.

Thouless looked at him, and there was a question in Thouless's eyes. He would not put the question into words, but it was there to be read: Are we to abandon ship now?

Henderson had no answer. He had come to no final decision, though he had given a deal of thought to the matter. Was there any possibility of bringing this half ship into port? If this had been the Western Approaches there might have been a good chance of doing so. A deepsea tug would have come out to take the hulk in tow. But in these northern waters there were no deep-sea tugs waiting to be called upon for rescue operations.

The Russians? Captain Henderson shook his head. It was no good expecting help from that quarter even if it had been possible to get in touch; and at the moment that also was out of the question, since the wireless aerial had been carried away at the time of the break-up. It might be possible to rig up an emergency aerial; he would have the radio officers on that job. Yet, even if an emergency aerial were erected, would it be wise to send out a signal? Might it not attract the kind of attention that was not wanted — enemy submarines, enemy surface ships, enemy aircraft? The *Rosa Dartle* — as much of her as was left afloat — had only a single Oerlikon on the starboard side and a trough projector for defence. It would need no more than a solitary bomber to finish her off. It was a bad situation, whichever way you looked at it.

'See that the boats are ready, Tom.'

He saw the rapid upward jerk of Thouless's head; he saw the question that was not put into words.

'We will not abandon yet,' Henderson said. 'It may become necessary later, but for the present we stay.'

Thouless nodded. There was a certain mute approval in the nod. Henderson knew Thouless's code: Never abandon a ship while there is the smallest possibility of saving it. And that applied to the part of a ship.

Henderson agreed with that up to a point. But with him the question of men's lives was one that could not be ignored. Save the ship if possible, yes; but do not throw lives away needlessly. So where Thouless saw his duty plain without complications, Henderson saw his not quite so plain and with a hundred and one complications and balances and counterbalances. Above all, he wished to lose no more lives. Meanwhile, it would be as well to find out just how many there were left to lose.

'We'll have that muster right away,' he said. 'See to it, will you, Tom?'

They mustered on the starboard side under the shelter of the boat-deck, and Henderson was shocked to see how few there were; no more than eighteen all told, not counting the two Germans. In those eighteen there were three radio officers, three gunners, three Americans, and two stewards; there were the carpenter, the bosun, the cook, and one AB. The third mate was there, but the second was missing, and missing also were all the engineers and all the rest of the crew. It had been a drastic thinning out indeed.

Mr Thouless took the names: Third Mate Matthews, First Radio Officer Clore, Second Radio Officer Barnett, Third Radio Officer Jones, Chief Steward Peters, Second Steward Stebbing, Bosun Jaggers, Carpenter Toresen, AB Parkin, Sergeant Grant, Gunner Bowie, Gunner Sime, Chief Cook Tarbat, Carson, Kline, and Muller. At the end of the list he added Mohr and Fehler.

No need for more than one boat, Henderson mused. He wondered what had happened to the second mate. There seemed to be no reason why he should have been down aft when the ship cracked in two. But the fact had to be accepted. He was glad it had not been Thouless. Matthews was a good man too.

He spoke to them briefly. 'I do not have to explain the situation to you. You can see for yourselves. It is bad, but it could have been worse. We are at least afloat and the gale has died down.'

Jaggers, with his bandaged head, holding his belly with both hands, said hoarsely: 'When do we launch the boats?'

He wanted to get away from this hulk. He did not trust it. It might sink under you any minute. Let them get away now while there was still time.

Henderson looked at him. It was exactly the question one might have expected from Jaggers.

'We launch the boats when there is no longer any chance of saving the ship.'

'No chance now, if you ask me,' Jaggers said. 'She's done for, finished. We ought to get away now. That's my opinion.'

'I do not recall asking for your opinion,' Henderson said acidly. 'However, the point is this: quite apart from the fact that it is our duty to remain until there is no further hope of saving what is left of the ship and the cargo, it is in our own interests to do so. Conditions on board may be rough, but they are not nearly as rough as an open boat. Another thing, the trawler that was with us yesterday will be searching the area. It is more likely to sight an object the size of half a tanker than something as small as a ship's boat.'

It did not occur to him, it did not occur to any of them, that the trawler might have seen the explosion of the after part of the *Rosa Dartle* and have taken it for the destruction of the entire ship. They could not tell that the trawler was at this moment steaming to rejoin the convoy and bearing the news of their destruction. If they had known they might have been less hopeful; they might all have thought, as Jaggers thought, that now was the time to get away, that it was madness to risk even one more night on board this floating death-trap.

But it was only Kline who supported Jaggers. 'How do we know,' Kline said, 'that the trawler ain't down at the bottom right now? How do we know it's out there looking for us?'

'We don't know,' Henderson said. 'We have to act on probabilities.'

'Maybe we don't all go for them probabilities,' Kline said. 'Maybe we say to hell with probabilities. Maybe we — '

Carson's voice cut in on him sharp, like a whiplash. 'Maybe you pipe down, feller. You said your mouthful. You do what the Cap'n says.'

Kline swung round on Carson, but again the glint in Carson's eye stopped him. This was no time for the showdown. Some other time. Not now. Some better time.

'Okay,' he said. 'Okay; let's all die. Let's all sing hymns and die for freedom. Okay.'

★   ★   ★

The day passed slowly. The sea, as if weary of its efforts and now wishing to sleep, became calm, its surface undulating gently, stirred only to harmless ripples by the light wind. The *Rosa Dartle* drifted south-eastward, turning slowly upon her axis, a great slab of iron buoyed up by the pockets of air trapped within her. The clouds moved away and the sun came to peer coldly down upon them, not warming the air, not melting the ice that clung to the ship like a glassy sheath.

Mr Thouless climbed to Monkey Island above the bridge and searched with his binoculars all round the wide circle of the horizon. There was nothing to give him hope.

Sergeant Grant and the two gunners took watches on the starboard Oerlikon, which was the only surviving gun, and waited for a German plane to come flying up from the south in the clear, cold light of the day. And no plane came.

The ship was cold and silent. There was no steam for the heating system, no electricity, no vibration of engines. In the wheelhouse the abandoned wheel seemed to bear mute testimony to the helplessness of this ungainly, wallowing craft. Captain Henderson, going into the wheelhouse, experienced a strange feeling as he looked at the wheel. It was as though that silent, motionless piece of joinery were accusing him. Never before in all his long life as a sailor could he remember walking on the bridge of a ship at sea and finding the wheel unmanned. Always there had been a helmsman keeping his gaze fixed on the compass, holding the ship to its proper course. But now there was no helmsman and no course; only this slow drift before the wind and the tide, the end of which no man could foresee.

Henderson, his leg creaking, pain coming up through the stump, moved to the wheelhouse window and looked down at the foredeck. The sea was no longer foaming across it. Indeed, everything was so quiet now that it was almost eerie. He did not think there had been any deterioration since he had last looked at the situation. There was still the list to port, but it had not, so far as he could judge, increased. This half ship was still down slightly by the head, but not dangerously so.

There was a shadow on the deck, a wide shadow thrown by the bridge structure. As the ship turned slowly, the shadow moved away and sunlight glinted on the ice. As Henderson watched he saw Thouless and Toresen appear on the catwalk. He watched them walk to the forecastle and examine the wreckage of the Heinkel; then they came down the forecastle ladder and went into the storage space below.

Henderson turned away. He could rely on

Thouless. Thouless would leave nothing to chance. He thought suddenly of the two Germans and wondered how they were taking it. The irony of the situation struck him, and his lips curved into a smile. He passed a hand over his face and felt the rough bristle and the salt. He could taste the salt on his lips. Well, that was how it should be, for salt was the true mark of his calling.

* * *

Mohr was cold and angry. He rubbed his hands together, trying to warm them. Fehler believed that Mohr was also afraid; the anger might be a reflection of his fear. Fehler, too, was afraid; he admitted as much to himself, but he was not so afraid as he had been during the night. That had been a terrible time, when the light had gone out and there had been the fearsome movement of the ship, and the noise and the uncertainty of what was happening.

They had tried to get out of the cabin, but the door had been locked against them, and all their efforts to shift it had been futile. Then, after a long time, a man had opened the door from the outside and had told them that the ship had broken in two. The man was carrying an electric torch, but he used it

234

sparingly, as if in the knowledge that it might be needed for a long time to come. And they could tell from the sound of his voice that he, too, was afraid.

Fehler said: 'What is going to happen? What was that explosion? Are we sinking?'

'As to sinking,' the man said, 'I don't know about that. We may be or we may not be.' He switched the torch off and spoke to them from the darkness. 'That explosion was our other half going up in flames.' There was bitterness in his tone. 'All the men too. Shipmates. All gone. We'll be lucky if we don't go the same way.'

'What do we do?' Fehler asked. 'Do we take to the boats?'

'In this sea? Some chance of that. Might come to it later though. My orders are to leave your door unfastened. Not much damage you can do now. It's been done.'

He had gone away then, leaving them to listen to the storm and wait. And so they had waited through the long hours of darkness as the warmth gradually went out of the ship and the chill of the Arctic crept in, even into the heart of the accommodation.

Fehler had not expected to see another day. He did not imagine that half a ship could long remain afloat — in such conditions. It was with a feeling of intense relief, therefore,

235

that he saw the light of morning coming through the plate glass of the porthole, and knew that the night was over.

Fehler listened to the sound of Mohr rubbing his hands together, and wondered whether the pain in his own left wrist was getting worse. When he moved the fingers of his left hand little needles of pain stabbed at him. Perhaps the bone had been splintered.

Mohr said bitterly: 'I suppose they're going to let us die of cold.'

'Perhaps there is nothing to be done about it,' Fehler said. 'I suppose they are cold too.'

'They could bring us food. Are we to starve?'

'Have patience, Konrad.'

'Patience! You talk to me of patience.' He put his hands in his pockets and turned his back on Fehler, staring moodily out of the porthole. Fehler could hear him muttering: 'Such bad luck. Only a little more and we should have been away. Such luck.'

'If you ask me,' Fehler said, 'we're lucky to be alive.'

Mohr answered coldly: 'I did not ask you. But what luck is it to be alive in such a situation as this? If we do not lose our lives we are prisoners for the rest of the War. What indignity.'

'It is not the indignity that worries me.'

'No. Because you have no proper spirit, no pride. But for a man like me it is different.'

'A man like you should, of course, have been immune from capture,' Fehler said ironically. 'Perhaps the Fates had not been suitably instructed. Possibly there was some clerical error at Party headquarters. Or possibly, though I hesitate to make the suggestion, our Führer's influence does not extend to the gods.'

Mohr swung round, anger flaming up in his face. 'Martin Fehler, you forget yourself. One does not make jokes about the Party; even less does one make jokes about the Führer. It may be my duty to make a report on your conduct when we get back to our squadron.'

'Konrad Mohr,' Fehler said, 'has it not occurred to you that we stand very little chance of ever getting back?'

'Then I may have to punish you myself.'

'Don't be a fool. How can you punish me?'

'That you may discover — to your cost.'

They stared at each other for a few moments, and then Fehler shrugged his shoulders and turned away. 'We are both being fools. It is possible that neither of us may live through another day. What are we quarrelling about? A few words. It is senseless.'

'Words have killed men,' Mohr said. But he

too turned away and went back to the porthole, staring out on to a bleak sea and rubbing his hands for warmth.

It was Muller who brought them their cold food. Muller was nervous, rather like a man who has been sent to feed a pair of newly captured wild beasts. He did not know how they would react. Perhaps they would set upon him and maul him.

He said, standing in the doorway with the tray of food: 'It's cold, I'm afraid. It's the best they can do.' And then he repeated the statement in German.

Fehler said with some surprise: 'You speak our language then?'

'My father was German. He emigrated to the States.' He spoke almost apologetically, thinking that they might consider it a reprehensible act to leave Germany and go to America.

But Fehler said: 'He was a wise man.'

Mohr, however, broke in harshly: 'Why did he leave the Fatherland? Was he a Jew?'

'No,' Muller said, 'he was not a Jew, but he could not make a decent living in Germany, so he went to a country where he could.'

'A soft, fat country,' Mohr said contemptuously.

'My country,' Muller said. 'And not soft.'

'Your country? But you are German.'

238

'I am an American,' Muller said.

Fehler began to eat a corned-beef sandwich, sitting on his bunk and looking at Muller. 'If you are American, why are you on board a British ship?'

'It happened that way.'

Muller liked the look of Fehler, but he was apprehensive of Mohr. Mohr really looked like the newly-caged wild beast. He supposed that they were both Nazis. He had read so much about Nazi atrocities that it gave him a queer, unreal feeling to be so close to two of them. He had hardly expected them to look like ordinary men.

'I'd like to go to America,' Fehler said. 'I always did think it would be worth a visit. Might even be the place to live. Somewhere new, away from the old ideas, the old chains.'

'It's a great country.'

Mohr scowled at Fehler. This talk sounded to him very like disaffection. Fehler would bear watching.

'Do you think there would be a chance there for a man like me?' Fehler said. 'Perhaps I could teach.'

'There are chances for anyone who is willing to work.'

'I shall have to think about it.' He grinned at Muller, his jaws working steadily. Muller felt that he ought to go, but still he hesitated in the doorway. There was a curious fascination in watching these two men who had fallen out of the air, men who ought really to have been dead. There was a fascination in the contrast between them.

'Of course,' Fehler said, 'I may never have the opportunity of going to America. We are all in a dangerous situation. Is that not so?'

'Very dangerous.'

'How would you estimate our chances of survival?'

'Better than they were four hours ago,' Muller said.

'But not good even now?'

'No, not good,' Muller said. He did not believe that any of them would escape. He did not see how they could. They might postpone their fate, but the sea would have them in the end, all of them. He was scared, but if it was all to do over again, he would do it. For his own self-respect he would do it again.

'But the weather is improving. I imagine when the sea has calmed down enough we shall take to the boats? That is the only way left.'

'Not yet. We are staying with the ship for the present.'

'Foolishness,' Mohr said. 'The ship is finished.'

Muller wondered whether he was thinking that a U-boat or a bomber might locate this remnant of the *Rosa Dartle*. There would be hardly any defence, and there was still plenty of cargo to make a good fire. Perhaps that was what was worrying Mohr. It worried Muller too, but he said only: 'Not quite finished yet.'

'No stern. No engines. No rudder. Of course it is finished. It is a matter of time only.'

'You had better tell the captain,' Muller said. 'He is the one who makes decisions.' He turned towards the door. 'You will be told if it is decided to abandon ship.'

'I hope so,' Mohr said. 'I hope so.'

* * *

Mr Thouless was seeing to it that the boats were well fitted out with provisions for a long, cold voyage. He had the stewards, Peters and Stebbing, as well as Jaggers and Parkin and Tarbat, working on the transfer of canned food and biscuits and condensed milk from the store-room to the boats. He had extra blankets put in them, tins of tobacco and cigarettes, and a paraffin stove in each boat with drums of fuel. He added carpenter's tools and axes, leaving nothing to chance. In the starboard boat he put a rifle and two

241

bandoliers of ammunition.

There was plenty of room in the lifeboats, for each one was designed to carry some thirty men. Even if they took only one there would be room to spare.

Jaggers was grumbling to Parkin: 'We ought to go now. There'll never be a better time. Look at that sea — dead calm. We get another storm and it'll sink this bit of a ship and there'll be no boats launched. We ought to go now.'

Thouless had sharp ears; he heard part of Jaggers's complaint and guessed at the remainder. He walked up to Jaggers with his springy step that even weariness had not subdued, and he thrust his beard at Jaggers's heavy face.

'If you're so keen to go, we could arrange it. Give you a raft. One big raft all to yourself. Nobody to worry you. How about it?'

Tarbat laughed, his whole, massive body shaking with the laughter. 'That's right, Mr Thouless. He'd have no worries then. Do his own cooking too.'

Jaggers looked savagely at Tarbat. 'Stow it, you fat poisoner. You keep your nose out of what don't concern you, see? Else you might get it hurt.'

'Not by a runt like you,' Tarbat said.

Jaggers was carrying a canvas bag full of

stores. He swung it back-handed at Tarbat's head and the stiff canvas jabbed Tarbat's eye. Tarbat reacted to the pain with a rapidity that was surprising in so bulky a man. He swung a fist at Jaggers that had developed its strength from pounding dough. Jaggers went down flat on his back, and his bandaged head struck the deck boards.

'That'll learn you,' Tarbat said.

But Jaggers was up in an instant, made wild by the pain in his head. He hauled out a long sheath-knife and came at Tarbat, his face wicked. If Thouless had not intervened then Tarbat might have felt the point of that knife in his big stomach. But Thouless clamped a hand on Jaggers's wrist.

'You can cut that out. What in hell's got into you? There's eighteen of us left and you want to start carving each other up. Put that knife away.'

Jaggers put the knife back in its sheath, but he still glowered at Tarbat and muttered to himself. Here was one more to add to the list of his hates.

★ ★ ★

The sun was a silver disc glowing with a fire that did not warm them. The cold crept down from the Pole, flowing between them and the sun; and the ice hung upon the rigging and did not melt. The ship moved before the wind, turning slowly, and the shadow of her superstructure lay now upon the port side and now upon the starboard, and the shadow undulated with the long, slow undulation of the water.

Bowie stood by the Oerlikon, the one remaining gun, and wished he was out of it all. He wished he was on dry land, somewhere warm, anywhere but in this present situation, which was certain to end in disaster. He thought of Rankin and Brennan and the rest of them who had perished with the other half of the ship, and he almost envied them. They were dead, but they were out of it. As for him, was he not likely to be dead also — today, tomorrow, or the next day? For him the agony was being spun out longer, that was all. And yet he wanted to live; with every fibre of his being he wanted it; the desire for life possessed him completely and utterly, so that he felt that he would have accepted a life sentence in prison if only thus could he have escaped from death.

He leaned on the edge of the gun-box and looked at the sunlight glinting on the sea; and as he looked, he heard a sound, and it was the faint sound of aero-engines a long way off. And in those waters he knew that there was only the one kind of aircraft — hostile.

There was a pair of binoculars hanging from a strap about his neck. He lifted them to his eyes and searched the southern horizon, and found the plane. He did not know whether it had seen the ship, but he did not wait to find out. He began to blow his whistle, the alarm signal, urgently, repeatedly.

Grant was on the gun when the plane attacked. For a while they had hoped that it was going to leave them unmolested, that it had not seen them. It was flying in a westerly direction, and it had become a minute black speck on the pale blue background of the sky before it turned and came back, and they knew that they were not to escape so easily.

Grant clipped the harness about his back and eased himself into the shoulder-pieces and moved the gun-barrel round and watched the plane through the spider-web of the sight. And this was the same again, the same, but different; for now he was alone where before he had been one of many; and now the forest of guns that had pointed skyward from the decks of the convoy had been whittled down to this solitary twenty-millimetre cannon.

As he stood there, balancing himself against the slight roll of the ship, he felt the burden of his responsibility; and yet he felt it.

not so much as a burden but as a spur. He did not experience fear, but a kind of invigorating excitement such as a runner feels while he waits for the starting-gun. He was keyed up, ready to go, and his only regret was that beside him in the gun-box was Bowie and not Brennan. But Bowie knew his job. He was small, but he could lift a magazine into position, and that was all that was needed from him. All the same, it would have felt better with Brennan.

The plane grew in the sight. It had four engines; it looked like a Focke-Wolfe Kurier, the kind that plagued the Western Approaches. Grant let it have a burst at a thousand yards and was wide. He saw bombs dropping from the belly of the plane, and he brought the gun on and gave another burst, and a piece of wing chipped off the Kurier, and the ship seemed to leap out of the water as the bombs exploded. Grant heard the sudden whoosh of the rockets going up from the trough, and saw them burst in the air; but they were nowhere near the Kurier.

He yelled to Bowie: 'Change this mag. We'll give him a real doing next time.'

'You better,' Bowie said. 'Another shaking like that and the bloody ship'll fall apart.'

Bowie was thinking that he could have done better with the gun. Sergeants were all alike; thought they could shoot; you couldn't tell them anything. He would have liked to have a go in the harness himself; he would have shown Grant a thing or two. But he whipped the old magazine off and hoisted the full one on its place.

'You better get him,' he said, 'before he gets us. By Christ, you'd better.'

The Kurier circled and came in again. It came in over the bows of the half ship, and a bomb fell where the stern of the vessel would have been if there had been a stern, and the blast thrust against the bulkheads that stood between the sea and the tanks of alcohol, pressing in upon them and feeling for the lines of weakness.

Grant fired at the plane coming in and swung the gun as it thundered overhead and took it again going away, emptying the magazine and yelling for Bowie to change it.

'When you going to hit him?' Bowie said. 'When you going to cut that bastard down?' But he said it under his breath, not letting Grant hear.

★ ★ ★

Mohr and Fehler had heard the plane coming in, and Mohr had looked out of the porthole and had seen it and recognized it.

247

'Kurier,' he said.

So this was it, Fehler thought. This was what it felt like to be on the other end, the receiving end. He felt sick. He wanted to be out there; he wanted to signal to the Kurier: 'Do not bomb. Do not bomb.' Where was the point in attacking a ship that was already dead? Could they not see that it was unnecessary, a waste of bombs?

And then he heard the Oerlikon firing and the swish of the bombs, and suddenly he realized that Mohr was lying flat on his face with his hands clasped over his head, shivering.

He heard the hollow ringing of the ship as the bomb blast came, and he thought: This will finish the job; this will finish us all. And he stood there, not moving, holding on to the side of the upper bunk and looking down at Mohr and listening to the sounds of battle between one small anti-aircraft gun and a bomber, and waiting for the great blast that would send them all to destruction.

★ ★ ★

It was the third mate, Matthews, who was operating the trough projector. There was not a great deal you could do with the trough; it was simply a rack of fourteen rockets which

248

were fired by a small electric battery. You waited until the target came into your sight, then you pressed the trigger and up went your fourteen rockets, spreading out like the pellets from a shotgun. If you carried out instructions carefully it should theoretically have been easy to register a hit. But between theory and practice was a great gulf, and Matthews, at his first attempt, discovered that it was at least as easy to miss.

He was still reloading the trough with Parkin's help when the Kurier came in on its second run, and he had no chance to fire at it again.

He yelled at Parkin: 'Come on, man, hurry. Let's have them.'

Parkin's hands were cold and he was scared, and the rockets were greased. One of them slipped from his grasp and fell to the deck.

Parkin, closer to the explosion, was killed instantly. He was more fortunate than Matthews. A jagged fragment of metal gouged its way into Matthews's stomach, ripping through the hot entrails and leaving a path of bloody havoc.

Matthews began to scream. He went on screaming for what seemed a very long while. Mr Thouless, who had come running from the bridge, was glad when he stopped screaming, because that meant that Matthews was dead.

★ ★ ★

The Kurier took a fast run over the ship, but there were no bombs left. It raked the decks with machine-gun bullets, and made a line of holes in the bottom of the starboard lifeboat. Henderson stood on the starboard wing of the bridge and heard the swish of the bullets and the whine of ricochets. He heard them very close to him, ripping into the bridge timbers and shattering the windows of the wheelhouse; but he did not move. A splinter of wood gashed his cheek and the blood ran down towards his collar, and he stood there with his hands resting on the stout teak, waiting for the crisis to pass.

★ ★ ★

Thouless was lying flat on the deck, with the body of Parkin on one side of him and the body of Matthews on the other. There was a horrible smell of warm blood and of something else coming from Matthews. It caught at Thouless's nose and throat, making him sick, nauseated. Matthews was lying full in his line of sight, and there was steam rising from the gouged entrails hanging from the stomach. Thouless closed his eyes.

★ ★ ★

Grant scored hits on this last run. He put a shell into the nose of the Kurier and another just behind the wing root, and he saw the sudden flash and glitter of the high explosive bursting. This time the Kurier did not come back; it flew away to the south with a thin trail of smoke coming from it. And then the smoke faded and the Kurier became smaller, and at last it was gone and there was no longer any sound of its engines, only the soft lapping of water against the sides of the ship and the faint creaking of woodwork.

'You got him that time,' Bowie said. 'By God, you got him that time.'

'I ought to have had him sooner,' Grant said. 'I ought to have knocked him into the sea. But he's away now.'

He could feel the heat coming from the gun-barrel, and the smell of burnt cordite pricked at his nostrils. The brass cartridge-cases jingled in the collecting-bag when he touched it.

'Better get this cleared and those mags filled up. We may have another visit.'

He wondered whether the Kurier would

251

get back to base. He was dissatisfied with himself because he had not made sure. The target had been big enough. He ought to have made sure.

He heard the creak of Henderson's leg, and then Henderson's voice behind him: 'You did well, Sergeant. Damn well.'

He turned and looked into Henderson's face with the blood drying on the cheek, and he thought how tired the Old Man looked.

He said bitterly: 'Not well enough, sir. I ought to have had him first go.'

'You did damn well,' Henderson said.

★　★　★

They buried the two dead men before nightfall, letting them slip almost silently into the cold, dark water. Lashed in canvas and weighted with iron, they went down into the depths, leaving only a vanishing ripple as the mark of their going.

And the ones that were left looked at the dark sea and the darkening sky and wondered who would be the next to follow in the wake of those who had gone.

11

The Night

Henderson awoke from a brief sleep to find someone tugging at his shoulder. He felt stiff and old, and more tired than he had ever been. He heard Thouless's voice, and detected the note of urgency in it.

'Are you awake, sir? Are you awake?'

Thouless was holding an electric torch, and the beam from it made a pool of light on the cabin floor, reflected and diffused, to cast a faint radiance over the whole cabin.

'All right, Tom,' Henderson said. 'Don't pull my shoulder off. I'm awake.'

He was aware that something was wrong, very much wrong. The bunk on which he was lying was tilted at an acute angle, so that he lay, as it were, in a trough between the bunk and the bulkhead to which it was fixed. It was a measure of his weariness that this tilting had not awakened him before Thouless had come into the cabin.

He struggled off the bunk now, fully clothed yet shivering in the cold that had penetrated everywhere.

253

'What's happened, Tom?'

'Some bulkheads must have given way. Those last bombs perhaps. Hard to tell. But she's going this time. No doubt about that.'

'We'll have to take the port boat.'

'The only one we can take. You're all right, sir?'

'I'm all right,' Henderson said. 'See that everybody is at the boat station. I'll be there.'

Thouless went away. Henderson felt under the pillow and found his own torch, left there in readiness for just such an emergency as this. He switched it on and wedged it on the bunk while he did what he had to do. The slope of the deck beneath his feet made it awkward for him. He felt the deck shift with a kind of jerk. She was going fast.

He pulled a coat on and slipped his arms into a kapok-padded lifejacket. He found the waterproof bag in which he had put the ship's papers, and slung this by its strap over his shoulder. Moving with difficulty, he went to the desk. He opened a drawer, found the picture of his wife, folded it, and thrust it into an inner pocket.

He opened another drawer and looked down at the revolver lying there. For a moment he hesitated. Then the thought of Mohr, of Kline, of Jaggers, of eighteen men in one boat impinged on his mind. He picked up the revolver and dropped it into the pocket of his coat. He took two boxes of .38 ammunition and dropped them into the pocket also.

★ ★ ★

It was Muller who went to fetch Mohr and Fehler, hurrying through the sloping alleyways behind the pencil beam of a pocket torch, and scared that the ship might go down before he could get back from his errand and up on to the boat-deck. There were noises in the alleyways, strange, furtive noises that all carried with them the same note of warning. Something ran past Muller on scampering, tiny feet; he saw the rat's eyes glowing in the light of the torch, and he shivered, not from cold, but because of the presence of the rat. The rat ran past and Muller hurried on, and he could feel the ship move.

The idea came to him that the ship was about to capsize, and he halted for a moment to make sure whether this was so. But the movement had stopped, and only the furtive noises remained to whisper to him of this calamity that was pressing close upon him. Somewhere he heard the sound of water trickling, as though a tap had been left running in an empty house. The ship smelled cold, dead, so that one might have imagined it already at the bottom of the sea with this one last pocket of enclosed air waiting to be engulfed.

Mohr and Fehler were asleep when he came to them. He was amazed that the ship could have gone so far on its way to destruction without waking them. He would have supposed that no one could have been unawake, unaware of the danger that was threatening.

He shook them roughly, letting the fear that was in him have its outlet in the wakening of these two heavy sleepers. They roused themselves reluctantly, as young men do, and Muller yelled at them: 'The ship's going. Hurry. The port lifeboat. Hurry!'

Waking in the cold, tilted cabin, with the strange whispering noises, they caught the infection of Muller's terror. They cast off the webs of sleep and started up from their bunks.

'You've got to follow me,' Muller said. 'No time to waste.'

Fehler said: 'Wait. Let us put our boots and coats on.'

Muller was in an agony of impatience, but he waited in the doorway, showing them the light so that they could put on their thick outer clothing. The ship gave another lurch.

'Hurry,' Muller begged, almost weeping. 'Hurry!'

When they were ready he turned and led them up the sloping alleyway and two flights of stairs and out into the bitterly cold air of the Arctic night. The sky was cloudless, and by the starlight they could see the dark outline of the ship's structure. They went up the ladder to the boat-deck, and the ladder was leaning so acutely to one side that they had to pull themselves up with both hands on the left-hand rail. Fehler, his left wrist useless, was at a disadvantage, but it would have taken more than that handicap to prevent his climbing the ladder.

The boat-deck was sloping down towards the water on the port side and it was sloping aft as well, so that it seemed as though the non-existent stern had dipped below the surface of the sea and was in the process of pulling the rest of the vessel after it.

By the lifeboat a group of men had gathered, blurred figures, their white faces showing palely, like ghosts in the darkness. Muller heard Thouless's sharp voice calling out names, and he could see a pin-point of light where Thouless was holding a shaded torch close to a sheet of paper.

'Grant.'

'Sir.'

'Bowie.'

'Sir.'

Muller could see the men move as their names were called, as if eager to get to the boat, eager to leave this ship that was surely sinking under them. Yet what awaited them out there in the Arctic in an open boat? The wind was freshening. It fluttered the paper in the mate's hand; it made a low, mournful whining among the shadowy obstructions of the boat-deck; it was cold, with the bitter cold of the polar wastes. And from this wind there would be no shelter.

'Carson.'

'Present.'

'Kline.'

'Sure, I'm here.'

'Muller.'

'I'm here, sir. I fetched Mohr and Fehler.'

'Good.' Mr Thouless folded the paper and stuffed it into his pocket. He switched off the electric torch. His voice was edgy; it seemed to cut through the darkness. 'Toresen, Carson, Grant — get into the boat. Don't forget the plug. You other men, stand by the falls.'

The deck was sloping more acutely. They could hear the water lapping over the rails below. Grant looked over the gunwale of the boat and knew that the sea was coming up to meet them, coming in long, slow undulations which moved along the side of the ship with a soft, chuckling sound that had in it all the menace of this grim and deadly ocean.

He heard Kline's voice, hoarse, grumbling. 'What we waiting for? Why don't we go?'

Thouless said curtly: 'Captain Henderson is not here yet.'

'Well, why don't he get a move on? What's he doing? Saying his prayers?'

'Cut it out,' Thouless snapped. He himself was wondering just what could be keeping the Old Man. Perhaps he ought to send a man to find the captain. But Henderson would resent that. He listened to the splash of water moving along the deck below. Time was running out. It would be well to get clear of the ship before she went down. He shifted his weight from one foot to the other and heard Kline's voice again, low, mumbling. 'Ought to go. Hanging around. Damn captain. Maybe go down with the ship.'

There was a restlessness in them all. The two groups of shadowy men clustered by the falls shifted; the sound of shuffling feet came from them; white faces turned to peer at Thouless questioningly. He, by his authority, was holding them there when they would have gone; one man holding sixteen. And still

Henderson did not come.

Thouless said suddenly: 'Muller, go and see what's keeping the captain. Tell him we're ready to go.'

Muller hesitated. Did it have to be him again? Must he be the one to go inside the ship — back into that trap? But the hesitation was only momentary. Muller was a man who obeyed orders and did not question them. He turned and made his way along the tilted boards to the head of the ladder leading to the deck below. And there he hesitated again, hearing the sound of the sea coming to claim the ship, hearing the slap of water against the foot of the ladder. How could any man be expected to go down into that?

But the mate had told him to go, and the mate's voice was the voice of authority, the voice that Muller obeyed. He took a grip on his courage and pushed a tentative foot down towards the first step of the ladder.

As he did so he heard a voice rising from just below the foot. 'Look out there. I'm coming up.'

Muller drew back, almost sobbing with relief. It was Captain Henderson himself. Then he reached down and took hold of Henderson's arm, helping him up. Henderson seemed to be carrying quite a load of kit.

'I was just coming to look for you, sir. The

mate said to hurry.'

'He did, did he? What's the rush?'

Muller did not answer that one. If Henderson could not see any reason for haste it was not for a man like Muller to point it out to him. But he was glad he did not have to go down that ladder.

Thouless said as soon as he saw Henderson: 'All present, sir. Everything ready to go. Will you get into the boat before we lower? Be easier for you.'

He was thinking of the artificial leg, of Henderson's age. And Henderson knew it and resented it.

'I will not,' he said.

Thouless thought the Old Man was being obstinate. He was sticking to the form, refusing to leave until everyone else was off. That was all very well, but in a case like this, what did it matter? He knew better than to try to shift Henderson, though. He only hoped there would be no old-fashioned ideas about going down with the ship.

'Lower away steady,' Thouless commanded. 'Keep her level.'

The boat went down with a sudden rush.

'Steady! Hold it aft. Pay out for'ard. Steady now.'

The boat had been tilted. Now it levelled off and took the water with a smack. Grant

261

could feel the impact, as though the bottom boards had struck something solid.

'Keep her clear,' Toresen growled.

They were level with the accommodation. Grant seized an oar and poked it out into the darkness, feeling for solidity. The oar found a resting-place and he pressed on it, trying to keep the heavy boat clear of the ship while Carson did the same with another oar. There was more movement in the sea than he had supposed; the boat rose and fell, threatening to crack its timbers against the ship's side.

Men began to slide down the ropes suspended from the davits, stumbling over the thwarts and producing a confusion of shadowy bodies.

'Down,' Toresen said. 'Get down.'

Fehler came down, using his legs and his one good hand to grip the rope. He landed on another man, and the man swore. 'Get your bloody feet out of my guts.'

They did not waste time. Now that the signal to go had been given they went quickly, slipping down the ropes and tumbling into the boat. The water was still rising in the ship. She could not last much longer. Even now she might suddenly roll over on her side and swamp the boat. It was time to be going.

'You now, sir,' Thouless said. He and Henderson were the last ones left on deck.

'Get into the boat, Tom, and don't argue,' Henderson said.

Thouless grasped the rope and slid down into the boat. It was not a long drop now.

Henderson, one hand on a davit to steady himself, took a last look at the shadowy outline of the bridge of his ship, shrugged his thick shoulders, and turned away. It was as though his command had been gradually whittled down, from a ship to half a ship, from half a ship to an open boat. Well, that was how it went, and a man was a fool these days if he allowed such things to affect him. They had to be taken with resignation as the results of war. In any case, he had never had any great sentimental attachment to the *Rosa Dartle*; he had not loved this ship as he had loved some. As a younger man he might have felt the loss more keenly; now he thought only of the destruction of one more British ship and the waste of another valuable cargo. He regretted this in so far as it was a success for the enemy, but he did not weep for the loss of this ship as for the loss of a friend. He took a last brief look and turned his face to the sea. The task that lay before him now was the task of keeping himself and seventeen other men alive in conditions that were inimical to human life. It was a stark problem of survival.

He heard Thouless's voice, more urgent

now: 'All ready, sir. Only waiting for you.'

He let go of the davit and gripped the rope in his strong, gloved hands. As he dropped, the boat came up to meet him. He landed awkwardly, and his artificial leg betrayed him. He stumbled and fell forward. His good leg was caught as he fell across a thwart, and the breaking of the bone sounded sharply like the cracking of a stick.

Even with the pain surging up in him, it was anger that he felt the more, anger that this should have happened at a time when he needed two good legs, and now had not even one. He struggled to raise himself, and the pain leaped in him again, surging up from the fractured limb.

And then there was Thouless's voice again: 'Are you all right, sir? Are you all right?'

He gripped the thwart with his hands while the pain lashed at him, and he snarled, forcing the words out through his teeth: 'I'm all right. Cast off. Pull away. Get away from the ship. Get away.'

He heard them releasing the shackles. He heard the oars creaking in the rowlocks. He heard the splash of the blades striking the water. And he felt the boat move away from the ship's side, move away into the darkness and the bitter wind, move out over the huge, heaving back of the Barents Sea.

They did not see the ship go down. That last sinking of decks and superstructure, that final engulfing of hatches and rails and ventilators was hidden from them by the darkness. They saw only the blurred outline of one another's shoulders and the pale glimmer of faces, and above them the revolving stars shining with an intense, cold brilliance and glittering in red and yellow in the great arch of the sky. They did not hear the sound of water rushing in to fill the gulf where the ship had been. They heard only the rattle of the rowlocks and the grunting of the rowers as they strained their backs to the work. And they smelled no longer the paint and the oil that had been the ship's smell, only the tang of sea-drenched timber and of tarred rope and canvas.

They hauled strongly, warming themselves at the labour, while the mate at the tiller set a course that should carry them to the Kola Inlet some three hundred miles to the southeast. It was a long journey for an open boat, but not impossibly long. There were two things that worried Mr Thouless above all others: one was the possibility of another gale such as the one that had scattered the convoy and in which no boat could hope to live, and the other was the likelihood of striking the coast too far to the west and falling into German hands.

The second possibility had occurred to Mohr also, but to him it was a matter for hope, not fear. As he pulled at his oar he turned over in his mind vague plans of escape. Surely there must be some way. He would wait and watch for his opportunity. And Fehler must help him.

The wind was westerly, and towards morning they hoisted a sail, resting from the labour of rowing. The sail filled and the boat moved sluggishly south-eastward, and the water froze on the shipped oars, and in the east the sky turned grey and the stars faded one by one.

With the coming of daylight they were able at last to see one another clearly, to read upon each other's faces the signs of hope, of fear, of weariness. It was as though until that moment they had never truly looked at one another, or, looking, had not seen what there was to see. Now, huddled in this one small boat, imprisoned by the confining ring of the sea, there could be no more dissembling, no more hiding of weaknesses or hatred or terrors. Here they were men revealed in all the nakedness of character, and here in the mirror of the sea they saw themselves reflected.

Henderson had said nothing about his leg until the morning. He had fought with the pain and had endured. Now it was impossible to pull the leather jackboot off and they had to cut it away with a knife. The leg looked bad, with a splinter of bone sticking through the skin and all around it the flesh black with bruising and clotted blood.

Peters, the chief steward, looked at the leg, pursed his thin lips, and shook his head doubtfully.

'I don't like the look of it. You ought to have told about this sooner.'

'Can you do anything with it?' Henderson asked.

Peters said slowly: 'I'm not a bone-setter. I can put splints on. But I don't like the look of it.'

'I'm not asking you to like it,' Henderson said acidly. 'Do what you can before the leg is frozen.'

Peters did what he could. Henderson bit his lip and gripped a thwart, and the sweat came out on his forehead. Peters's fingers were so cold he could hardly feel the bandages. He was afraid Henderson was going to lose another leg; but they might all lose more than that before this trip was over.

With the coming of morning, clouds had gathered, spreading from the west until there was nothing overhead but an opaque lead-grey covering. It hid the sky and blotted out any slight warmth that the sun might have given. The wind blew steadily, and the yellow sail drew them slowly southward, moving them imperceptibly nearer to the bleak and frost-bound Murman Coast. Now and then a thin cascade of water came over the gunwale and froze where it fell. At midday it began to snow, and the sail turned to a white ghost, and they went on through the drifting snow, with the cold piercing down to their bones and their faces numb.

They had rigged a canvas shelter over the fore part of the boat, and under this they took turns to huddle and try to sleep. But, weary though they were, sleep came with difficulty and was brief and unsatisfying, and when they woke it was to feel again the sickening motion of the boat and the cold and the hope-destroying sense of desolation.

'We are dead men,' Stebbing said; and he put his gloved hands to his pale face and tried to draw warmth into the frozen cheeks.

Jaggers cursed him for voicing the fear that was in his own mind also. 'You shut your big trap. We ain't dead yet.'

'It is only a matter of time,' Stebbing said softly. He put his hands on his knees, and his eyes were sick with the fear of death. 'Only a matter of time.'

Jaggers struck him across the mouth, and Thouless barked sharply: 'Cut it out.'

Jaggers mumbled: 'Him and his dead men. He asked for it.'

Stebbing's shoulders began to shake. He was weeping in a muffled, inward way, and the soft sound of his weeping mingled with the sighing of the wind in the rigging.

'That soft son-of-a-bitch,' Kline said contemptuously. 'Listen to him. Sounding off like a spanked kid.'

Kline was angry and bitter. It had all gone wrong, just as he had known it would right from the start, from the moment when he had stepped on board that Limey tanker in Philadelphia. If he had had any sense he would have walked straight off again. He had known how it would turn out; he had known it would turn out bad, and he had not had the basic horse-sense to follow his hunch. That steward was soft, but he was right: they were all dead men, dead as so many slabs of canned meat. He looked at Toresen and hated him for the humiliation that Toresen had forced on him.

Toresen noticed Kline looking at him, and said: 'Hello there, kiddo. How are you feeling?'

'Don't give me that kiddo,' Kline said. 'You think I was born yesterday?'

'Somebody had a hard time with you if you were — to judge by the face.'

Kline said savagely: 'Okay, be smart. Be as smart as you damn please, but don't be smart with me. I don't like it, see? You be smart with some other guy, some guy that appreciates it. But not me. I don't go for that stuff.' The breath came hard through Kline's flattened nose, and it came like spurts of white smoke. Kline's face was dark and unshaven under the peaked leather cap with the ear-flaps, and his body was squat and thick and massive in the padded coat that he was wearing. 'You just remember that, see?'

'I'll remember,' Toresen said. 'I won't talk to you at all if that'll make you happy.'

'Nothing's going to make me happy, but that'll help.'

'All right then, kiddo,' Toresen said.

Kline began to beat his hands together, thumping one gloved fist in the palm of the other. He felt the tingle of blood in the fingertips, and his mind swung back to the old days, the days in the fight game, the good days before it had all gone sour on him.

* * *

270

Henderson sat with his back against a thwart and his broken leg stretched out in front of him. The leg did not pain him quite so much now; it had become numb. It was as though he had two dead limbs, two stiff and useless appendages to the heavy, muscular body that was now immobilized. He blamed himself for carelessness; he ought to have been prepared for the sudden lift of the lifeboat as he slid down the rope from the davits, but in the darkness he had made an error of judgement, and this was the result: a broken leg to keep company with the artificial one.

He looked over the gunwale, and the sea was almost at the level of his eyes. So he had been brought low — from the bridge of a ship to the bottom boards of a lifeboat. He looked at the sea and saw it moving in long, low ridges that were the same drab colour as the sky. It was a colour that had no warmth in it; there was no warmth anywhere. But still, inside him, there burned the small, bright flame of hope; for he was a man who did not give way easily to the dark forces of despair.

When it began to snow Thouless suggested that he should go under the shelter, but Henderson refused. He watched the snow falling, and he saw the dry, white powder lying on his leg and upon the lockers, and he saw it dropping into the sea and dying, as a man might die from that same immersion. And yet not dying either, but altering, changing into a new form, so that there was no death. So, for man also there might be no death but only a sea-change, no death but a release from pain and fear and the unquenchable longing for the unobtainable.

He watched the snow falling, and his eyes felt hot with the sharp, stabbing pain of utter weariness. He closed his eyes and in a moment was sleeping, his chin fallen upon his chest, his hands deep in the pockets of his coat where the revolver and the boxes of .38 ammunition were.

★ ★ ★

The sea moved around them like a serpent, mocking them with their helplessness. They were cold and damp and wretched, drifting so slowly towards an inhospitable shore that might kill them even if the sea should spare them. And yet there was not one man of the eighteen who did not shield his small and flickering lamp of hope.

★ ★ ★

The rifle lay under the shelter, and there were two canvas bandoliers of cartridges beside it.

Sometimes Mohr looked at the rifle and speculated, but he did not touch it. He kept away from the rifle, but he knew that it was there, and the knowledge revolved like a wheel in his brain.

Grant also looked at the rifle, but he did touch it. He slipped the bolt out and looked through the bore, and shook his head sadly because the metal was dull. He took the pull-through and the oil bottle out of the butt, and he cleaned the bore and the mechanism so that the rifle was ready for use. Then he reassembled it and laid the rifle down in its place.

And Mohr watched him without appearing to watch, peering from under his lowered eyelashes and thinking of a time that should come when he would find a use for the rifle. And Fehler must help him.

But Fehler was not thinking of the same things as Mohr. Fehler talked to Muller. He talked in low tones and in English, so that Mohr should not understand. It was of America that Fehler talked with Muller, and of the American way of life. He listened to what Muller had to tell, and it sounded good to a man who was sick of the old world. But he did not speak of these things to Mohr, for Mohr would not have understood.

And so the boat moved on with its eighteen men and their hopes and their fears and their schemes and their memories. And the day faded into night, and there were no stars, but the wind blew steadily and coldly, so that the sail filled with the wind, and the mast creaked under the pressure. They were a tiny island drifting across the face of the sea, and no man knew of their existence.

12

The Boat

Stebbing was the first to die. On the third morning he did not wake. When Toresen touched Stebbing's arm he found that it was stiff. The light was coming slowly, creeping out of the east, and in that grey light Toresen could see the snow powdering Stebbing's coat. He pulled back the hood of the coat and looked at the face. The eyes were closed and the face was like stone. Toresen put a finger on one of the cheeks and felt the hardness of frozen flesh. He pulled his finger away, wondering when Stebbing had died. But it did not matter; he was dead, and there was an end of it. Stebbing, who had been so soft and now had become so hard. Toresen was not surprised that he should have been the first to die; he had been a man lacking in courage, lacking endurance. He might have lived longer, but he had given up hope and had let his life slip away because he had not the spirit to hang on to it.

Toresen pulled the hood over the face and crawled away to tell Mr Thouless.

They were surprised to find how heavy Stebbing was. And yet, when they pushed him overboard, the body floated, perhaps buoyed up by the air trapped in the clothing. They were a long time leaving that bulky, floating shape behind. It seemed to follow them. They could have turned their backs to it, but there was a fascination about it that compelled them to look. It was as though they feared that if they did not watch it, it would creep up on them unobserved. They felt that it was Death himself floating there, mocking them, taunting them with their helplessness.

'That's how we'll all be,' Bowie said. 'That Stebbing — he knew. He said we was all dead men. He was right.'

'You can stow that talk,' Thouless said sharply.

'I got a right to say what I like,' Bowie grumbled.

'Not in this boat. You can think what you damn please. But keep it to yourself. Don't give us the benefit of your reflections. We don't want them. Understand?'

Bowie turned his pinched face away from Thouless and looked over the stern of the boat; and there was Stebbing, still floating.

'Damn him! Why don't he sink?' Bowie muttered. 'Threatening us. Why don't the bastard sink and have done with it?'

The wind was light; it scarcely filled the sail. They put the oars out and rowed, trying to get away from Stebbing, away from death. But they tired quickly, and they drew the oars in again, and the water froze on the blades where they lay along the sides of the boat. And Stebbing was still in sight.

'He don't want to leave us,' Jaggers said softly. 'He don't want to be alone.'

To Jaggers it seemed a fearsome thing, that awful loneliness of the great waters and the great deeps beneath those waters. What was there down below in the darkness? What evil creatures lived in that vastness, waiting for the dead bodies to drift down to them? Suppose, though you were dead, you still felt pain, still could feel the flesh being torn from your bones by ruthless jaws. What horror then to die and be frozen and be tumbled overboard and left alone to sink slowly down through layer after layer of ice-cold water, down into the mud and the slime and the shadows, where the skeletons lay for ever, waiting.

Jaggers looked at the others in the boat, hunched in their thick clothing, their faces dark with unkempt beards, and he thought of them as murderers. It was they who would lift him out of the boat, they who would fling his frozen body into the sea. He hated them, each one of them, for this thing that they would do to him if he should die. Therefore, he would not die; he would outlive them all. Even though all the others should die, falling away one by one, yet he would live on. He would not be tumbled over the gunwale like so much deck ballast. Not he. Not Herbert Jaggers. He made a promise to himself that it should not happen. But he was very much afraid.

★ ★ ★

Henderson lay with his broken leg stretched out in front of him and the artificial leg discarded, put away where he could not see it. There was a blanket wrapped around him, but he felt the cold. He was always cold now, with the leg numb, and yet paining him in sudden spurts and darts of agony, like knives thrust into the flesh, and afterwards a dull ache that continued without ceasing in a kind of harmonic variation of greater and lesser suffering.

He was not sure whether he slept, but he knew that there were periods of unconsciousness which might have been sleep or might have been something deeper. He did not know how long these periods lasted, but he knew that when he awoke he awoke always to the same feeling of cold, to the pain, and the sound of men's voices, and the creak of the mast and the slapping of water against the sides of the boat. Had it not been for Thouless, he might have lost track of time, but Thouless kept him informed, coming for instructions, conferring with him about rations, about the course, about every other matter that concerned the welfare of eighteen men, and then of seventeen, and soon of fewer. For he was still captain, still in command, crippled though he was; and in the last resort it was his decision, his word, that counted.

They navigated by the compass in the boat, and they hoped to find the Kola Inlet; they hoped to reach Murmansk, at the head of the Murman railway, that long, meandering line which carried the sea-borne supplies to Leningrad. But it would be fatally easy to miss so small a target, easy to go too far east and fall somewhere upon the bleak Murman Coast and perhaps die there of exposure and starvation; easy also to make their landfall too far to the west on a coast now controlled by the enemy. One way might be as bad as the other, and the margin for error was small.

★   ★   ★

The third radio officer was the second to die. He had been a sick man before they had taken to the boat, a sick man with a cough and a thin, pale, graveyard face. He was easy to roll out of the boat, weighing little, and he sank quickly without fuss, as though glad to be gone, glad to be released from a life that had become painful to him.

'There's a good boy gone,' Toresen said. 'He never whimpered. He took what was coming to him and never let out a yelp.'

'He died, though,' Jaggers said. 'He died, didn't he?'

'So what if he did?'

'I ain't dying,' Jaggers said. 'He died, but I ain't going to. You ain't going to tumble me over the side like that. Not never.'

Toresen stared at Jaggers, and he could see a kind of madness in Jaggers's eyes, and an inch or two of dirty white bandage under the Balaclava that he was wearing. There was something queer about Jaggers, some fever burning in him.

Toresen said softly: 'You might die though. It might happen that way.'

Jaggers held his sagging belly with his two hands in the old manner that Toresen knew, and he pushed out his heavy scrubby chin in a gesture of defiance. He was defying, not Toresen, but fate, the sea, shipwreck, death itself.

'It won't then. I'm going to live. I'm going to live longer than any of you. I ain't going to die.'

'All right,' Toresen said. 'Good luck to you.'

He wondered where Jaggers had found his guts. He had never had any before; but he seemed to have scraped some up from somewhere. Well, you never knew. Perhaps Jaggers would live longer than any of them, just as he said. Who could tell?

★ ★ ★

Sime did not die from natural causes. He was killed. And it was Kline who did the killing.

Sime was a man who loved to eat. The quality of food did not greatly concern him, but the quantity of it was a matter of supreme importance. He wanted a lot of food and he wanted it often. In the lifeboat food was strictly rationed, and though, all things considered, it was a reasonably generous ration, it was not nearly generous enough for Sime. He was hungry. He was cold, too, but it was the hunger that worried him most.

On the second day he tried to wheedle an extra allowance from Mr Thouless. He might as well have saved his breath. Thouless stared at him bleakly.

'You'll have as much as the others, no

281

more. Is that clear?'

'I'm hungry,' Sime grumbled.

'It'll do you good to be hungry. Get your fat down.'

Sime did not wish to get his fat down. But though as a rule he was not very quick to learn anything, he learned quickly enough that the mate meant what he said. There was to be no extra allowance for him or for anyone else.

Bowie laughed mockingly. 'Try catching a fish, Sharkie. You scared of an empty belly?'

Bowie was hungry too, but he knew better than to try for more than his share. It just got you into bad odour, and all to no purpose. Mr Thouless was as tight as a clam.

Sime showed no resentment of Bowie's ridicule. There never had been any way of getting under his skin. He just said again: 'I'm hungry.' And it was only Grant who guessed that when Sime was hungry there was no telling what he might do. Those eyes of his — dead as stones. What went on in the mind behind them? For certain, it was no normal mind.

There was one time when Sime tried to snatch a biscuit from Toresen. Toresen hit him once, hard, with the flat of his hand. Sime did not try that trick again.

'Mind your manners, kiddo,' Toresen said.

He said it quietly, but there was a warning in the voice that even Sime took heed of.

But there were other ways. Thouless did not watch the food all the time. There were nights when it was dark and the boat was a drifting prison, with men sleeping and perhaps only the helmsman awake, and he intent on keeping a steady course, while the wind came cold out of the west to fill the sail and drag them nearer to that iron-bound coast that was their only hope of salvation.

It was on such a night that Sime dipped into the biscuit-tin and crammed the food into his mouth and chewed ravenously. And it was then that Kline found him, for Kline too was awake. He had been awake for some time, awake and thinking; and when he thought, he became bitter and angry, so that the anger was already in him when he heard Sime breaking into the biscuits.

Kline picked up the first weapon that came to hand in the darkness, and it happened to be the rifle. He swung the rifle with a short, jabbing movement, and the barrel came down slantwise across Sime's forehead, and Sime did not even cry out. He went over the gunwale and into the water, and the sea and the night swallowed him as if he had never been.

In the morning they could see the blood on

the rifle barrel, the dark smear of Sime's blood, but the man himself was gone.

Kline made no secret of the affair. 'Hell, he was stealing the food. I hit him and he fell overboard. He got what was coming to him, that guy.'

Thouless said icily: 'You murdered him.'

Kline's breath came hissing through his flattened nose. 'Murder! I don't call it murder to hit a goddamn bastard that's stealing other men's grub. Say we was to starve just through him hogging the rations — who'd be a murderer then?'

'This will have to be reported when we get back,' Thouless said. 'A thing like this cannot simply be overlooked. It's a serious matter.'

Kline's face was hard. 'Sure, sure — when we get back. When'll that be, for Christ's sake? This year, next year, some time, never. You make me sick. Kicking up a stink about one rotten son-of-a-bitch that's better out of the way. Lucky for all of you there was somebody awake that had the sand to deal with him. Now we don't get no more trouble like that, not from anybody, see?'

Thouless said in his thin, biting voice: 'Even in a ship's boat it is not for anyone to take the law into his own hands. It will be reported.'

'Okay, then. Report it. See where that gets

you. Report it till you spit blue ink — if you get the chance.' He took a cigarette out of his pocket and lit it, and he watched Thouless through the smoke, and his eyes were hard and angry and black with hatred. He added softly, 'But maybe you don't get the chance. Maybe you don't — not ever.'

★　★　★

Nobody saw the first and second radio officers go. At least, nobody admitted the fact. They disappeared on a night when the wind was blowing strongly and the clouds were so thick there was nothing but blackness overhead and all around the boat; darkness and the mournful sound of the wind that came with ice in its teeth, and the water smacking against the sides.

The helmsman saw nothing, and heard nothing but these sounds; and yet there must have been a splash and perhaps a cry; but how would he have known that these were not the splashing of the waves and the crying of the wind? And even if he had known, what could he have done in such a night? A man who went overboard was lost; from that journey there was no return. And so, when morning came, there were thirteen men left in the boat.

'Somebody else ought to go,' Bowie said. 'This is an unlucky number. No chance with thirteen.'

One might have supposed that he was joking if there had been any sign of laughter in his voice or on his face; but there was no laughter in Bowie, not any more.

'Cut it out,' Grant said. 'Silly superstitions. Old women's tales. Cut it out.'

Bowie said: 'There's truth in superstitions. It don't do to go against them. One less would make things safer for the others.' He glanced at Mohr and Fehler, and glanced away again. He said in a low voice, mumbling: 'There's people in this boat that ain't our people.'

★ ★ ★

On the fifth day, when the sky cleared and the sun made a shadow of the boat's mast upon the water, they saw a ship hull down upon the horizon, and hope rose in them. But the ship came no nearer, and soon it had vanished below the rim of the sea, and they were alone again in the immensity of the Arctic.

On that same day they heard the sound of aircraft engines very faintly, and they looked at the sky and saw a speck moving like a fly on a high ceiling. And behind the speck a

286

vapour trail floated out like a white banner. They did not know what kind of plane it was, for it was too far away for them to discern the shape of wings and tail-plane and fuselage, but again they had their brief moments of hope, and again the hope died as the speck disappeared from the face of the sky. The vapour trail endured for a time, but the wind caught it and tore it into shreds, and it disappeared like the ship and the aircraft, leaving only the boat and the moving shadow of the sail.

'They didn't see us,' Jaggers muttered. He put his hands on his belly and massaged it gently. It felt empty, hollow as a drained barrel. He thought of hot stew and hunks of bread, of plum-duff steaming from the saucepan, of rounds of roast beef and Yorkshire pudding, of bacon and eggs, fish and chips, steak-and-kidney pie — there seemed to be no end to the dishes that came to torment his mind with their unattainability.

'I'm hungry,' Jaggers said. 'I'm that hungry I could eat a whale.'

'I'll cook it for you if you catch it,' Tarbat said, and he laughed softly.

★ ★ ★

Mohr stretched out his legs one after the other. He stretched and bent them, flexing the muscles, keeping them exercised, so that when he needed to use them they should be ready. In the cramped area of the boat you could become so inactive that the limbs became weak from lack of work. Mohr did not intend that this should happen to him. Freedom, even life itself, might depend on the ability to use one's legs. When this sea voyage was finished there might still be a long journey ahead, a land journey. He would need all his strength then and all his endurance.

So he exercised his legs, and looked at the rifle and the bandoliers of ammunition, of clipped-up .303 ammunition, for which he might one day find a use, even as he would find a use for his strength. But he must make sure of Fehler. Fehler, who talked too much to Muller, as if he had lost all pride.

★ ★ ★

Bowie sat and brooded on the fact of thirteen men in one boat, and the more he brooded on it, the more it seemed to him that no good would come of it. Thirteen always had been an unlucky number, always would be. Call it superstition if you liked, but an idea of that

288

sort did not grow up without any sound foundation. There must be something in it. And in a situation such as this you could not afford to take risks. If nobody else was prepared to do anything about it then he, Bowie, would have to.

So he looked at Mohr and at Fehler, and weighed one against the other, trying to decide which of them must die to save the others. And after much thought the choice fell upon Martin Fehler.

He also looked at the rifle, but in the end he rejected that weapon. It was not suited to his purpose. What he needed was something quiet and something swift. A knife? No, a knife was messy and might not be effective. He shrank from using a knife. And then his hand, moving in the pocket of his coat, fell upon the perfect implement for his task — a length of cod-line taken from a hammock.

He lay back with his shoulders resting against a locker and a smile twisting his thin, bitter mouth. And he waited patiently for the coming of darkness.

★　★　★

Muller was sleeping next to Martin Fehler, and Muller awoke in the night with Fehler's knee driving into his back, and he heard the kind of grunt a man makes when he is exerting all his strength on some object. Muller rolled over in the darkness and stretched out his hand and touched a man's face, but he did not think that it was Fehler's.

He said with a quiet urgency, sensing that here was something wrong, yet not knowing what it could be: 'Martin; are you all right? What's the matter, Martin?'

And then he heard Bowie's voice hissing in his ear: 'Lay down, you bloody fool! Lay down!'

And suddenly Muller knew what was happening, for he had felt the cord, and he knew that Bowie was strangling Fehler. He thrust his fists up into Bowie's face and began to shout. Bowie went over backward, and the cord slipped from Fehler's throat.

And then there was a light shining on them from Mr Thouless's torch, and Bowie was cursing and screaming like a man gone mad: 'I'd have had him. Number thirteen, I tell you, number thirteen, and I'd have had him. I'd have made it twelve. Now we'll all drown, all of us, every last one. You fools! Now we'll all drown.'

Thouless struck him with the side of his hand, and Bowie's voice choked suddenly and died away into a whimper, and he crept away from Thouless and lay down in the bottom of the boat, shivering and sobbing and cursing, not troubling to control himself.

Thouless said to Fehler: 'Are you all right?'

Fehler answered: 'All right now. Nearly all wrong, though. I did not think any man would have done such a thing.'

'If he tries it on again,' Thouless said, 'I'll put him overboard himself.' He raised his voice. 'You hear that, Bowie? We're thirteen. We stay thirteen. If any man gets killed the one who kills him goes over the side too. Fishes' food. You got that?'

Bowie did not answer.

★ ★ ★

To Kline's way of thinking, what Bowie had done, or had attempted to do, had been only right and proper. If Kline had had his way both Mohr and Fehler would have gone overboard to feed the sharks. That was the right place for damn Nazis. The time might yet come when that would happen. Kline's opinion of Bowie went up. There was one Limey who had the right idea, anyway. If it came to the pinch there was a man who might be in Kline's own camp. He moved over to talk to Bowie.

Henderson apologized to Fehler for what had happened, and to Mohr also as the senior

291

of the two Germans.

'Disciplinary action will be taken, of course,' Mohr said.

'When the time comes.'

Henderson was tired. His body ached, and pain flowed up from the broken leg. This voyage seemed endless. There was no rest, no comfort in the boat, and the cold wrapped them like a blanket of ice.

Mohr was thinking: This old fool, hanging on to the trappings of command when everyone can see that he is as good as dead. A dead man still clinging to what is no longer his.

So Mohr thought, but there was a capacity for endurance in Henderson of which Mohr did not dream.

Only Thouless truly understood Henderson, understood him now as he had never done on board ship. It was as though adversity had drawn these two men closer together, had shown them with a brilliant clarity the virtues in each other's characters, and had invoked a more charitable view of their unquestionable faults. Thouless now took strength from Henderson's mental toughness. Now that Henderson could no longer give any physical assistance, Thouless leaned upon his authority and was glad to have him there, and prayed that he would not die. And Henderson came to love Thouless as a son, loved him as he would not have thought possible just one week ago. And Thouless was his right hand, doing for him what he could not do for himself.

Peters, the chief steward, and Tarbat, the cook, dealt out the rations under the supervision of Mr Thouless. Peters was a dry husk of a man out of whose body the years seemed to have sucked every drop of moisture. He had a dry, husky voice, and his words were like specks of dust floating out of the dusty recesses of his throat. He was so small, so tough, so wiry, that one might have supposed him to be as immortal as the carved figurehead of an old sailing-ship, with no more wants than a coat of paint now and then to keep out the weather. But he took his full share of the food, and as much went to serve the needs of his wizened body as disappeared into the cavernous bulk of Tarbat.

Tarbat thought this was all wrong. 'By rights, the rations ought to be allotted according to weight of subject receiving same. I ought to have three times what you do. Look at all I've got to feed.'

Peters said: 'This is an excellent opportunity for you to take a course of slimming. Haven't you heard that fat men die young? No insurance company would accept you as a first-class life. You want to think about that.'

'Come to that,' Tarbat said, 'I doubt whether there's an insurance company in the world what'd take on any of us as first-class lives. Not to say first class. We ain't A1 at Lloyd's, if you see what I mean.'

'I follow the trend of your reasoning,' Peters said; and the dry dust of the words fell softly on Tarbat's ears like a dust of death. 'We are not good risks.' He looked round the boat with his prying, bird-like glance, letting it rest momentarily on each of the dark, hunched shapes that were the survivors of the *Rosa Dartle*, and then he brought it back to Tarbat. 'No, not one of us,' he said. 'Not even I.'

★ ★ ★

Twice a day they had a hot drink, heating it on the squat paraffin stove under the shelter of the canvas in the bows of the boat. They warmed themselves briefly with the drink and the stove, but afterwards the cold crept in again and the memory of warmth was gone.

They rubbed fish-oil into their frost-bite, and the stench of the fish-oil clung to them and became part of the character of that voyage, as the bitter cold was, and the creak of the mast, and the sound of the wind, and the lift and fall of the boat, as the faces of their companions in misfortune, as the brief dreams of dry land firm under their feet, and the waking again to the beat of the sea and the long, dull ache of frozen limbs.

And so the boat moved onward with its human cargo, and all the hates and hopes and fears of those thirteen men. And each day was a repetition of the last, so that one was distinguished from another only by the death of a man or the sight of a ship, the strength of the wind or a fall of snow. And many times they looked over the bows, hoping for the sight of land, and as many times they were disappointed.

'Perhaps there is no land,' Peters said. 'Perhaps the land is gone and we shall sail on for ever like The Flying Dutchman. Perhaps we are dead men already and do not know it. Perhaps this is the meaning of Purgatory.'

But Mohr did not believe that they were dead. Mohr believed in reality, the reality of life, of hope, of the rifle lying on the locker, and two unused bandoliers of .303 ammunition. And plans went round in Mohr's brain like a squirrel in a cage.

★　★　★

One day it became warmer. The sun shone upon the boat and the ice melted from the oars. Their hopes rose with the rising sun and the warmth; but all day the keel moved softly through the water and the land did not appear on the horizon; nor any ship, nor life of any kind, except a lone bird flying strongly on white wings that flashed in the sun.

And then it was night again, and when the sun vanished the warmth vanished also, and the cold seemed worse by reason of that short period of relief. But still the variable wind filled the sail, and still the boat moved on, drawing ever nearer to a coast that must somewhere break the line of their voyage.

'Unless the world has turned upside down,' Toresen said. 'Maybe there's been a great flood and the land is gone, like the steward said. Gone for good.'

'Or bad,' Carson said.

It was a fear that was in them, a fear that took no note of reason, of science, of geography; a fear that there might be no more land for them, ever.

'I'd give a thousand pounds,' Jaggers said, 'just for one square yard of Liverpool pavement.'

'It's worth more than that,' Tarbat said. 'Where would you get a thousand quid, anyway?'

★ ★ ★

Mohr did his exercises, keeping his legs in trim for the time when they should be needed; and Kline watched him, and the thought that was in Kline's mind was that with two Germans gone there would be that much more food for the others, that much better chance of survival. But he made no plans. Mr Thouless had given warning to Bowie and to the the rest, and Kline believed that Mr Thouless meant what he said. So Kline glowered at Mohr and Fehler and hated them, but he did not touch them. Grant did not like the look of Kline. There was a wicked gleam in Kline's eyes. This was a man who could work mischief. But there were others too who might make trouble — Jaggers and Bowie and Mohr. When you were close with men in a boat like this you came to know which were the bad ones, the ones that could bear watching. Bowie might look cowed, Jaggers might seem scared, but they had the capacity for evil. And Mohr — perhaps Mohr was the most dangerous of all, because he was a fanatic, driven by some passion that he had borrowed from a madman.

Grant kept as near the rifle as he could. He cleaned it and looked along the sights, and he felt the good solid wood of the butt nestling under his arm, and the weight of the weapon lying in the palm of his hand, and he liked the feel of it. He had drilled with just such a rifle as this, a Short Lee-Enfield, years ago when he joined the Army; he knew it like an old friend. And like an old friend, he knew that it would not let him down.

★ ★ ★

Muller talked to Fehler in a low voice, so that the others should not hear. Fehler knew that Mohr was watching him. but he cared nothing for Mohr. Let him watch. Fehler had finished with him, he did not even look upon Mohr as a comrade in arms, not any more; all that was finished, blotted out by events and the passage of time. It was as though a curtain had fallen between him and Mohr, cutting them off, one from another.

★ ★ ★

Henderson was like a god watching over the boat. He would sit motionless for hours, with his thick torso bent slightly forward, and the strong face, grey-bearded now. the white hair visible on his forehead. He had the loaded revolver in his pocket, and no one knew about that except himself. That was his secret. He kept it there as the ultimate argument, the final warrant of his authority. He hoped there would be no need to use it, but if the need should arise, it was there, ready. And he was ready also.

Thouless came to him and talked with him, and moved away again, resenting the lack of space that curbed his natural activity. Peters came also to inquire in his dust-dry voice about the broken leg.

'Is there much pain, sir?'

'I can stand it,' Henderson said.

'You should be in hospital. Bad for it here — very bad.'

'There's nothing to be done about that.'

Sometimes he wondered whether he could stand the pain; he felt like crying out with the agony of it. But then the pain ebbed, and he was glad that he had controlled himself, that he had not shown weakness before these men.

'If there is anything I can do — ' Peters said.

'No. Nothing. Nothing.'

★ ★ ★

Jaggers's head ached under the bandage. Perhaps it was the cold wind breathing upon it that made the wound ache. Peters had had the bandage off and had looked at the wound and had muttered something under his breath that Jaggers could not hear. After that he had dressed the gash with something from the first-aid kit that had stung like mustard, and then he had bandaged it again with a clean bandage.

'How's it doing?' Jaggers asked.

'We may have to take the head off,' Peters said. 'Nothing serious.'

Jaggers supposed that this was meant as a joke, but there was no smile on Peter's face, and Jaggers did not smile either.

'I'm a sick man,' Jaggers said. 'By rights I ought to have extra grub. I'm an invalid.'

'No sense in feeding a man who's going to die,' Peters said. 'Just waste of good grub.'

Jaggers's eyes went wide with fear, and there was a mad look in them that startled Peters. There was a mad screech in his voice too that made all the others turn and stare at him.

'I ain't going to die. I tell you I ain't going to die.'

Peters put a hand on Jaggers's arm, trying to soothe him. 'Of course not. It was only a joke. Just a joke.'

But he was thinking that if ever a man had the graveyard look, that man was surely Herbert Jaggers.

★ ★ ★

And so, as the boat moved on, each man watched his neighbour, looking for signs of weakness, of treachery, of approaching death. Cold and hunger were the enemies, and against such assailants the rifle was no defence. But there were other enemies too, the enemies that crept into men's hearts and made war from within; and against these also there was no weapon of steel that would prevail, but only the high spirit of endurance and the bright, white flame of hope.

★　★　★

They did not see the land from afar off. There was no thin cloud of mist low on the horizon that was to harden slowly into a line of coast. There was no eager cry of 'Land-ho!' For they came upon it in the night when most of them were sleeping or huddled, sleepless, in damp blankets through which the cold forced its way and would not be denied.

Carson was at the tiller, steering half by instinct. He felt the wind gradually dropping, and then he saw on the starboard side of the boat the faint white outline of hills, very close. He looked over the port gunwale, and there were hills on that side also, and he thought for a moment that this must be some hallucination, and then he feared that the hills were hills of ice, great bergs that had floated into the path of the boat and had surrounded it. But he looked again in the starlight, and now he was sure that these were no hallucination and no ice-bergs, but solid, snow-clad hills. He knew that at last, after so many days and nights of sailing, the boat had made its landfall.

He began to shout then, rousing the others to this great news. 'Hi, there! Wake up! Land! Land, it is, my boys! Stir yourselves! We've made it, made it!'

He drummed on the boards with his feet. 'Look at the sweet land, my fine boys. Wake up and look at it.'

He found Thouless beside him, and heard Thouless's voice. 'It is so. Thank God, it is so.'

And Thouless went for'ard under the shelter to tell Henderson the great news; and found him awake in the darkness, as he had been for a long time, lying there with his pain.

'We've made it, sir.'

Henderson said quietly: 'It is a good thing, Tom. But what land is it, do you think?'

For the moment Thouless had not considered this point. it had seemed enough that they should have found the land at all. But Henderson had gone immediately to the crux of the matter. Though they had beaten the sea, there might still be other enemies to overcome.

He could hear the eager voices of the other men. It was the land fever that had fallen upon them, the fever that would come and burn itself out in a brief bout of excitement. For a while they would forget all their petty hates and jealousies, united for this one short moment in the knowledge that the sea was not to have them.

Thouless knew that it would not last. The mood would pass, the moment of brotherliness, of comradeship, would fade away as the fear of the sea faded, and the bitterness would return, the hate and the envy and the pettiness. He had seen it all before.

He found Toresen beside him. Toresen's voice had a tremor in it, even Toresen's, as if he were having difficulty in keeping his excitement under control.

'Where are we, sir, do you think?'

The wind had fallen away altogether now. The sail hung lifeless and the boat drifted sluggishly.

'Is it Murmansk?'

Momentarily that thought had come into Thouless's mind also, a hope that by some miracle of navigation and good fortune they had sailed in the darkness across Kola Bay, up the mouth of the Tuloma, and into the very gateway of Murmansk. The briefest reflection told him that this could not really be so. They would not have been able to penetrate so far into the narrows, passing the defences without detection, without seeing a ship or a boat in the entire passage. Even in darkness it would not have been possible. This must be some other indentation, some inlet in a coast that had yet to be identified.

'No,' he said. 'It is not Murmansk.'

'I didn't think it could be,' Toresen said. 'There'd have been an air raid going on. We'd have seen the searchlights. Always search-lights in Murmansk. But where are we?'

'Your guess is as good as mine. It's land, anyway, and that's something.'

'It's a whole lot if you ask me. Just now I'm not so fussy about the exact character of the land, just so long as it's firm under my feet.'

The boat had almost ceased to move. There was scarcely a ripple on the water, and the silence was strange to them after the incessant wind, the creaking of the mast, and the splash of the sea against the sides.

Thouless ordered the sail to be lowered, and it came down, stiff with frost. They stowed it away and unshipped the mast, and took up the oars with a new energy born of the new hope that was in them.

Thouless himself took over from Carson at

the tiller, and Carson took one of the oars. Thouless steered the boat in towards the shore on the port side, staring into the darkness for any sign of life, and seeing only the white outline of the low hills. There seemed to be little or no current flowing, and for this reason he did not think they could be in the estuary of a river. He believed that this was no more than a narrow opening in the coast-line, a kind of fjord, tapering towards the tip.

He saw a radiance beginning to show along the line of the hills, and the silver horn of the old moon appeared and grew slowly into a crescent. It shone coldly upon a cold world of snow and water, and it shone upon the silver drops that scattered from the blades of the oars.

No life, Thouless thought; a dead coast. As far as he could see in that pale light it stretched away in its bleak desolation, offering no shelter and no comfort. It was a cold welcome after so long and hazardous a voyage.

They had been rowing for perhaps half an hour when he saw the hut. It stood some fifty yards back from the water's edge, and there was no light showing from it. It looked black under the moon and the shadow of the hills. Nevertheless, Thouless's heart gave a leap as he saw it, for where there was a hut there must be human life; the very fact of that building proved that they had not been cast up on some Arctic island inhabited only by seals and sea-birds. Here was the mark of man's work — four walls and a roof — protection from the elements.

'We'll land here,' Thouless said. 'There's a hut.'

The rowers, with their backs to the prow of the boat, had not seen the building. Now they all turned and stared at the black shape of it.

'The Ritz Hotel,' Tarbat said. 'Neon signs and all.'

'Bacon and eggs for breakfast,' Toresen added. 'A hot bath and clean sheets. Lovely, kiddo.'

But Peters said softly, breaking in upon them with his dust-dry voice: 'Might be the shotgun from the bedroom window. Might be keep off the grass.'

'No grass,' Tarbat said, and shook with laughter.

The keel grounded on shingle. They waded through the shallow water and the crust of ice at the edge, and made the painter fast to an outcrop of rock.

Thouless said: 'Grant, Toresen, come with me. The rest of you stay by the boat.'

Grant asked: 'Do I bring the rifle?'

Thouless considered for a moment. He looked at the dark outline of the hut. Then he said: 'Yes, bring it.'

Grant ripped open one of the bandoliers and pushed two clips of ammunition into the magazine of the rifle.

'All right,' Thouless said. 'Let's be moving.'

Their legs were stiff, and there was a queer feeling of weakness about them, as though they had been made of rubber. The shingle sloped upward steeply and became rock. The snow was crusted in ridges that were iron hard under the feet. There had been a thaw during the day, and water had run down the slope, and then night had come with the temperature dropping to zero, and where the water and the slush had been were now these jagged ridges as hard as the rocks with which they mingled.

The hut stood on a kind of platform where the slope flattened out before rising again up the side of the hill. Their breath steamed in the moonlight as they moved upward, and the cold air was harsh in their lungs. Grant looked back and saw the others grouped on the shingle, and behind them the boat; and in the boat was Henderson with only one leg, and that broken. It would be well to have Henderson where he could rest in comfort. He needed a bed, medical attention, good

307

food, warmth. It was not likely that he would find all those here, but there might at least be warmth.

The hut was built of logs, roughly jointed at the corners. There was a small window in the side facing the water, and, farther on, a door. Grant lifted the butt of the rifle and thumped with it on the timbers. The door was not fastened; it opened with a creak of hinges. A dank smell of decay met them.

Thouless switched on his torch and shone the beam into the interior of the hut. There was one room only, with a rough table, a wooden form, and a rusty iron stove. Fixed to the far wall was a bunk.

'Ritz, sure enough,' Toresen said. 'A nice warm welcome.'

They moved inside, and the smell of decay was all around them. Thouless walked over to the bunk and the beam of light splashed upon it. There was a little mould clinging to it, and nothing else.

'No visitors lately,' Toresen said; and the sound of his laughter echoed hollowly, then ceased abruptly. 'No welcome on the mat neither.'

'The inhospitable shores,' Grant said.

They had come a long way for such a welcome.

13

The Hut

Mohr and Fehler were standing side by side and staring at the water. There was a cold wind blowing up the inlet and there was no sun. The wind rippled the surface of the water, and the ripples splashed over the fringe of ice that clung like a broken pie-crust along the shore. Behind them were the low hills, with here and there a stunted pine-tree thrusting up through the snow; and in front of them, a hundred yards across the water, were more hills, more snow, more stunted pines. To their left, possibly a quarter of a mile away, was the end of the inlet, a shore curving in an almost perfect semicircle. To their right lay the open sea. Nowhere was there any sign of the work of human hands except the small log hut which they had made their refuge.

Mohr said: 'I shall need your help. You understand that?'

'I cannot do it,' Fehler said. 'We have given our parole. Have you forgotten?'

Mohr kicked impatiently at the stones.

309

'That is of no account. Our duty to the Führer, to the Fatherland, demands that we take any steps to make our escape.'

'Even the breaking of parole?'

'What is parole? A word. Do you imagine I had any intention of remaining tamely in captivity, perhaps of being sent to Siberia? If this Henderson is such a fool as to believe that a word can take the place of a locked door, so much the worse for him.'

'And how do you mean to escape? Where will you go?'

'We will head westward. I have considered the matter carefully, and it seems to me that we have landed to the west of Kola Bay. You realize, of course, what that means?'

'If it is so, it means that we are within quite a short distance of our own forces. Is that what you mean?'

'Exactly,' Mohr said. 'It is even possible that we are at this moment in German-held territory. In any case, the thing to do is to head westward.'

'And suppose we are on the Murman Coast to the east of Kola Bay. What then? By heading west you would go straight to the Russians.'

'That is a risk that has to be taken. In any case, we should do no better by going east. But there is no more to say. I have decided. We start tonight.'

'No,' Fehler said.

The colour flamed into Mohr's face. 'Have you forgotten that I am your superior officer? I order you to go with me. You have a duty to your Fatherland.'

'I have a duty to myself,' Fehler said. 'I am on parole.'

'You defy me, then?'

'On this point, yes. There is no more to be said.'

Fehler turned away and began to walk back to the hut. Mohr watched him go, rage making his lips tremble.

'Traitor!'

He was certain now that Fehler intended treachery. So he would have to deal with Fehler.

* * *

Henderson lay in the bunk where the others had laid him. They had brought their remaining food and equipment from the boat and had piled it in the hut. They found some wood and made a fire in the iron stove that was falling to pieces with rust. Smoke poured into the room, but it drove out the smell of damp and decay. For the first time in many nights they slept without the sound of the sea in their ears, without the constant movement of the boat under them.

Peters took the splints and bandages off Henderson's leg and was unhappy about what he saw underneath. He wondered how any man could have endured the pain.

'We ought to get this into hospital,' he said.

Henderson did not disagree, but he wondered how many miles away over frozen, snow-covered country the nearest hospital lay. Grant and Toresen had climbed the low hills above the hut and had gazed out over a desolate land. They had seen no sign of human life, nothing to indicate where they were. They returned to the hut, sliding down the snowy hillside in their thick, clumsy boots. Henderson and Thouless listened to their report. It was not hopeful.

'We shall have to use the boat,' Henderson said. 'None of us is strong enough to go overland. We shall have to sail along the coast until we come to the Kola Inlet.'

'Which way?' Thouless asked.

It was that question again. Were they to the east or to the west of Kola Bay?

'I think we must go east,' Henderson said. But he knew that he could be wrong, and that eastward might lie only the bleak Murman Coast and the thickening ice. Yet to head west might mean only to fall into the hands of the enemy. They must go east.

But when they went to look at the boat on the second day they found that it was useless. It was lying half under the water, and there was a great hole smashed in the bottom.

Thouless looked at the hole and at the splintered timbers, and he looked at the rocks on the shore, but he knew that a rock had not done this work. It was the work of an axe.

'Somebody did this,' he said. He stared at the others, his eyes hard. 'Somebody sneaked out in the night and did this. Some madman.'

It was the insanity of the act that appalled him. By this piece of sabotage perhaps all their lives had been forfeited.

'Who?'

Kline burst out savagely: 'Them sons-a-bitches. Them damn Nazis. They're the ones.'

Mohr was standing a short distance behind the others, looking on with an expression of disdain. Kline ran at him and struck him on the jaw. Mohr went down, and Kline kicked him furiously.

'Stop that,' Thouless said sharply. 'We don't know he was the one.'

'Who else?' Kline snarled. He drew his foot back to kick Mohr again, but Mohr had rolled away agilely and was on his feet, breathing hard and dabbing at the blood on his lips. Kline would have attacked him again, but Carson put a hand on his arm and held him back.

'Hold it, boy!'

Kline simmered down slowly, but he still glowered at Mohr. 'You going to let him get away with that?'

Thouless said again: 'We don't know that he did it.' He turned to Fehler. 'Ask him if he holed the boat.'

Fehler put the question, and Mohr answered disdainfully: 'Why should I do that? Let them look among themselves for madmen. I did not do it.'

Fehler believed that Mohr was lying. He believed that Mohr would stick at nothing to gain his own ends. He meant to go overland — westward. He did not intend to go in the boat, and he meant to make sure that no one else went in it. But Fehler said nothing of his suspicions when he translated Mohr's answer.

Thouless also thought Mohr was lying, but there was nothing to be done about it. To punish Mohr on suspicion would not improve matters. The boat would remain useless.

'Get back to the hut,' he said harshly. 'We shall have to go overland.'

★ ★ ★

314

As darkness gathered in the hut Mohr kept apart from the others, who were huddled round the pitiful fire in the stove. He kept apart and watchful. He no longer trusted Fehler. He believed that Fehler had gone over to the enemy and might betray his plans of escape. Although Fehler could not know that it was he, Mohr, who had made the boat useless, he might suspect that also. No man could be sure that Mohr had done it, because he had done it under cover of darkness when the others had been asleep. They might all suspect him, but no one could prove it. And now, standing apart from these others, Mohr felt spiritually apart also. He was alone. He would have to fight alone. For the Führer he would do that also.

He saw two men go out of the hut, and he noted that those two men were Fehler and Muller. Suspicion flared up in him again. So Fehler was about to betray him. His hatred of Fehler was now mingled with the feelings of a true patriot, a man who had imbibed the Nazi creed from his boyhood, who acknowledged no other god. Fehler was a traitor, and there was only one punishment for traitors — death. He, Mohr, must be the executioner.

He moved softly to the door, and saw the rifle standing in the corner. When the door was opened inward it would hide the rifle from the rest of the room. Mohr opened the door and took the rifle. He went out into the gathering dusk and closed the door behind him.

Grant was squatted close to the stove, half dozing. He felt the cold air flowing in from the open door, and he looked up and saw the door swing shut. He wondered who had gone out, and he looked at the other men, checking them over in his mind. Muller and Mohr and Fehler were missing.

Grant thought nothing of it. If they wished to go out into the cold that was their affair; yet it was strange that it should be those three — the two Germans and the American of German descent. Could there be any treachery afoot, or was that too fantastic an idea?

He turned the matter over in his sleepy mind, and then he looked towards the door again, and into the shadow beyond the door where the rifle stood. But he could see no rifle because it was too dark in the corner. Yet, suppose there was no rifle? Nonsense. Who would want the rifle?

But then he thought again of Mohr and Fehler and Muller, but especially of Mohr. And after a while he moved away from the stove and went to the far corner of the hut to look for the rifle. And it was not there.

Grant was no longer half asleep; he was suddenly very wide awake. He opened the door and went out of the hut, and the cold struck him like a blow. Outside there was still a trace of daylight remaining; the snow made a white background and was crisp underfoot. Grant looked up the hill, but he did not think Mohr had gone that way. He went down the slope to the shore of the inlet and saw the tracks in the snow leading away to the left. He began to run.

And then he saw Mohr, and beyond Mohr, Fehler and Muller. He heard Mohr shout something, and the other two swung round and faced him. And then he saw Mohr go down on one knee in the snow and bring the rifle up to his shoulder. He saw the spurt of flame like a red flower blossoming from the muzzle, and Fehler dropped where he had stood.

Grant had stopped for a moment, but now he began to run again, crunching through the snow, his feet sliding under him. He saw Muller look down at Fehler, and then move towards Mohr. Muller was shouting something, but Mohr made no answer. He worked the bolt of the rifle and fired again; and Muller spun round so that his back was to Mohr. And Mohr worked the bolt again and fired again, and Muller dropped with his face

317

in the snow, and lay there.

Mohr did not hear Grant coming. He was looking down at Muller's dead body. Grant came up swiftly behind him and put his arm round Mohr's neck and jerked the head back. Mohr tried to bring the rifle up, he tried to free himself, but he could not do it. Grant had learnt unarmed combat in a tough school, where the order was to make sure your man was dead before you let him go. And Grant was angry.

The rifle dropped from Mohr's hands and made a nest for itself in the snow. And Mohr never knew who it was who had avenged Fehler and Muller, because he never saw Grant's face.

★ ★ ★

Mr Thouless was worried. His forehead was puckered in a frown. 'You should not have killed him.'

'He was a murderer and he deserved killing,' Grant said. 'He smashed the boat and he murdered Muller and Fehler. He is better out of the way.'

'He was a prisoner-of-war, and he should not have been killed — not without trial.'

But Thouless was not sure of himself. He could not honestly condemn the sergeant for what he had done. Might not he himself in the heat of the moment have done a similar thing? Who was he to judge? But there had been too much death. He wondered where it would end. He wondered whether any of them would escape.

Grant cleaned the rifle and stood it again in the corner of the hut. Mohr would not take it again.

And Kline and Jaggers and Bowie crouched in a little group by the stove when the others were asleep, and talked together in low voices, and understood one another.

★   ★   ★

Light was creeping faintly into the hut when Grant awoke. But there were others awake before him. He heard Kline's hoarse voice, speaking low.

'Okay, fellers. Start loading up.'

Grant, only half awake before, raised himself from the floor on one elbow. The bed on which he had been sleeping was a sheet of canvas from the boat; a lifejacket was his pillow. Kline's voice had brought him to full wakefulness. Something was happening here, and he did not like the smell of it.

He said sharply: 'What's going on?'

'Shut it,' Kline said. And Grant saw Kline

then, a squat, thick figure standing by the door, whence he could command a view of the whole room. And in Kline's hand was the rifle.

Grant yelled to wake the others. 'Hey there! Rouse up! Stir yourselves — all of you!'

Kline growled at him from the doorway. 'Okay, kick up a rumpus. See where it gets you. You want trouble, you'll have it, plenty trouble. Get them rations, fellers.'

Grant saw Jaggers and Bowie stowing the remaining tins of food and milk from the lifeboat into two bags. He stood up.

'What do you think you're doing, Bowie?'

'What's it look as if I'm doing?' Bowie snarled. 'Picking daisies?'

The others were awake now — Thouless, Toresen, Peters, Carson, Tarbat, and Henderson. Kline menaced them with the rifle.

'Keep right where you are, all of you. Else this gun's going to start popping. Get me?'

'What's the game, Kline?' Carson asked. 'You running out on us?'

'That's about it,' Kline said. 'Me and the two smart boys. We figure it this way — three stand a better chance of getting through with that amount of provisions than ten, especially when one's a cripple.'

'So that's the way it is?'

'That's the way.'

'I always reckoned you were mean, but I never figured you were that mean.'

'Don't try to break my heart,' Kline sneered. 'The man ain't living that could do that. How's it going with them rations, boys?'

'All ready,' Jaggers said. He swung one of the bags on to his shoulders, and stood there with his hands supporting his belly. He grinned maliciously at Peters. 'You thought I was going to die, didn't you? But it's not me that's kicking the bucket this time, not Herbert Jaggers.'

Peters said in his dust-dry voice, lacking all emotion: 'I think you may beat me to it yet.'

'Not me,' Jaggers screeched. 'You're done for, finished — all of you. But us three, we're going to live. We're going to live, do you hear?'

Kline broke in impatiently: 'Stow the talk. We gotta be going.'

Grant made a move towards him, and looked down the menacing barrel of the rifle.

'Don't try it, son. I got blood on my hands already. A bit more won't worry me.'

'All rations stowed,' Bowie said. 'All ready to go.'

'Take that canvas sheet and them extra blankets,' Kline said. 'We'll be needing them. They got a nice warm hut; don't need blankets. Get up, all of you.'

The four men who had been lying on the floor got to their feet. Jaggers and Bowie began to roll up the blankets in the canvas.

Kline looked at Toresen with hatred in his face. 'I got a scar on the wrist,' he said. 'I guess this about pays that off. What you say?'

'Maybe you think so, kiddo,' Toresen said. 'Strong man with a gun, hey? Not so strong without it.'

'Strong enough.'

'So you're going with the jackals at your tail. You'll all die in the snow.'

'I ain't going to die,' Jaggers yelled.

'You're afraid to, aren't you?' Toresen said contemptuously. 'You were yellow right from the start. A damned yellow drunken rat.'

Jaggers had stopped rolling the blankets. He seemed to be getting ready to rush at Toresen, but the courage to do so was not in him.

'Get on with it,' Kline snarled.

Jaggers got on with it.

Kline looked at Toresen again, and brought the rifle up to his hip, pointing it at Toresen's chest.

'There's another score to settle. You thought you beat me once, remember? You don't know Joe Kline. He's the boy that makes everything even in the end. So right now, before we go, I mean to do just that. You got any last words?'

Bowie looked up from the floor. 'What you doing, Joe?'

'I'm going to shoot this big guy,' Kline said. 'Just for my own pleasure.'

'Don't be a fool,' Bowie said sharply. 'What good'll it do you? He'll die anyway.'

'I aim to make sure.'

His finger began to tighten on the trigger.

'Now, see here — ' Bowie said.

And then there was an interruption. A quiet, almost conversational voice came from the bunk that Kline had not even troubled to watch, because he knew that in the bunk was only an old man with one broken leg and the stump of another — a man who could not harm him.

'Drop that gun!'

Kline swung towards the bunk and saw the revolver in Henderson's big hand. For a moment he seemed to be stupefied by the sight of that muzzle staring unwaveringly at him, as though he could not understand what had gone wrong, how this plan of his had been upset.

He still held the rifle in his thick, scarred hands; the barrel had moved away from Toresen when Henderson's voice had caught him like a hook and pulled his gaze to the bunk. The rifle was at his hip and his fingers were coiled tightly about it, but for the moment all ability to act had been taken from him.

There was a hush of expectation in the hut, no man moving, so that the low whine of cold air blowing through the cracks in the door could be plainly heard, and even the distant sound of seawater falling upon the shore.

Jaggers, still down on his knees, his hands on the half-rolled blankets, let his frightened gaze move from Henderson to Kline and back to Henderson. He moistened his lips with his tongue and waited. The others waited too, all frozen into the positions in which they had been when the quiet voice had altered everything in one single moment of time.

And then the command was repeated, but this time the voice was raised a little and there was the bite of authority in it. It was the command of a man who did not consider the possibility of disobedience.

'Drop that gun!'

The second order acted on Kline like a goad jabbing into his flesh; it pricked him out of his momentary immobility. He swung the rifle full round and fired without taking aim, and the bullet tore into the wall an inch above Henderson's head.

Henderson's hand appeared to spurt flame.

The rifle slipped from Kline's grasp and clattered to the floor. On his battered face there appeared a look of surprise, of bewilderment, as though he could not understand this thing that had come to him. His legs bent, crumpled under his weight, and he fell to the floor with a .38 bullet embedded in his heart. It was the end of the road for Joseph Kline, the end of a long, bitter, angry road which he had trodden with savagery and violence until at last he had died by violence, reaping the final harvest of his sowing.

Carson's breath came out in a long, hissing sigh, like steam from an engine.

'By hookey, you played the trump card, Cap'n. It was a close call, but you had the ace of trumps all right.'

Henderson was staring at the revolver in his hand. He could smell the harsh odour of burnt powder, and it was a bitter scent, the scent of death and futility. He felt no triumph at having beaten Kline, only a deep sense of disgust that this should have been necessary. They had been delivered from the sea only, it seemed, to die one by one in this forsaken, inhospitable land. It was senseless.

He slipped the safety-catch on and put the revolver away where he could no longer see it. He lay back in the bunk and felt the pain coming up from his leg like a steel wire probing his body, feeling for the weakness in him. In the timber of the wall he could see the slanting hole that the rifle bullet had gouged. He had been near to death in that moment when the bullet had whipped past his head. For himself he would not have cared if it had found its intended mark; it would have been a release from pain. But for the sake of the others he was glad that he had won the duel with Kline, for Kline would have robbed them also of the chance of life. They might yet die; the odds were still against them, but at least they had a better chance than Kline would have allowed them.

Henderson closed his eyes. It was better as it was.

Jaggers and Bowie were like men who suddenly perceive a chasm opening beneath their feet. They stared at Kline's body with frightened eyes. Jaggers got up from his knees and his trembling hands went to his sagging belly, as if feeling for reassurance in familiar things.

Toresen flicked him with the back of his hand, and Jaggers shrank away, whining.

'Bastard!' Toresen said.

Mr Thouless cut in swiftly. 'Enough of that. It won't do any good. Leave him alone.'

'I ought to croak the swine,' Toresen said.

Peters muttered softly: 'He'll croak without your help, Chippie. He'll croak sure enough.'

Grant stooped and picked up the fallen rifle. He snapped the bolt back, and the brass cartridge-case flew out and fell with a faint clink to the floor. Mechanically he began to clean the rifle; there was no longer any danger from Bowie and Jaggers now that Kline was dead. They were jackals that had lost the hyena.

'You, Bowie,' he said. 'You can put that bag down. You won't be needing it — not this trip.'

Bowie let the bag drop. He was biting his lip and he looked vicious, but he knew who had the whip-hand now.

'I'd make you clean this rifle,' Grant said, 'but somehow I don't trust you with firearms. Not any more.'

'That Kline,' Bowie snarled; 'I wish he'd shot the whole bleeding lot of you. I wish he had.'

'You're a nice boy,' Grant said. 'You have the nicest thoughts.' His voice hardened suddenly; it had the parade-ground bark in it. 'But watch your step, Bowie. Watch it.'

Carson stirred Kline's body with his foot, rolling it over until it lay on its back, and the hole where the bullet had entered his chest was visible. Kline stared sightlessly up at the ceiling of the hut, and his mouth looked twisted, as if he had died cursing.

'Fella, you had it coming to you,' Carson said. 'You had it coming a long, long time.'

They were all startled by the sound of Henderson's voice again. He spoke without opening his eyes, almost as though he were talking in his sleep.

'You must start today. Every day that you remain here reduces your chances of survival. There is not much food left. Therefore, you must set out today.'

'And you, sir?' Thouless asked softly.

Henderson's voice was firm; he had evidently given the matter full consideration. 'I shall stay here.'

Thouless broke out vehemently: 'No, sir. We will not leave you. It is unthinkable.'

'It is for the good of the greatest number.'

Thouless had began to pace up and down the room as though feeling the need for some outlet for his emotion.

'No, no, no, no! I will not — I cannot agree.'

Without raising his voice, without opening his eyes, Henderson said: 'That is an order, Tom.'

Thouless stopped his pacing and stared at the bunk. The others watched him silently, not making any attempt to sway him one way

328

or the other. They knew that their fate might hang on his decision, but they knew that it was a decision for him alone to make.

Henderson's head turned, his eyes opened, and their steady gaze rested on Thouless. Henderson looked at Thouless as a father might look at his son, loving him. And Thouless gazed back at Henderson and knew that he loved this man also.

'That is an order,' Henderson repeated. 'You understand, Tom?'

Thouless's eyes were bright; it was as though a fire were burning in them. A nerve jumped in his cheek.

'I will not accept that order, sir. I refuse to accept it. We will not go without you. Order or no order, we will not do it.'

There was a mutter of approval from the men in the hut, from all except Jaggers and Bowie. It was like a breeze rustling through a bare forest.

Henderson heard the sound. He sighed.

'So then — it's mutiny?'

'You can call it that,' Thouless said.

14

The Journey

It took Toresen a day to make the sledge. Grant and Carson helped him, using the tools that had been in the smashed boat. They cut timbers from the boat, and Toresen shaped them to the purpose they were now to serve. The boat had made its sea journey; now it was to travel overland.

The sound of the sawing, the sound of the axe, and the sound of hammering were lost in the vastness surrounding them; they were the sounds of men striving to break out of a prison.

And then in the distance they heard the low rumbling of gunfire, coming like faint thunder from a storm very far away.

Toresen stopped hammering and cocked an ear. 'There's life somewhere,' he said.

'And death,' Carson said.

'Could be the Murmansk barrage. Could be an air raid.'

'Could be.'

The sound came from the east, or south-east.

'That's the way we'll have to go,' Grant said. 'I wonder how far?'

'We'll find out, kiddo.'

Toresen was not pleased with the sledge. He looked at it with the critical eye of a craftsman, and could see no good in it. But to the others it looked an excellent sledge, better than anyone could have expected from such material and in such conditions of manufacture.

Thouless walked all round it, examining it from every angle. He congratulated Toresen on his work.

'You've done it well, Chips. Have you ever made a sledge before?'

'Never,' Toresen said. He stared at the sledge also. 'It's a rough job, but maybe it'll serve.'

'It'll serve. No doubt about that.'

Toresen had attached towing-ropes and shoulder-harness. Thouless pulled on the ropes and the sledge moved smoothly over the packed snow, the runners squeaking.

'Couldn't be better.'

'It won't move as easy when it's loaded,' Toresen said. 'What we need is a team of huskies.'

'We've got men,' Thouless said.

Darkness was falling; the water of the inlet looked cold and sullen. Above the hills the

331

first stars were appearing, and the colour was draining out of the sky. Frost gripped the land in an iron claw. They retreated from the night into the hut.

Thouless reported to Henderson. 'It's finished, sir. We start tomorrow.'

'Very well, Tom. Very well.'

Grant slept with the rifle sling attached to his belt. He did not think that Bowie and Jaggers would try any more tricks, but he was taking no chances. Now that Kline was dead the other two were without a leader. They were resentful but cowed, and he believed that they would stay with the main party, not having the courage to go off on their own. They must know that retribution awaited them at the journey's end, but they would prefer that to almost certain death in the snow.

Grant awoke in the small hours of the night and lay for a while listening to the breathing of the other men. One man was snoring loudly and Grant guessed that it was Tarbat; no one else in the hut was capable of snoring quite so resonantly as that.

He got up quietly and groped his way to the door. When he opened it a few flakes of snow drifted in. He went outside and closed the door behind him. The snow fell thinly, silently, but there were clear patches of sky where the stars were visible, and he could see the Great Bear and the Little Bear and the constellation of the Bull.

Again he heard the distant rumbling of gunfire, and saw three successive flashes to the south-east, like the leaping flames of a fire reflected in the sky. He thought he could detect the faint drone of aircraft engines, but could not be sure. Closer and more certain was the low murmur of water rolling against the ice fringe at the shores of the inlet; it was a cold, mournful sound, like the whisper of death.

Grant shivered; he could feel the tips of his ears tingling in the freezing air. He turned and went back into the hut.

★　★　★

In the morning the new sprinkling of snow lay like a thin dust of icing-sugar over the landscape. They carried Henderson out of the hut and put him on the sledge, wrapping him in blankets. Henderson's shoulders rested against a pack of supplies tied up in canvas. The stove and the oil drum were there also. He felt sick and tired and in pain.

'You should have left me,' he said to Thouless. 'This is madness.'

Thouless said: 'If we had left you we should

have deserved to die.'

Carson, Toresen, and Peters adjusted the harness about their shoulders.

'You too, bosun,' Thouless said.

Jaggers put a hand to his bandaged head, whining: 'I'm a sick man. I ain't fit to drag no sledge. It'll kill me.'

'I hope it does,' Toresen said. 'I just hope it does.'

'Get hold of that rope,' Thouless ordered. 'You'll do your share.'

The others stared at Jaggers without pity. He looked at Bowie for moral support, not hoping to find it in any other quarter, but Bowie turned away and spat in the snow. He was finished with Jaggers.

Jaggers picked up the rope and harnessed himself to the sledge with the others. Toresen was just behind him, and Toresen would see that he did his stint with no slacking.

Thouless carried the revolver in the pocket of his coat, and Grant had the rifle slung on his shoulder. Bowie and Tarbat had small packs.

'All ready?' Thouless said. 'Let's be on our way.'

They set out, a tiny group of men, weakened by privation, reduced by hatred and violence, searching for life in a dead and frozen land.

To avoid the indentations of the coast-line they headed inland at first, southward. Later they would turn eastward, hunting for the Tuloma river, for Minkino and Murmansk — if these towns did indeed lie in front and not behind them.

Thouless, Grant, Tarbat, and Bowie went ahead, breaking trail for the sledge and keeping between the ridge on the left and the shore of the inlet on the right. The others followed, straining at the ropes, with the sledge sliding and squeaking after them. The snow crunched under their feet, and their breath came like smoke. And so they went on, driving into the unknown; and the hut dwindled behind them, and the skeleton of the boat, and the dead bodies of those who had finished their journey.

The light hardened as they went on; the air was clear and crisp and cold. The sun came up, a pale disk that rested for a while on the top of the ridge with a black pine-tree cutting it in two and throwing a long shadow on the snow; then it climbed hand over hand up the pale blue ladder of the sky and covered its head in a veil of cirrus cloud.

Grant trampled the snow with his leather jackboots, seaboot stockings rolled down over their tops, and felt the blood stirring in his feet, felt them thawing out, coming to life again from their frozen state. He eased the sling of the rifle on his shoulder, and stared at Mr Thouless's back. Thouless was striding forward springily, his head pushed out like a dog pointing. In his eagerness he was going too fast, forgetting the others, forgetting that they could not all travel as quickly as he. A shout from Toresen reminded him.

'Easy on, sir. Have a heart. We ain't all Olympic runners.'

Thouless looked back then and saw the gap that had opened between himself and the sledge party. He waited for them to come up, and then continued at a more moderate pace. Yet even now he would momentarily forget the need for patience, and would go striding ahead for a few paces at a fierce, eager rate until another shout reminded him that this was to be no brisk morning walk but a long and bitter struggle against odds.

It took them nearly an hour to reach the head of the inlet, and they paused there to change places. Toresen took the rifle from Grant, and Carson became leader. Grant, Bowie, and Tarbat harnessed themselves to the sledge while Thouless bent down to speak to Henderson.

'Are you all right, sir?'

'Fine, Tom, fine.'

He did not speak of the pain in his leg or

336

the icy coldness creeping through his body like a slow paralysis. He only regretted that they should be taking so much trouble to drag a doomed and useless carcass over so many miles of snow, expending their own failing strength to no purpose. But he knew they would do it, so he spoke no more of that.

'How far inland, Tom?'

'Two days' journey at this rate, I should think. Then eastward.'

'How long can you hold out on the rations?'

'As long as necessary,' Thouless said grimly. 'We are not going to die.'

Henderson's lips were stiff, but they creased into a smile. He gripped Thouless's hand, and his grip was still a powerful one.

'You're a good man, Tom.'

He lay back on the sledge, hating his body for being so helpless, for needing to be dragged by these others instead of marching boldly at their head. He should have been the leader, not a dead load trailed at the end of a rope like a disabled ship behind a tug.

Carson was already moving on ahead. Thouless picked up his rope.

'Right-ho, men.'

They leaned their weight on the harness. The sledge resisted for a moment, then slid forward.

Henderson listened to the sound of the runners hissing under him. He could see the men's boots sinking into the snow and slipping as they strained at the ropes. Behind them the water sparkled in the pale sunlight, and now they were leaving this last probing finger of the sea, this last reminder of their ordeal by shipwreck.

The ridges on either side closed in on them, and the way became steeper, so that it was as much as they could do to drag the sledge. But after a time the ground levelled out and they travelled on across a wide valley, seeing in the distance ahead more hills, more emptiness, and the glittering carpet of the snow.

There was no mark upon the snow, no sign that other men had ever travelled this way before them. They might have been explorers breaking into a new world, but that the guns muttered now and then from the distance, and they knew that where guns were, there were men also — men killing men, rending the flesh, letting the blood flow. It was towards the guns that they must go.

Grant was pulling beside Bowie. Now and then he glanced at Bowie's pinched, bitter face and wondered what was passing in the man's brain. Above his ragged beard Bowie's nose looked as sharp as a pen and his eyes had a feverish brightness. Grant watched for any sign of slacking, but Bowie was pulling his weight; he seemed to be bearing up as well as any of them, certainly better than Jaggers, who stumbled often and was moaning wretchedly.

'Your pal doesn't like it,' Grant said.

Bowie said contemptuously: 'He's no pal of mine, that jellyfish.' And then he was silent again.

At noon they halted in the middle of a great waste of snow. There was a wind blowing from the east, not a strong wind, but icily cold; it seemed to needle its way in through their clothing to prick at the flesh beneath. It made no sound; it was like the pallid ghost of a wind drifting over a white and ghostly land.

They ate biscuit and corned beef. They lit the paraffin stove behind the shelter of the sledge and melted snow for cocoa. The ration was small; it seemed to do no more than aggravate their hunger, reminding their aching bellies of what food was.

The guns stopped muttering; clouds banked up over the sun. It began to snow lightly, and the snow was an added irritant, a further discomfort.

They were not sorry to be moving again, for the exercise warmed them, and they travelled southward still, navigating by a pocket compass that Thouless carried. Only Henderson, incapable of exercise, could not get warm. He lay on the moving sledge like a slab of meat, and felt the pain moving up his thigh, and the sickness in his body and in his mind. He watched the towropes slackening and growing taut, easing and tightening, as the men stumbled onward. And here, as in the boat, it was as though they were caught in a nightmare, for ever pressing on, yet never making any impression upon the miles that had to be conquered and left behind them.

Soon the snow stopped, but the air seemed to become colder. The silent, invisible wind came like a river of ice out of the east. The men's breath was laboured and their lips were stiff with cold.

'See the world with the Merchant Navy,' Tarbat said. 'And what a world. By God, what a world!'

'It's clean,' Grant said. 'All nice and white and clean like a new sheet. What are you grumbling at?'

'I'm not grumbling. You never heard me grumble. If I was the grumbling sort I'd tell you how cruel bad my feet are. But that's not my character. I just suffer in silence; I sit like Patience on a flipping monument, smiling at grief.'

'With a smile like yours you'd scare the wolf from the door.'

Grant thought Tarbat looked bad. He had shrunk; the skin of his face hung in loose folds, like secondhand clothes on a man too small for them, and he walked with a stumbling, shuffling gait as if near the end of his endurance. Yet he would need to hang on for a few more days; there was nothing for him here but death.

And if Tarbat was bad, Jaggers was undoubtedly worse. If he had not known what Jaggers was Grant might have been moved to pity him. But Jaggers had forfeited all pity.

When dusk came they made camp, erecting a tent with the canvas and spars which they had brought from the boat. In this rough shelter, huddled together for warmth, they slept or tried to sleep, while the slow hours of the Arctic night crept away on leaden feet and the cold came up from the ground on which they lay.

At daybreak they took their meagre breakfast and set out again, divided as before into two four-man teams and still heading inland. Midday found them in a sparse belt of stunted pine-trees. They halted there and cut timber with the axe and kindled a fire. They stowed more timber on the sledge, and when they had eaten and rested they went on again.

The trees were half a mile behind them when they saw the plane. It came from the west, flying slowly and at a low altitude, as though searching the ground. They stopped and looked up at the plane and waved their arms, thinking that perhaps here was deliverance come from the sky.

Jaggers began to yell hoarsely, oblivious of the fact that his voice would be lost in the racket of the aircraft's single radial engine.

'Help!' Jaggers yelled. 'This way! Help us!'

The plane appeared for a time to be passing by them; it was on a course that would take it to the south of their position. But suddenly it altered direction and began to fly directly towards them where they stood in a little, scattered group.

'He's seen us,' Tarbat cried. 'Thank the Lord for that. He's coming for us. We're saved.'

Grant had said nothing; he had not waved his arms or shouted. He simply looked at the plane and noted the fixed undercarriage — two spatted wheels hanging on unbraced struts — and his mind worried at the memory of a plane that looked like that, a radial-engined monoplane with a high, umbrella wing, strutted from the fuselage. It was very much like a Westland Lysander, the standard reconnaissance plane of the British Army. Yet how could there be a Lysander here? He had never heard that any had been supplied to the Russians. There was a Hurricane unit based in North Russia, but no Lysanders; yet here was the very image of a Lysander flying straight towards him.

And then the pieces of the puzzle clicked into place and he knew that this was no Lysander but a German Henschel 126, so similar to the British plane in appearance, yet so much less welcome.

He shouted to the others: 'Get down, you fools. It's a Jerry!' And he ran away from the sledge and flung himself full length in the snow just as the Henschel tilted its port wing to give the observer a sight of the target and a spray of bullets came lashing down from the cockpit.

Grant heard a scream, the thin sound lifting above the roar of the Henschel's engine. The rattle of the machine-gun ceased abruptly, and he raised his head and saw that it was Jaggers who was screaming. Slowly the screams died away into a low moan of pain. He got up and went to Jaggers and saw a red stain of blood on the snow. Jaggers was bleeding from the neck, but a closer examination showed that it was only a graze.

'Stop that noise,' Grant said harshly. 'You

aren't killed. It's nothing more than a scratch.'

'My leg,' Jaggers groaned. 'My leg's smashed.'

Grant saw then that another bullet had gone into Jaggers's thigh just above the knee, and this was a far more serious business. Jaggers would not be walking any more.

'You've had it, bosun,' he said. 'Sure enough, you've had it this time.'

He heard the Henschel approaching again. It had swept round in a wide arc and was coming in from the north.

'Get down!' he yelled.

They flopped down and tried to dig themselves in. There was no shelter. They were in open country, and the snow was a white background that revealed and would not hide them.

Grant lay on his back and fired his rifle at the Henschel. He had thrown off his gloves so that he could work the trigger and the bolt, and his fingers were freezing. But he fired five rounds as the Henschel came in and roared over them, and he heard bullets from the observer's machine-gun slashing into the ground just by his head. When he was able to look he could see the dotted track of the holes not six inches from where his body lay. It had been a close call.

Twice more the Henschel came in machine-gunning, and they were as helpless as dead men lying on the dead white carpet of the snow. The bullets came like hailstones, and they waited shivering for the impact.

Only Bowie ran away — stumbling, falling down, rising again, and running on — desperately on — anywhere to get away from death. But the Henschel chased him and shot him down, drilling his body with bullets until the blood poured out of the holes in dark rivers.

Bowie lay with the blood gushing from his wounds and cursed the men who had killed him: 'Bastards! Filthy bastards!'

And he died — cursing.

The others lay in the snow and feigned death, and the Henschel swept over them for the last time and flew away to the east and faded into the emptiness of the Arctic sky. They stood up then and shook the snow from their clothes and looked at one another to see who was left.

Peters was dead. A bullet had struck him in the back of the head just at the base of the skull, and had gone through the brain and had come out above the eyes. And so for him also the journey was ended.

For the rest, only Jaggers was seriously injured, though Toresen had a scratch on the hand, and the heel of Carson's right boot had been half torn off by a bullet. The remainder had escaped without injury.

Thouless went to the sledge where Henderson was still lying, where he had lain throughout the action.

'Are you all right, sir?' Thouless's voice was anxious.

'I think so, Tom. But there's a most unholy smell of paraffin.'

Thouless looked at the paraffin drum and saw that it had a bullet-hole through it. There was scarcely half a gallon of the precious liquid left.

'You're lucky, sir. They hit the sledge. It was a near thing.'

'I know, Tom, I know.'

Jaggers was trying to drag himself to the sledge, a constant, sobbing gibber of pain and fear dribbled from his mouth.

'What in hell's wrong with that bosun?' Henderson asked.

'He caught one in the leg,' Thouless said. 'Now we're going to have more trouble with him. The damned, useless swine.'

Jaggers's trouser-leg was soaked with blood. They had to cut away the trousers with a knife so that they could get at the wound to dress it. Jaggers kept letting out little yelps of pain until Toresen threatened to bash him on the head if he didn't pipe down. But the agony of his shattered leg was stronger than his fear of what Toresen might do to him, for the bullet had splintered the bone and left a pulp of torn and bloody flesh. Jaggers was really in a bad way.

'What do we do with that joker now?' Torsen asked Thouless. 'By rights we ought to leave him. He would have left us.'

Jaggers heard the suggestion and let out another yelp. 'You can't leave me here; you can't go off and leave me. I'm your shipmate. You couldn't go away and leave a shipmate to die.'

'Couldn't we?' Toresen said. 'What makes you so sure?'

Thouless was worried about the problem of Jaggers. It was obvious that the man could not walk. Equally obviously they could not follow Toresen's suggestion and leave him to die. Much as he might deserve such a fate, to do so would have been inhuman. Somehow they would have to pile Jaggers on to the sledge as well as Henderson. The question then would be; could they drag the sledge with this added weight now that there were only five of them left to do the job? Well, they would have to try; there was no other course.

He gave orders concerning what had to be done.

Henderson said: 'You'd do better to leave the two of us. You could give me the revolver.'

Thouless glanced at him and saw the big, weather-beaten face set grimly. So it had come to that. But not yet, not if he had anything to do with it. He would drag Henderson through hell itself, but he would get him to safety. If not he would die also. He would not leave the Old Man.

'We're taking you with us,' he said.

Henderson sighed. 'Well, if that's the way you feel.'

'It is the way.'

They piled snow over the bodies of Peters and Bowie, since they could not bury them, and they went on, grimly hauling the heavy sledge, but moving so slowly and painfully that the little mounds of snow marking the abandoned dead remained visible for a long time, reminding them when they looked back of their own mortality.

Henderson lay on the sledge packed close to Jaggers and listened to the bosun's groans. He gazed up at the sky and saw the heavy clouds that hung like lead above this little party of struggling, weakened men. There was more snow in those clouds, and snow would not help them. He wondered how many more miles lay ahead, and what lay at the end of those miles. There was no telling. He heard the hissing, laboured breath of the men pulling the sledge, and he knew they could not go on much longer; they had not the strength. He and Jaggers were a drag on the others, robbing them of their own slender chance of survival; it was not right that this should be so. He thought of the revolver that Thouless carried, the revolver that had already disposed of one man. If he could regain possession of it, it might dispose of two more. But he could not ask for the revolver; Thouless would be suspicious. Therefore, he would have to get it in some other way — in the night.

Jaggers moaned suddenly: 'My leg! Oh, my leg!'

Henderson said softly: 'All right, bosun, we'll take care of your leg; we'll take care of it.'

When they pitched camp for the night Tarbat was near to collapse. Toresen, Thouless, Grant, and Carson were still strong; they were tough men, all of them, men of bone and muscle and sinew, able to face privation. But Tarbat's job on board ship had not kept him fit; he had allowed himself to become flabby and overweight. Much of the weight had now fallen from him, but he was weakened by the meagre ration and was finding the going hard. But he was willing; he was no shirker. Come what might, he would keep at it until he dropped; he would not give in.

'How are you feeling?' Grant asked anxiously. 'You don't look too well.'

'I'm fine,' Tarbat said. 'Corns on the feet, that's all. That damn corn doctor in Philly didn't do the job proper. Apart from the old plates of meat there's nothing wrong with yours truly that a good slap-up meal at the Savoy wouldn't cure — or fish and chips in the *News of the World*, if it comes to that.'

He gave a laugh, but the laugh seemed to be too much of a strain on his constitution; his legs crumpled under him and he collapsed in the snow. Grant went to lift him, but he waved his hand impatiently, refusing help.

'Them corns — just them corns.'

It was snowing before they had the shelter erected, and the wind was blowing the snow in a great swirling curtain across the bare, lifeless, undulating country. All night the wind rattled the canvas, and snow drifted in upon them, sprinkling them with sugared whiteness. They slept and dreamed of better things.

But Henderson did not sleep; sleep did not come to him easily, for the pain was with him always. Soon, though, there would be no more pain; no longer would he be a leaden weight holding the others back — neither he nor Jaggers.

Thouless was lying on one side of him and Jaggers on the other — he had made sure that it should be arranged so. It made his task easier. He could hear Thouless's steady breathing. The mate was asleep. This was his opportunity. He reached for the revolver. It would not take long — one shot for Jaggers, through the head, and another for himself. Tomorrow the five that were left would be able to go on unhindered.

His hand moved over Thouless, feeling for the weapon. He found the pocket in the coat where the revolver lay. He drew it out of its resting-place very carefully and gently, so that he should not awaken the sleeping man. Thouless stirred, but did not wake.

Henderson found Jaggers's head and pushed the muzzle of the revolver close against it. He squeezed the trigger.

He had tensed himself for the blast of the explosion, but all he heard was the sharp click of the hammer. He squeezed the trigger again, and again there was nothing but the click of an empty gun. He knew then that Thouless had forestalled him, had guessed what he might wish to do, and had unloaded the revolver.

He gave a low growl of frustration, and felt

a hand close over his own. He heard the whisper of Thouless's voice in his ear.

'No, not that way. You are coming with us. That isn't the way out.'

He surrendered the revolver and let his hand drop by his side.

'It would have been the best way.'

'No, sir. No way at all.' He thought he detected a catch in Thouless's voice. 'Don't you see that we need you? If we lose you we lose all. Don't you see?'

He did not see, but he accepted it. He had done what he could, and Thouless had blocked the way. Now things must take their course. He could do no more.

'God, Tom,' he said. 'Just listen to that wind.'

* * *

Grant woke to the sound of the wind weeping outside the darkened tent. But it was not the wind that had aroused him, nor even the cold. It was Jaggers's hand gripping his chest, tearing convulsively at his clothing.

From Jaggers's throat a dreadful rattling sound was coming. Grant had never heard such a sound before and he never wished to hear it again. It was the voice of death coming out of the darkness.

Then it ceased abruptly, as if strangled, and Jaggers's hand stopped scrabbling at Grant's chest.

Grant said: 'What's wrong, bosun?' And then more urgently: 'Bosun, what's wrong with you?'

There was no answer. Jaggers was not even moaning any more. Grant put his ear close to Jaggers's mouth, and Jaggers was not breathing any more either. He too had come to the end of the journey.

★　★　★

On the following day they turned eastward and made better progress. The land was covered with a new, smooth layer of snow that dazzled their eyes, and the wind was bitter. But there was only one man on the sledge and four to haul it. They excused Tarbat; it was as much as he could do to carry his own weight. Tarbat protested that he was ready to haul a rope, but Thouless was adamant, and in the end Tarbat was glad enough to fall in behind the sledge and walk in the tracks that the others had beaten.

In the afternoon they saw marks in the snow, stretching away to right and left and cutting across the line of their route. They halted.

'Skis,' Grant said. 'Maybe an Army patrol.'

It was the first sign they had had that there was really human life in this forsaken land, and their spirits rose.

'Let's hope it's the right army,' Carson said.

'You mean the Left Army — the Reds.'

'The Red Army's the right one for us now.'

They debated whether to follow the tracks of the patrol, but decided against it. Instead they pushed on eastward. They came to another thin wood, and they rested there and heard aircraft flying overhead. But they remembered the Henschel, and made no attempt to draw attention to themselves.

The planes flew on and the engine note faded, but after a while they felt the ground tremble under them as though an earthquake had shaken it.

'Bombs,' Grant said. 'We must be getting near civilization.'

But they were becoming weaker, and the sledge was a nightmare weight that held them back. Ahead were low hills which had to be climbed or skirted, and either way it was a dreadful labour. Once after toiling upward for an hour they slipped and went rolling back down the slope to lose in a minute all that they had gained. But they would not leave the sledge, would not leave Henderson. With all of them it had become an article of faith that Henderson must be carried back alive, and each one of them would have died rather than forsake him.

* * *

The days passed in a long-drawn-out agony that seemed to have no end. The food dwindled; the paraffin was exhausted. They jettisoned the useless stove and went on. When they found a tree they cut firewood and carried it on the sledge. But they were travelling so slowly that every yard they gained was a minor triumph. The hills met them one after another; they crossed frozen lakes; they found treacherous ground where their feet sank in deeply and they were forced to draw back and find another way. And still the snow came and the wind, and they struggled on, on, on, endlessly, wearily on.

One day they came to the gutted ruins of a village, but there was no life left there; nothing but charred timber, some snow-covered piles of rubble, and a few pieces of twisted iron. Once men had lived there, but it was impossible to tell how long ago, impossible to tell how long it was since death and destruction had visited the place and burned and ruined it.

'Where there's a village there should be a road,' Toresen said. But the snow had obliterated any sign of what might once have been a way; now there was only the wide plain, the hills and desolation.

'Let's get on,' Thouless said. 'There's nothing here.'

They had travelled perhaps another half-mile when Thouless glanced back and discovered that Tarbat was missing. He took Toresen with him and went back. Tarbat was lying just on the outskirts of the charred remnants of the village. He did not move when Thouless shouted to him.

They rolled Tarbat over on to his back and rubbed his cheeks and hands. Tarbat's breath came very faintly, but he was alive. After a while his eyes fluttered open, but he seemed at first quite unable to realize where he was. Then he gave a little apologetic grin.

'Sorry, sir. Didn't mean to be a bother. Be all right in a minute.'

He made a pathetic attempt to get up, but there was no strength in his legs. He sat in the snow looking strangely childlike and helpless.

'We'll make camp here,' Thouless said. 'You'll be better tomorrow.'

But he did not think that even after a night's rest Tarbat would be fit to go on; it looked to Thouless as though the cook had come to the end of his tether.

★　★　★

Early in the night they heard wolves howling. It was a mournful, eerie sound. Grant, lying awake and listening to the howling, wondered whether wolves had plundered the dead village; there might have been bodies there once. The charred posts stood up like black tombstones behind the tent; the camp had been pitched in a graveyard, and only the wolves and the phantoms of the dead were there for company.

There was no more food, and they could not tell how much farther they had to go; there was no way of telling. Perhaps after all, Grant thought, they had been wrong; perhaps they were merely heading out into the wilderness, into unknown wastes of snow-covered tundra. But there had been a village once; he grasped at that evidence of civilization, holding it as the promise of life — even a dead village.

One thing only was certain: Tarbat could not go on under his own power. Could four starving men, however tough, drag the other two? He doubted it.

He was turning these matters over in his

mind when he heard the sound of the aircraft, the heavy beat of the engines vibrating overhead. Then the guns began to mutter — and they were closer than they had ever been before.

There was a light in the sky that shone on the canvas of the shelter, so that the dark shapes of the men lying there were faintly visible. Grant wondered whether it was the aurora, but when he got up and went out he saw that the light was man-made, for away to the east were the silver beams of searchlights weaving an intricate pattern that changed from moment to moment. He stood by the tent and watched the barrage going up, the red balls of tracer, the glittering jewels of the shell-bursts. He felt the earth tremble beneath him and knew that bombs were exploding. A fire leaped up and splashed a crimson stain upon the sky.

Toresen, Carson, and Thouless had come out of the tent also.

'That's Murmansk,' Grant said. 'That's the Murmansk barrage sure enough.'

'Could be,' Toresen admitted.

'Could be! It couldn't be anything else.'

'How far off would you reckon?' Carson asked. 'You've seen more of this stuff than I have. How far away would you say that lot is?'

'Five miles, maybe ten,' Grant said. 'I

shouldn't think it was more.'

'We could walk that.'

'You bet we could. You bet we will.'

They started at daybreak — Grant, Toresen, and Carson. Thouless insisted on staying with Henderson and Tarbat, although Henderson urged him to go with the others.

'There's nothing you can do here, Tom.'

'I'm not leaving you,' Thouless said, and there was a finality in his tone that invited no argument.

The three men travelled light, carrying no weapons. It was a clear, frosty morning, and the snow squeaked under their boots. As the light changed from a dull grey to brilliant white, slowly turning from night to day, they saw the snow and the hills ahead of them. Here and there from the hills, like dark candles stuck in an iced Christmas-cake, pine-trees pointed to the sky; along the ridges the trees were like a gapped, irregular fence.

They went forward in the direction from which the guns had flickered in the night, but the deep snow hampered them and tired them, and their stomachs were empty.

The sun came up, showing a pale face through thin cloud, and the snow glittered, crystalline, glassy, making the eyes burn. They went in single file, taking it in turns to lead. Three fighter aircraft flew over their heads, very high up, and a vapour trail hung for a time in the sky like a long roll of cotton-wool.

With Toresen leading and Carson in the middle Grant watched the snow scattering from the other men's feet. He looked at his watch and saw that they had been travelling for three hours, shuffling on across this endless desert of snow, on and on, getting nowhere.

At the end of each hour they rested briefly and then pushed on again. They did not want the night to overtake them; the journey had to be finished in daylight, for they had no tent and no blankets. But the hours passed, the sun reached its zenith and began to sink towards the western hills, and still they could see no signs of human life.

Perhaps, Grant thought, they were going in the wrong direction; perhaps they were travelling in a circle, as he had read that men did in the open; perhaps soon they would come again to the tent, to Henderson and Thouless and Tarbat, and the sledge that Toresen had made. But then he told himself not to be a fool, for they had the sun to guide them and the compass; they could not have lost the way. It was farther than he had reckoned; that was all. But supposing it was too far. They were all weak now, and this was no marching pace, unless it were a dead march. The words 'dead march' began to beat in his brain like a drum. Dead march, dead march, dead march. And then they altered to another refrain: Dead men, dead men, dead men.

He was becoming light-headed; sometimes the earth and the sky seemed to whirl round him, so that he almost fell. His eyes were burning, and there was a dull, sick feeling in his belly that nagged at him unceasingly.

He began to imagine things. He imagined he saw a table laid out with steaming roasts of meat, with great boiled puddings and thick sauce; he imagined a fire burning in an open hearth, warmth and good cheer just ahead of him, just beyond his reach. But he knew that all this was foolishness, that there was no table, no food and no fire, nothing but the hills and the meagre trees and the everlasting snow.

He imagined he heard a ship's siren.

Toresen shouted: 'There's a ship.'

'Imagination,' Grant said. 'No table, no fire, no siren. Just imagination.'

'To hell with imagination,' Toresen said. 'That was a ship's hooter. You couldn't mistake that sound.'

'Sure thing,' Carson said.

They had stopped walking; they stood in a little, silent group, listening for a repetition of that sound. The hills and the dark pines seemed to be hushed and listening also. The very air was motionless, frost-laden and silent. It was as if the whole world were holding its breath and listening.

And then it came again, unmistakable, a rude and strident sound tearing the silence apart as a man might tear a curtain. It came from the east, from beyond the ridge in front of them, and to their listening ears it sounded like the sweetest of all sweet music.

'What are we waiting for?' Carson shouted. 'Let's go.'

They found new strength to climb the last hill, new hope drawing them onward and upward, until they reached the crest and stood there staring down at what lay below them.

It was the river.

'Look at them goddamn ships,' Carson said, and his voice cracked and broke into laughter. 'Just take a look at them ships. Oh, boy, them ships!'

They were lying at anchor in the river, ten, perhaps twnety of them, warships and merchantmen; and from their jackstaffs fluttered the White Ensign, the Red Ensign, and the Stars and Stripes.

'Our ships,' Toresen said. 'Our bloody, lovely, darling ships. Christ Almighty, there's a sight for you. You never saw ships as pretty as them, I bet — never.'

They were grey, drab ships; they floated there, swinging idly to their cables, and the cold Tuloma flowed past them on its way to Kola Bay and the Barents Sea. They were drab ships, trying to hide themselves under a camouflage of grey paint, trying to sink into the background of cloud and water; they were drab ships with here and there a streak of rust, a streak of salt, a streak of soot, their anti-aircraft guns pointing upward at the sky and thin wisps of smoke drifting from their funnels. Ships not built for beauty; designed and constructed only for the purpose to which they were dedicated — to fight or to carry merchandise. And yet, in the eyes of those three men standing motionless on the hill above the river, they were so beautiful that the heart almost burst with the wonder of them.

'Let's get moving,' Grant said. 'Let's be on our way.'

Sliding and stumbling in the crisp, frozen snow, they went down the hillside, down to the river and the ships.

15

End Of The Trail

The walls of the hospital ward were painted white, but the paint had yellowed with age. Thouless followed a plump nurse down the long aisle between the rows of iron beds. The nurse had high cheekbones that came up close under her eyes, giving her a vaguely Mongolian look, and her hair was braided on either side of her head in two flat coils like ear-muffs.

Thouless wondered whether she could hear anything. Not that it mattered so far as he was concerned; he spoke no Russian, and he did not suppose she understood English. Yet she would need to hear what doctors and patients said to her, and if the coils of hair excluded sound it would make matters difficult; all kinds of mistakes might happen. The question worried Thouless a little, because it might affect Henderson's welfare, and he was concerned about Henderson.

The nurse stopped at the foot of one of the beds and turned and smiled at Thouless.

When she smiled the eyes seemed to disappear altogether, but she had good teeth — very even and very white; she would have served as an advertisement for toothpaste in a capitalist country.

Thouless saw Henderson lying in the bed, and he thought Henderson looked younger. That would be because the beard had been shaved off. Henderson looked clean and spruce, but thin. He grinned at Thouless.

'Good to see you, Tom. Thanks for coming.'

Thouless went up to the bed and the nurse went away.

'She's a decent kid,' Henderson said. 'They all are.'

Thouless said awkwardly: 'You don't have to thank me. How are you feeling?'

'Fine, Tom, just fine. Couldn't be better.'

'They treat you all right, then?'

'Oh, yes, they treat me well. Wish I knew Russian though. It'd make things simpler.'

'Yes, I suppose it would.'

Thouless looked at the next bed and looked away again. A man was lying there with his head swathed in bandages; he was quite motionless; he might have been dead. Thouless wondered how he had been injured. In an air raid? In battle? In an accident? Or a drunken brawl?

'When do you leave for home?' Henderson asked.

'In a couple of days,' Thouless said. 'I may not be able to come again, but I'll try to look in tomorrow.' He sat gingerly on the foot of the bed. 'Is there anything I can do?'

He was staring at Henderson, as if trying to engrave the imprint of that big, white-haired head on his memory. Henderson. They had pulled him through in spite of everything; but those last days in the tent before rescue came had been the worst. There had been wolves; he had had to shoot two of the brutes, and the others had dragged them away and eaten them.

And all the while he had known that Henderson was in agony, and that there was nothing he could do but wait, not even knowing for certain whether the others had got through or were lying somewhere out in the snow — dead. It was the passive waiting that had been the hardest to bear.

But it had all worked out right in the end. The Russians had wasted no time; they had acted quickly on the information given them by Toresen, Grant, and Carson. They had known where the ruined village was, and they had come swiftly — men of the Red Army on skis. He had seen them coming like ghosts in their white coats.

'I'd like you to go and see my wife — Freda,' Henderson said. 'That's if it wouldn't be too much trouble.'

'Of course,' Thouless said. 'Of course I'll go.'

'Tell her I'm all right. Tell her I'll be back for the summer, eh? She'll be worrying. They always worry — women.'

'I suppose so,' Thouless said.

He looked down at the bed-clothes. Henderson seemed to be occupying only the top half of the bed. Where Thouless sat there was nothing, just — flatness. He looked up and saw Henderson's eyes fixed on him, and he was embarrassed. But Henderson's mouth twitched into a smile.

'They took the other one as well, Tom. They made the two of them match. Tidy-minded people, you see.'

'Oh,' Thouless said. 'I'm sorry.'

'It doesn't matter. Maybe they'll fix me up with a couple of tin legs. If not there's always the wheeled chair.'

Thouless tried to imagine Henderson in a wheeled chair, and failed. He hated to think of its coming to that. There was no room for wheeled chairs on the bridge of a ship.

Henderson seemed to read his thoughts.

'I've finished with the sea, Tom. One more voyage, and that'll be the last.'

'Oh,' Thouless said, and then was silent. It seemed a dreadful thing to him that Henderson should never again be able to go to sea as master of a ship. He tried to imagine himself in the same position; it would be like the end of all meaning in life.

Henderson said: 'I think I shall try my hand at painting — oils. I shall have plenty of time now.'

'Yes,' Thouless said. 'You'll have plenty of time.'

★ ★ ★

The post-office in Murmansk smelled of damp plaster, melting snow, wet floorboards, cigarettes rolled in newspaper, steam heating, and human bodies. Behind the counter a number of women clerks were busy, their plump, round faces innocent of make-up. In front of the counter a drab collection of people waited patiently to be served: men in quilted jackets and felt boots, soldiers of the Red Army, two sailors from the North Fleet, and in one corner an incredibly wrinkled old woman who might have come inside simply for the warmth. On the walls were pictures of Lenin, Stalin, and Kalinin.

Grant and Toresen were buying postage

stamps for souvenirs, stamps with pictures of Russian heroes, of Russian tanks, Russian aircraft, Russian guns. They paid for the stamps with grimy rouble notes, and went out of the fetid atmosphere of the post-office into the cold, crisp air outside.

A motor lorry ground its way past over the hard-packed snow, and behind the lorry came a sleigh drawn by a pony, an old man kneeling in it, the reins in his right hand. It was the old way following behind the new; in this northern outpost the two still mingled; there were log houses and concrete building blocks, street loudspeakers and black bread.

Grant and Toresen walked to the Arctica Hotel and went up the wide staircase and into the dining-room. Thouless, Carson, and Tarbat were there, sitting at a table and drinking tea. They made room for the others and ordered more glasses of hot, sweet tea and a plate of greasy cakes.

'You got what you wanted?' Tarbat asked.

His hands were bandaged. He had had three fingers amputated because of frost-bite, and had lost some toes also. The skin of his face still looked too big and loose for what it contained. But he was cheerful; he was lucky to be alive, and he knew it.

Grant showed him the stamps.

'Just bits of coloured paper,' Tarbat said. 'Beats me why anybody troubles with those things.'

'Pound notes are bits of coloured paper, and I'll bet you trouble with them.'

'That's different,' Tarbat said. 'Pound notes are British.'

'You can give me dollar bills,' Carson said. 'That's the paper for me.'

Thouless felt that, rightly speaking, he ought not to be sitting here with these men. He was a stickler for convention, and it seemed to him that it was wrong for an officer to hobnob with the crew; it was bad for discipline. But the feeling was not strong; it was a hangover from the past. He had been through too much with this little band of men, these few survivors, to be aloof now. Nevertheless, he could not relax as they did. Even now there was still a curtain of reserve between him and them.

Toresen appeared to sense as much. He tried to draw Thouless into the conversation.

'So the ship's sailing tomorrow, sir.'

'Tomorrow,' Thouless said.

'When the War's over,' Tarbat said. 'I'm going to leave the sea. I'm going to have my own little bakery, and I won't even go to Southend for a paddle. I never want to smell seaweed again as long as I live — never.'

'You'll be back,' Toresen said. 'You won't be able to keep away.'

'Not me. Not ever. I've had my bellyful of it. I've got enough salt to last me out.'

'Me,' Carson said. 'I got no other way of making an honest dollar. Been a sailor since I was so high. Only job I know.'

'Come in with me. I'll teach you to bake.'

Carson grinned. 'Me, a baker! You want to poison somebody?' When they left the Arctica it had begun to snow. Winter was making a fight of it before retreating. They walked through the falling snow down the long slope to the docks, over a level crossing, and past gaunt sheds, past piles of cargo that had come in with the convoys and now lay rusting or rotting on the quayside because the Murman railway could not cope with it, past sentries in long, grey coats with long, Russian rifles slung on their shoulders, past a line of trucks, past cranes, past dock workers in greasy quilted clothing, past the hissing steam of winches and slings of munitions swinging out over the quay, past one ship and then another, and a third, until they came at last to the one that was to take them home.

And they said goodbye to Carson and went up the gangplank. And when they were on deck they looked back and saw Carson standing there.

And Carson gave a flip of the hand and a grin, and turned and walked away, and was lost in the swirling curtain of the snow.

THE END

FINAL RUN
THE WILD ONE
DEAD OF WINTER
SPECIAL DELIVERY
SKELETON ISLAND
BUSMAN'S HOLIDAY
A PASSAGE OF ARMS
OLD PALS ACT

We do hope that you have enjoyed reading this large print book.

Did you know that all of our titles are available for purchase?

We publish a wide range of high quality large print books including:
Romances, Mysteries, Classics
General Fiction
Non Fiction and Westerns

Special interest titles available in large print are:
The Little Oxford Dictionary
Music Book
Song Book
Hymn Book
Service Book

Also available from us courtesy of Oxford University Press:
Young Readers' Dictionary
(large print edition)
Young Readers' Thesaurus
(large print edition)

For further information or a free brochure, please contact us at:
Ulverscroft Large Print Books Ltd.,
The Green, Bradgate Road, Anstey,
Leicester, LE7 7FU, England.
Tel: (00 44) 0116 236 4325
Fax: (00 44) 0116 234 0205

Other titles in the
Ulverscroft Large Print Series:

MERMAID'S GROUND

Alice Marlow

It's been five years since Kate Williams' beloved husband died, leaving her with two young children to raise. Now she's built a good life in one of Wiltshire's prettiest villages, and she has her dream job, as gardener at Moxham Court. For the last year, Kate has had a lover, roguishly attractive Justin Spencer, but he won't commit to more than a night here and there. When she takes in a male lodger, Jem, Kate's secretly hoping his presence will provoke a jealous reaction in Justin. What she hasn't reckoned on is exactly how attractive Jem will turn out to be.